Xavier

A Hero No More

by

Kenneth R. Harvey

authorHOUSE®

AuthorHouse™
1663 Liberty Drive
Bloomington, IN 47403
www.authorhouse.com
Phone: 1-800-839-8640

First published by AuthorHouse   04/20/2011

ISBN: 978-1-4567-4669-8 (e)
ISBN: 978-1-4567-4670-4 (hc)
ISBN: 978-1-4567-4671-1 (sc)

Library of Congress Control Number: 2011902843

Printed in the United States of America

Dedication

I would like to dedicate this book to two very special people and my dearest friends, Drew and Angela Starke.

I would like to thank Drew for pushing me to write this book and forcing me to stay motivated until it was completed, you are a friend and mentor.

I would also like to thank his lovely wife Angela who helped me from the very beginning to mold and shape the story into something that was readable. Angela is a great reporter and friend and I hope I did her feedback justice in the book.

Angela and Drew, I cannot thank you enough for all the hard work and dedication you gave me when, at times, I wanted to give up.

Your friend,

Kenneth Ray Harvey

Chapter 1

Warren and Martha Morgan stood in front of the Washington Monument in awe. Martha gazed at its height and pointed a slender finger towards the sky, as Warren focused intently on the map he held in his hand. He began reciting information as though he were a tour guide. He told her, in a matter of fact way, why the monument was a different color at the top than at the bottom.

She admired the way he lovingly described all the details and facts. Shivers shot up her spine as he spoke in a rich voice. His tone reminded her of Charlton Heston playing the role of Moses who barked out the Commandments. She, unlike the Israelites, would obey him completely and without question.

Warren and Martha had been married for more than forty years, and after all that time they had just now saved enough money to go on their first vacation. There was no question about Washington D.C. being their destination. It had been a dream of theirs since they had first said their wedding vows. They couldn't care less about Venice, Paris, Rome, or any other exotic European city they'd heard friends bragging about. They were Americans, and they wanted to see the heart of America.

Taking their tiny savings, they bought two airplane tickets from El Paso, Texas to Washington's Reagan National. It was the first time either of them had ever flown, and as much as Warren tried to put up a brave act, he was scared. When the plane took off, he held his wife's hand so tightly that she felt the blood stopping its circular journey and bunching up near the area that he was squeezing.

Martha, like a good wife, endured the pain and would do nothing to bring shame or embarrassment to her love. She leaned into his chest and allowed him to feel like he was squeezing her hand to protect her instead of showing his own fears. She loved him, and she knew he loved her, too. Their close bond allowed both of them to know that they'd do anything to lift the other one up, regardless of the situation. They trusted each other completely.

After an uneventful flight and landing, the couple sauntered to the baggage claim area. Warren manhandled the luggage with the swiftness of a twenty-year-old who was anxious to start his vacation. They waited for the bus to take them to their rent-a-car stop where Warren got an almost new Cadillac CTS.

He felt excited as he drove his bride around town in the upscale car. Martha protested about the cost, but Warren would hear nothing of it. Although time and life had taken their toll on Martha, her face now weather-beaten and aged, she was still his queen. After all these years, he wanted to treat her like one on their vacation.

They had planned to visit all the museums in D.C. first before touring the monuments and finally the White House. There was no particular order to see the other buildings, but they especially were looking forward to the National Museum of American History as part of their tour.

As they drove down Constitution Avenue, everything appeared grander than they had expected, and with each landmark there was a new sense of excitement. The traffic was thick and parking nearly impossible. After turning onto 18 Street and circling the block a few times, Warren found a legal parking spot and parallel parked his impressive rental.

Warren held his wife's hand and paused for a moment before opening the car door. There was no rush. They were on vacation. After the brief rainstorm had passed, they got out of the car and walked to the intersection. They waited. The light was not green and by no means would they jaywalk, especially in Washington. Martha looked at her husband and smiled. She loved that he loved his country so much. He was a good man.

Even though he couldn't join the military because of a bum leg, he believed in everything the country stood for. In the south during the 60s, when there were several groups fighting against blacks, he had always opened his home to welcome people of color.

He'd say, "As long as you're willing to be a man, then be a man."

Warren was known for hiring them to work for him, and he provided free supplies for their families.

Now even as hard work and time aged his body prematurely, he still had the deep fiery blue eyes that grew with excitement as he moved closer to one of the symbols he had often read about as a kid. Martha leaned in close and kissed him on the cheek, not able to control herself any longer. He was not a big fan of public affection, but he smiled and squeezed her hand to let her know that he appreciated her kind gesture.

As the sun began to fight its way out of the grayish, rain-filled prison, a young man with an oversized backpack hurried past them as if they were moving too slow for his liking. Two young Asian women talking loudly into their cell phones passed them also, as though Warren and Martha were invisible and they were the only people in the world whose conversation was worth hearing. A young fully-developed woman jogged hurriedly past them.

Martha glared at her and took notice of the skimpy running togs the woman wore that were at least one size too tight and revealed way too much skin. Martha wondered how much attention Warren would give her. She made a bet to herself that he would not linger to look at the young lady, and felt confident that he would prove her right.

Within moments, the young lady was down the street and around the corner. All the time, Warren never really took his eyes off the map that was in front of him. He only glanced upward to make sure he was not in the way of the jogger. Martha mentally gave herself a "high five" and smiled, proud of the fact that she knew her husband so well.

For the rest of the day, she leaned in close to him and regarded the tall buildings and people who walked hurriedly around them. Warren was her monument, and she felt blessed to be with him.

"We better find our hotel," Warren said, interrupting Martha's thoughts.

"Oh, do you think we have time for one more place?" Martha asked, her voice like the soft whine of a child.

She knew she could ask him for anything, and he would do what he could to deliver.

"What do you need, dear?" he asked smiling like a Cheshire cat.

Martha began to talk to him about a mall that one of her friends had told her about in a Virginia suburb close to D.C. The mall, Tysons Corner, was somewhat fancy but Martha had been told it would be worth the trip. Warren smiled and kissed his wife on the cheek.

"Anything for you, dear!" he replied.

While Martha knew she had a certain power over Warren, like the expensive jewelry that she hoped to see at Tysons, she also knew she should only use that power for special occasions.

Proceeding to the car, Warren looked over his shoulder, inhaled deeply, and smiled. He had done what he had wanted to do so many years ago—see the Washington Monument and White House in person. They would use the rest of their time in Washington to get to know the people and the history. They wanted to get a feel for what their tax dollars were being put to use for. However, on their first day in Washington, they had promised each other that they'd do something special.

The drive out of the district was a simple one. A taxi cab driver told them to follow Constitution Avenue west, which eventually ended up on I-66. The interstate would take them directly into Virginia, and then they were instructed to get on 267 West. They couldn't miss the exit signs for Tysons Corner.

Although there was a navigational system in the car, Warren didn't use it. He was not a man who liked too much technology, and he enjoyed doing things the old way. He often laughed when people came to him for help when there was a prolonged power shortage and the equipment they relied on so much was nothing more than a dead box.

Martha opened up a map that had been placed in the glove compartment and began to bark out directions. Like a good soldier, Warren followed. They both noticed several cars that whizzed past them or would blow horns as if they were doing something wrong. Unfazed, Warren drove the speed limit. The good thing about the Cadillac was it kept most of the sound out. Warren had never gotten a ticket and refused to start now.

The light in front of him turned red, and he eased to a stop. With both hands on the wheel, he turned and looked at his wife. She smiled at him, and he smiled back feeling a bit aroused by the way he was taking control.

He whispered, "I love you."

She smiled like a school girl with a crush. He was still the only one who could get her face to turn bright red just with a look. Warren veered onto Route 7. After resting at a signal light, he heard a honk from somewhere and realized the light must be green.

Before he pushed the accelerator to drive, Martha screamed. The only thing she saw was the front of a large black Hummer with chrome bars barreling down on them, head on.

The crash tore away most of the front of the Cadillac and killed Warren and Martha instantly. Several people gasped in horror at the sight and sound of the crash. Although the airbags had deployed, they didn't stop the force of the truck. The passenger side door was open and mangled almost beyond recognition. Warren's bloody body was wedged against the steering wheel. The accident could have been a commercial showing the durability and strength of the Hummer. Its front right fender and hood were damaged but not a mangled mess.

Several drivers brought their vehicles to a screeching halt, and about five men went into heroic mode, helping in whatever way they could, despite the chaos and car parts strewn everywhere. Black smoke began to billow out from the back of what was left of the Cadillac, which made it difficult to see. One man froze in horror as he realized that what he had just kicked out of his way was the head of Martha Morgan. It slammed up against the curb. Women on the street screamed, while two other men moved towards the Hummer to assist the driver so he could get out of his vehicle. The accident was clearly his fault, but safety came first.

The driver's door creaked and a large muscular black man tumbled out screaming. He was struggling at first but within a minute seemed to be able to stand up. The two men tried to help the driver, but he began to swing at them with the sheer might of his body. He knocked one would-be good Samaritan to the ground and tossed the other aside as if he wasn't worth the effort. He looked around like a crazed animal, and then took off running. Although he was easy to spot, no one was brave enough to follow.

Chapter 2

The buzzing sound of an alarm meshed into the dream that Charles Brown was having about his ex-wife, Deloris, yelling at him like always. Her voice turned into one long whining buzz like that of his alarm clock. Half asleep, he laughed, which was something he rarely did nowadays, but the dream's significance was too funny to ignore.

"Come on, Charles. Get up," he told himself as his conscious mind fought to reestablish itself.

Blinking sleepily, he found himself staring into the face of his little Beagle named X. From experience, X knew to let Charles sleep until the alarm went off. He got trained this way after an incident a long time ago when he made the mistake of barking before Charles was ready to get up and ended up with a shoe to the mouth. It's not that Charles had a quick temper, but there were certain moments when he should've let a sleeping giant sleep.

Charles reached out his arm, which felt like a thousand pounds, to turn off the old-fashioned clock's alarm. He liked the old-fashioned items and felt an affinity with time itself. Every night he had to wind the clock, and anyone in the room could hear it ticking as the springs did their job. To Charles, the ticking sound of a clock was a symbol of his very being. Every day he had to wind himself up. He hated his life, or at least what had become of it. During his marriage, his wife had given birth to a son whom they named Malcolm.

By the time Malcolm was five years old, Charles rarely got to see him, because his ex-wife and her new husband moved to another state. But even if they had lived in the same town, the judge would have made sure he only had a limited amount of time with his child. The reason that was given was that his job and his stress would not be a proper environment for raising a young boy. As much as Charles hated to admit it, deep down he knew the assessment was correct.

"What in the world am I doing?" he asked himself while shaking his head.

He didn't have to work today. In fact, he may not have a job at all. He screwed up big time trying to work a lead on a murder case. He took things into his own hands and didn't follow procedure. The woman was already dead, but as he unloaded his gun into the suspect, he knew it would get him into trouble.

Either way, life for him would get a lot worse but he surmised that at least one more bad guy would be off the streets. The male suspect was only twenty-two years old, white, rich, and good looking, a combination that spelled trouble from the onset.

His father owned several shopping malls, homes, and other real estate investments. Charles estimated that the suspect's father was worth close to 20 million dollars. After the autopsy, they said the woman died of an accidental death, but Charles believed otherwise—too many things didn't add up.

"Oh, well," he reassured himself, "at least I'm not spending time in some prison with a bunch of men that I put there. Life could be worse."

"What do you do at 4:00 a.m. when you really have nothing to do?" he thought to himself.

It was too early to jog, so he flicked on the TV that stood on a nightstand in his bedroom. He sat there in a daze and flipped through channel after channel. Nothing grabbed his attention. His dog, X, cocked his head to the side and whined. He appeared to look at Charles as though he were a worthless piece of crap.

Charles gave him a swift tap on the head. It wasn't hard but just enough to let him know not to look at him that way again. X growled for a second, lifted his head, and then walked away like a servant that had just been disciplined by his master but was powerless do anything about it. At least he would have his dignity as he seemed to lift his tail showing Charles where to kiss.

Charles made a mental note to himself to be overly affectionate to him later and maybe make up for his wrongdoings. Although he was not a big fan of the mushy stuff, he could turn it on if he had to. Heck, he figured he had even gotten married once because of it.

Flicking through the channels, he moaned at the selections.

"Is this what the weirdos watch late at night, or early in the morning?" he mused out loud.

One minute there was an infomercial for men who wanted to make their private parts bigger, and then a moment later, a large man was selling knives and exclaiming how sharp they were. Next, he happened onto a channel showing an old black and white movie that wasn't good during its time and still wasn't good today.

"I don't really know why I had the cable installed," he sighed.

Bored with watching TV, he decided to turn it off and pick up a book. He rationalized that at least he could read until around 5:30, before going for his jog.

Walking to the manmade office that he had constructed by placing a bunch of books on a table, along with a writing pad, laptop, and trash can off to one side, he took a seat on an old black worn-out chair that he had picked up from a garage sale for a few bucks. Pushing papers aside and thumbing through a few books, he finally decided to read something that would improve his mind rather than entertain him.

Scanning through the titles, he stopped at a book called, *The Principles and Power of Vision*, by Dr. Myles Munroe.

"I don't remember buying this," he said, but figured he may have to find another job soon and could use some vision.

Opening the book, he read a hand scribbled note on the inner page that said that he was destined for great things. It soon became the second time he laughed today as he thought about his current situation.

He felt it would be a pretty good read, even though it was one of those spiritual religious books.

"A man needs a dream; needs to have some sort of vision."

Not bad at all, Charles thought, as he examined a few pages. Some of the words he read came back to him as a book that he must have read a long time ago. The next few hours seemed to fly by quickly considering the amount of pages he had read. He noticed the sun coming up and plotted out his jogging route in his mind. Jogging had always been his form of religion, which revealed that he could push his body and in turn push his mind.

"Who knows, maybe when everything is all said and done, I could become a runner," he sarcastically thought to himself, still lamenting over his situation.

In the past, when he decided to participate, he had won several ironman events, and if he really focused, maybe he could make some money through running. Anything was possible.

After putting on an old pair of New Balance running shoes, grey shorts, and a white T-shirt, he whistled for his faithful dog and off they went. Although X had aged a little, he was still in good shape. They began to run around the neighborhood until they hit the main road at the end of the block.

Although there was very little traffic at this time of morning, he tried to keep alert. Birds chirped in the air and a slight fog rose off the ground in front of him. It was a good feeling, and the more he ran, the more energy he felt he had. Short of having a woman in bed with him, he felt this was the next best thing to getting the euphoric high that he got while being in love.

A late model Crown Victoria, with light blue paint and a small dent on the driver's side drove past him. He tried to memorize as much as he could, figuring that he never knew when he might need that information in his line of work. He squinted to try to get a glimpse of the driver—a woman in her early thirties.

Judging by how high she sat in her car's seat, either she was super short and had to boost the seat up, or she was a taller than average lady. He couldn't make out her eyes but he could see the details and shape of her face. In a moment, she was gone, but he figured he could pull her up out of a lineup anytime. Besides, he had memorized her license plate number.

He liked to push himself hard while running the last mile, as he thought of himself as something more than a cop. Maybe it was sheer determination, or maybe it was anger. Nevertheless, he did it because he could, and today he ran the last mile like a man on fire. His legs throbbed and his chest burned. His heart pounded wildly like it was going to pop out, but he kept going. His poor dog struggled to keep up, but X had little choice. Either he ran to keep up with his owner, or he would die and be dragged the rest of the way home.

Once back in front of their house, both man and beast bent over panting and tried to catch their breath. Several cars were out on the streets now and although most of them were his neighbors' vehicles, they still slowed down to make sure everything was okay.

Charles forced himself to stand rather than incline his body in a bent-over stance. He inhaled the crisp morning air deeply. He felt alive and ready to take on the world. X, on the other hand, would probably rather sleep the rest of the day. There was no guarantee that he would even awaken to eat.

Sweaty hands grasped the door, and he flung it open as though he was announcing himself to the world. But today there would be no cheering from the crowd and that was okay with him. The hardest part at the moment was trying to figure out what to do with the rest of his day, let alone the rest of his life.

The rest of the day part he figured would be the easiest; he could do nothing yet find simple things with very little substance to occupy his time. He went to the movies and watched a horror show that was hardly worth the price of admission. He hung out at a Starbucks and watched people. He did anything to waste time but nothing proved good enough to fill the void.

Looking at the sky, he realized it was finally getting dark. He thanked God for the mercy of night and the feeling that another day was ending. Placing his hands on his head, he felt that if this was going to be his life, then he wished he were dead.

Returning home, he walked towards his bedroom and flicked on the TV to give himself background noise while he took a shower. Undressing, he admired himself in the mirror, and figured that he didn't look too bad for a thirty-year-old. His strong musky scent was masked well by the sweet smell of jasmine deodorant that he had used earlier. But his body dripped with perspiration from the hot muggy day, and the deodorant's scent had evaporated. Now his skin was beginning to feel sticky.

The hot shower began to steam the mirror, which was his signal that it was time to get in. He imagined the hot water cascading down his back, and massaging his shoulder. X was already curled up in the corner of the room, and he barely lifted his head to acknowledge his master walking past him.

"Ha," he exclaimed, "just like my wife!" Then he corrected himself and said loudly, "my ex-wife."

A news flash on the TV grabbed his attention as a black woman in her thirties spoke with the energy of a twenty-year-old. She stood in front of several police cars as if she were trying to ready herself to shock the world.

"Xavier Wilson is wanted for vehicular manslaughter, running from the scene of a crime, assault, and several other charges. Police say he ran a light and crashed his car into what appears to be the mangled wreck of a Cadillac."

The camera widened to show the damage behind her and then it panned back in for a close-up.

"Both passengers in the other car are dead. Police officials stated that one of the victims was decapitated. Xavier is considered extremely dangerous. If anyone knows of his whereabouts, they should contact the police immediately. Angela Stark signing off."

The news channel was silent for a moment and then the announcers moved on to the next story. Charles stood motionless in front of his television set. He could not believe what he had just heard.

Xavier was his hero from long ago. In fact, it was him who had signed the book about vision that he'd just been reading earlier. Xavier was the football player that Charles had always wanted to be. He even named his dog, X, short for Xavier.

Chapter 3

Xavier's quick rhythmic pace slowed to almost a crawl as he shielded his eyes from the glare of the harsh streetlights. His thoughts challenged him to understand why he was running in the first place. He squinted and stared at the row of homes directly in front of him. It was at that moment that it dawned on him that none of the homes were his.

"What the heck is happening to me?" he said to himself, not sure of where he was or even if this was his neighborhood.

He lifted his wrist closer to his face to get a better view of what time it was on his gold and diamond, black, limited edition Rolex watch. Straining against the darkness, he realized that six hours had passed. His body ached all over as if he had just been in a game, which in a way felt good, but he knew was impossible. It had been thirteen years since he retired and his playing days were long gone.

He moved toward a row of townhomes that each had their own source of outdoor lighting. He glanced down at his tired body and noticed that his shirt was ripped and that he had blood on his hands. He wiped his forehead with his arm and saw more blood.

His mind began racing as he tried to piece the events together about what had happened and why he was running and not driving his Hummer. The last thing he remembered was that he was in his house, then he remembered the darkness, and now he was here.

He moved his hand to his back pocket wondering if maybe he had been robbed and because of the struggle, he had been hit and lost his memory. He doubted that was true since his Rolex was still on his wrist, but any theory was better than none. Reaching around to his back pocket he found his wallet, which was still there as he had expected. He would have been disappointed had it been otherwise.

He opened the wallet and saw several crisp hundred dollar bills, an American Express card, a MasterCard, Visa and several other discount cards. Everything was still there so he ruled out the theory about someone robbing him. He reasoned that there had to be a good explanation.

"Got to think, got to think," he mumbled.

His mind was like a blank canvas waiting for a picture to appear. He looked at his surroundings again and then realized that he was near Tysons Corner, which was nearly twenty miles from his home.

"Okay," he hollered, feeling like a mini detective figuring out a case. "That means I had to have driven here. I don't see my Hummer so maybe it was a carjacking."

Pride and cockiness jumped in as he imagined himself putting up a huge fight before being knocked upside the head. There was no doubt that there had to be more than one of them because he couldn't see himself being overpowered by one man alone, gun or no gun.

Looking around, he figured that it was best to let policemen do their jobs. He headed for the nearest house to use a phone after he realized his cell phone wasn't with him. That part worried him, but most of the important numbers on his phone were coded and he would cancel his number after he contacted the police.

Looking around he surmised that the mall was about two miles away and he could easily jog or walk to it, but he was worn out. He knocked on the nearest wooden door for no particular reason other than the fact that it was close.

He waited a few moments, not really sure that if he had been on the other side of the door and had seen a large black man through the peephole, that he would open the door. One more try and then he would just walk to the mall. He was sure that he could get help there. This was just simpler.

As he turned to walk away, the door opened, slowly at first, and then enough to reveal a small Asian woman. He never really had a thing for Asian women—too small and not enough meat on their bones, but with all things considered, she was pretty.

She looked at him cautiously but still curious to see what was wrong. Xavier thought that if she had lived in his old neighborhood, she might have been in for a world of trouble opening the door for a stranger. He rationalized that maybe she knew karate or something like that. He had seen the movies before and had a great appreciation for what somebody could do, and better yet, the knowledge of what the body could do at the command of a skilled master.

He tried to speak in a slow almost childish tone hoping that she would understand. He also didn't want to offend her.

"Phone," he said, stretching out the word for as long as he thought necessary for her to interpret.

She smiled at him, and he assumed that she was looking at his bloodied shirt. Then she bowed. Repeating his words, she took him by the hand and led him inside her home.

He almost hated the thought of taking advantage of her innocence, but he felt that it would be a great opportunity to educate her. He made a mental note that after he made his call to the police that he would give her a bit of his sage advice.

In his mind, it would go something like this, "There are a lot of bad people in the world. You should be more careful about whom you let into your home, including me."

Glancing at the sparsely furnished room, he quickly tried to figure out her life. From what he could tell, she was single, although that was just at a quick glance. A small TV stood in the far corner of the room on an all-black lacquered stand. He could tell it was something that would be found at a cheap knockoff store or maybe in the mall but certainly not at a high-priced furniture store.

Three pictures were hung neatly on the wall, each with an Asian woman performing a task—writing, smelling flowers, and bowing down as a giant Buddha faintly praised her in the background. A single black sofa was diagonally positioned in the middle of the room. That was it.

Xavier wondered where the guest would sit. He noticed her shoes were off to the side near the front door, and when he had entered her home, he had removed his shoes as a sign of respect to the owner.

The family room led straight into the kitchen and dining room area, which consisted of a glass table decorated with a vase of flowers, and four black chairs. An aroma filled the air, which had a scent that he was not quite sure what to make of it, but he liked it.

"Phone," she said, interrupting his thoughts.

She gently took him by the arm and led him towards the phone. For a moment, he was amazed at her unusual kindness. In his life experiences, kindness was just a ruse until either they worked up the nerve to ask for what they wanted, or it was merely a ploy to invade his inner sanctuary. Then they'd use him for all that he was worth.

She pointed a small childlike finger at the phone, which hung on the wall. Xavier smiled thinking to himself that she was so behind the times with her wall phone. Didn't she have a cell phone he could use? She returned the smile with a shyness that he felt was refreshing.

As he began dialing the number, she turned and walked towards the kitchen. He promised himself not to look, but he couldn't help glancing at her butt. It was not something he was proud of, but he liked what he saw. Not bad, a little flat, but not bad.

A female voice came on the line and said, "9-1-1, how can I help you?"

Xavier cleared his throat and then told her that he thought he had been mugged.

She responded in a condescending tone, "You *think* you have been mugged?"

Xavier rolled his eyes and wondered if his statement had sounded half-stupid. His biggest problem was that he was a nice guy and really didn't like to cause trouble. On the playing field, if there was a problem, he could hit someone in the mouth and the problem was solved. With that, he had no issue; they knew what they signed up for. But outside the game, he always tried to look at things from every perspective.

"I really don't know what happened," Xavier said, his confidence a little shaken.

He was now trying to picture how he would sound to himself if he were on the other end of the phone call. The young Asian woman returned with a bowl of hot water and a few herbs that were thrown in.

She took a cloth, dipped it in the water, and began to dab it on his head. Although the water was hot and he had no idea what type of herbs were floating around, he figured what the heck. How could he refuse when she had gone out of her way to make him feel comfortable?

The water stung for a moment, and then like a nice cool ice cube on a hot day, his skin began to feel much better. Xavier smiled and tried to bow in return, while continuing with his phone conversation. He wanted to show her his great appreciation. She smiled in return and continued what she was doing.

The female on the phone was not gracious like his host.

She repeated her question, "Sir, were you mugged or not? I don't understand how you wouldn't know the difference."

Xavier tried to explain that he didn't remember the last few hours and that when he apparently became conscious again, that he didn't know where he was. He further explained that he knocked on someone's door to use their phone with the intention of calling the police.

The conversation went on for a few minutes longer. Then she asked if he was feeling okay, and if he knew the location of where he was calling from. Her final question, in Xavier's mind, should have been near the top of her list.

"What's your name, sir?"

"Xavier. Xavier Wilson," he replied.

The phone went dead for a moment as if the call had been dropped. Xavier had to speak into the receiver to make sure that he was still connected.

"Are you there?" he asked, starting to feel a little bit annoyed.

The operator responded, "Sir, I'm glad you're okay. Did you say that someone was with you?"

Xavier sensed that her voice sounded shaky. Earlier she had given him the impression that he was bothering her by asking for help, but now it appeared that she was going out of her way to be overly kind.

Xavier replied, "Yes," but he still wasn't sure why her tone of voice had suddenly changed.

"Sir," she continued, "is the person you're with okay, and can you give us the person's name?"

Xavier felt foolish that he hadn't taken the time to find out his host's name.

He cupped his hand over the phone, and asked, "Excuse me, what is your name?"

After a few moments of trying to explain what he just said, she finally understood.

She said, "Name Le. Le."

Her name is Le, Xavier thought. He was even more impressed with her that she was able to live in a place alone from what he could tell and barely speak English.

He removed his hand from the receiver and told the 9-1-1 operator, "Her name is Le."

The operator sighed as if she were disconnecting a bomb and had just cut the correct wire.

"May I speak with her?" the operator asked, still sounding sweet and angelic.

Xavier started to hand the phone to Le and he told her, "The police want to talk to you."

He seemed to be striking out lately by saying all the wrong words, because as soon as he said, "police," the young Asian lady's face changed.

She thrust her hand forward, and hollered, "No police, no police."

Chapter 4

A small, two-bedroom stucco home nestled in the middle of a quiet cul-de-sac that was surrounded by homes with similar architectural designs produced a nondescript example of its occupants. All lawns were neatly groomed, all driveways had two parked vehicles, and all address numbers—made of cheap brass and found at any home improvement store—were affixed to each home's mailbox.

Breaking the silence of an all-too-common night, a dog barked. Its lone sound echoed through the darkness. The neighborhood was the type of place where everyone knew everyone yet no one really knew anyone. In fact, politeness was only a surface gesture that was used as a shield to keep people from getting to know each other on a deeper level. It allowed no one to peer into the darkness that could sometimes possess a man's soul.

A door slammed against its wooden frame with such a strong force that it brought an onslaught of even fiercer barking from the neighboring dogs. Several once-dark homes sprung to life with the quick flickering of a light that illuminated their front lawns, while other homes remained dark as if trying to hide in the emptiness of the night.

A young woman frantically waved her middle finger in the air, gesturing at the male figure standing in the doorway. His menacing stare and fiery eyes revealed his fearless and immovable stance.

With an ear-piercing wail, she screamed several curse words at him, yet he remained motionless. His rigid body didn't budge an inch, no matter how close she got and regardless of how loud she wailed.

Everything inside of him, the man named Harold Fisher, wanted to grab her and choke the life out of her, but he waited. He had trained for this moment, dreamt of this moment, and had planned out every phase of what would happen, but he had to focus. He couldn't ruin the outcome by giving in to his emotions.

The woman, Miriam Fisher, his wife, stood about five-foot-four, although she normally wore high-heeled pumps that made her appear several inches taller. Sandy blonde hair swept across her reddened face as she yelled the words that she believed could destroy the man in front of her.

"Why in the hell would I ever want to stay with you? You're a worthless piece of shit!" she said, in a loud voice that she hoped her neighbors would hear.

Harold stood still, like a mannequin. He just glared at her and didn't say a word.

Rage filled her body and all of her past insecurities came rushing to the forefront of her mind. Her natural pent-up response was about to explode. She lowered her body position like a linebacker getting ready to make a tackle. Then she rushed, full force, at her opponent who stood steadfastly in front of her. It appeared that she was determined to hurt him as a trained professional player would do to his opponent and that nothing could stop her.

To him, it was almost comical seeing her little feet running as fast as they could, while carrying her aging body. Nevertheless, he knew that she moved with the force of someone who wanted to cause pain.

As he sized up the situation, he cracked a slight smile realizing that what was happening at this very moment was not far out of the realm of what he had dreamt about two nights ago. In his dream, they were outside. She had begun to lunge at him, and just as she was ready to impact his body with her deadly blow, he had taken one step to the left. Then he grabbed her and the next thing he heard was her neck snapping. Then she fell to the ground.

In that flash of a second, time seemed to move in super slow speed— not quite slow motion, but like the slow frames that used to appear on the big screen in shades of ancient black-and-white silent films.

He could see her coming at him. He could see the hate in her eyes. When he held his breath, he knew that this was what he had been waiting for. He moved to the side just as he had planned and then, then, nothing. He took the full force of her blow as she knocked him to the ground.

This was the only part of the dream that had not come true. This was the part that no matter what he dreamt, it would never become a reality.

The point was that when everything had been said and done, at the end of the day, he was still a coward. He was afraid of her and now as if in some funny bizarre world, *he* was the abused spouse, and she was the one committing the crime.

Several more blows came across his head and he took them. In fact, he welcomed them. In his demented mind, this was part of his training. He had to learn how to endure pain. He had to learn how to separate his body from his mind—not separate, but embrace the pain from body to mind.

Sweat began to drip off her face, as she appeared to wear down. Both of them were out of shape, but she was more out of shape than he was. As newlyweds a few years ago, she had a drop-dead gorgeous figure—the kind that was not too skinny like high-fashion models, but the kind that you would see in a *Playboy* magazine or everyday book featuring real women.

Out of his dream-state mental fog, he heard her bellow, "I hate you. I hate you."

Harold calmly smiled, looked at Miriam, grabbed her arm, and for the first time in his life, he stood up for himself and said to her, "Then leave!"

Miriam appeared to be in shock—frozen in disbelief.

It was something she never really expected, although she undoubtedly understood why. They had fought like this many times in the past, and she would always be the victor. He had gone to jail once for domestic violence, and then at other times he was written up for drug charges. All she had to do was say that he had abused her again, or report his little secret, and he would be gone for a long time.

For him, that was his biggest fear—the fear of going back; the fear of what they would do to him.

She knew about his fears and up until now, she always used it to her advantage. However, tonight it was different. She knew that a deep emotion had been stirred up inside of him. For the first time since she had known him, he talked back.

"You heard me," he said in a weak, timid voice. "Go ahead and leave. I don't need you anymore."

Miriam was speechless, feeling a hurtful pride well up in her throat, but that quickly turned into anger. She was mad. In fact, she was downright pissed off. How could her little man tell her to leave? Their fights had become a habit. The physical abuse was a habit. But when he told her to leave, to her, he had taken their relationship beyond the imaginary line and boundaries she had created in her mind.

Quickly, she formulated a plan, because she never wanted to be outdone by that weasel of a man she had married. She looked at him with cold, piercing, blue eyes and walked calmly back into the house. It was as if she had somehow fallen into a trance, and was being pulled away from him by an unseen force.

He pondered what she might do, but for that matter, he feared for what he was capable of doing to her. Minutes passed. The silence grew large. Somewhere deep inside he wanted to believe that standing his ground would cause her to change, but in his heart, he knew better. She was not wired like that. Maybe that's why he fell in love with her in the first place, and maybe that was why he feared her.

Getting up from the ground, he followed her into the house. His greatest hope was that during their little fight, the neighbors had somehow magically slept through it.

He opened the door just in time to see her run face first into the wall. Her head made a sickening thumping sound as her skull crashed into the immovable stud behind the plaster wall. She stepped back, dazed, as a large, reddish-brown lump began to swell in the center of her forehead.

She shook her head to regain her senses and then ran into the wall again. This time she missed the beam but made a large hole where several pictures had once been hanging. Rolling out of the mess, she laid face up on the wooden floor.

Before she blacked out, she looked at him and smiled.

Chapter 5

As Xavier stood in Le's family room, he hesitated for a moment, not sure what to do. He expected that he might have a problem with trying to explain his sudden memory loss, but he certainly didn't need the police coming to a total stranger's home to help him. Xavier looked at her again and tried to say the words slower this time. He figured that it might have sounded like something else.

"Police," he said, letting the words form around his mouth and ease out in such a way that he thought would be more easily understood.

She reacted by bowing and smiling, which left him feeling frustrated.

The operator on the line was now yelling his name. Xavier hated being caught in between the two people—one yelling and the other smiling and bowing. He looked at Le and then placed the phone back against his ear.

"Yes, I'm here," he said, catching the tail end of her hollering.

"Is everything all right?" the operator asked, this time with a voice mixed with fear and desperation.

Xavier noticed the change in her voice, but he didn't think much of it. In fact, he figured it might have been because she recognized his name and was excited to be actually talking to him.

"She doesn't want to come to the phone," he said, trying to sound calm.

He always remembered something that a speech coach had taught him a long time ago. "If you talk calm, people will calm down around you." It was good advice and Xavier had used it during the years when he played ball and talked with reporters. Now he figured he would put the old charm on again and calm things down.

"No police," Le whispered, her voice filled with a mixture of fright and pleading.

Her eyes begged Xavier to hang up, but he knew that he couldn't just drop the conversation. After all, he had dialed 9-1-1, he was in trouble, and needed help. He lifted his hand as if to stop a young child from talking while an adult was on the phone.

Le stopped in mid-sentence, politely bowed her head, and stayed quiet, submitting to his request. The operator, on the other hand, was now pressing the issue and becoming somewhat rude, or at least it felt that way to Xavier.

"I have to go," he told the operator with the same tone of voice that she had spoken to him.

Holding his breath, he hung up the phone.

Le looked at him surprised but with great appreciation. She bowed to him several times, so much, in fact, that once more and he would stop her.

He wasn't sure what was going on but figured it was time to find out. No money or anything else seemed to be missing from his wallet. Whatever Le had put on his head seemed to be working, so he figured the police could wait.

"You okay. No police," he said, sounding like a poor white man's attempt at speaking Chinese.

She took his hand into hers and held it as if it were something of great value. He looked down and noticed the sharp contrast in color and size of their hands. His hand nearly engulfed the small, pale, white hand that cupped around his dark massive meat hooks. She searched his eyes as if looking to see if he would be someone that she could trust. Maybe she figured she had gone this far so why not trust him. Or maybe it was the fact that she sensed that she could.

Xavier was trustworthy even to a fault, and if she told him something in secrecy, then it would stay there.

"I…" she started saying, but then paused and squinted as if to squeeze the proper word out of her mouth. "I no citizen," she whispered.

Her English was still better than several American citizens he had known in his past. Xavier squeezed her hand gently to let her know that he understood. Although he believed that people needed to become citizens, he also believed that America was a land of second chances. Sometimes it took awhile to do everything right.

"Where are you from?" he asked, trying to make conversation while at the same time putting her mind at ease.

She looked at him and then cocked her head to the side, the way his dog X did when he didn't understand his orders completely.

"From?" she repeated, and then as if a light had suddenly gone on in her head, she smiled, and said, "Korea."

Xavier was now excited because he knew how to say hello to her in her language, and like Christmas, he couldn't wait to give the surprise.

"Annyong ha shimnikka," he said, almost shouting it into her face.

Her small eyes opened wide with the exciting possibilities of having someone to speak the same language as her. She began to talk rapid fire in her own language.

Xavier almost didn't want to be the one to stop her and ruin the excitement, but he had to. He had no idea what she was talking about, although it reminded him of some past girlfriends as they had spoken about their shopping adventures.

Interrupting her, he smiled and said, "That's it," to indicate that hello was the only word he knew.

At first, she didn't get it, but slowly it must have sunk in because her excitement faded to plain old politeness. Xavier began to study her, and they both stood in silence. He tried to figure out how a woman who could barely speak English was able to afford the nice townhouse, even if it was sparsely furnished. His mind raced with the possibilities.

Scanning the room once more, he looked for any sign that someone other than her might live in the house. He came up empty and decided to venture into other possibilities. Maybe she was one of those masseuses who he had always seen advertising their services in the newspaper at the bottom of the sports section. If that were true, then that would explain why she wanted no police. It seemed that most of those places did more than give massages.

He looked at her again and tried to figure if she fit the bill as to what one of those girls might have looked like. Naw, he told himself, almost embarrassed that he had even thought of such a thing. Maybe she was a kept woman. It seemed like Asian women were the big thing nowadays, and maybe someone was taking care of her. Again, he felt like he was not giving her any credit and tried to drop the issue.

"Maybe I should go walk to the mall," he said, feeling that the longer he stayed the more he would clump her into every stereotypical group he could think of for an Asian woman.

As he started to step back and pull his hand away, he felt a slight resistance in her hand as they separated. He bowed to her, feeling that in her house he should show respect and conform to her customs.

Without warning, both of them jumped as a loud squealing sound of sirens and flashing lights broke through just outside the front door. An immediate rush of blood pulsed from Xavier's heart into what seemed to be a direct shot to his brain.

Le appeared frightened and ran to his side for protection, like a child would run to her daddy. Several more cars swarmed in, as if out of nowhere, with their tires screeching to a halt.

Things were happening fast and Xavier felt as though he had been caught up in some sort of twilight zone. His mind tried to retrace the steps he had taken since coming into the house. He also tried to figure out just who this lady was who was now hiding behind his waist. What was she hiding?

A loud speaker came on with the thunderous voice of a man calling him by name.

"Xavier Wilson, this is the police. The place is surrounded. Come out with your hands up and let the hostage go."

Chapter 6

Charles had forgotten that he was standing naked in front of his television set watching the breaking news about Xavier. Although Charles wasn't modest, he still didn't like exposing himself if only to his dog.

Steam made its way outside the bathroom and began to cause a light gray overcast above his bed. He could care less about the moisture ruining his furniture or damaging the walls, but he had to face facts. He was a single man now, possibly without a job and definitely without a paycheck. Expenses such as wasted water were not something he could afford.

Deciding to chance missing a break in the event, he figured he could take a quick, two-minute shower and be back in front of the TV before anything else happened. Besides, he reminded himself that he wasn't on the case, and if he did miss something important, it would undoubtedly be played again during another newscast.

The hot water from the shower felt good against his body and completed the final segment of his day. He lathered himself as fast as he could but still enough to feel clean. Although he wasn't super self-conscious about his hygiene, he hated being unable to shower.

Perhaps it was the result of his years on the force and taking a shower was the only thing he could do to clean his hands of death, murder, and evil that surrounded him. He rubbed the soap over his chest and felt the scars where he had been stabbed, and then just above his right bicep where a small hole from a .22 had made a nice valley for resting water.

Every injury was part of who he was, yet the biggest injury was to his heart. As much as he hated to admit it, he was lonely...and tonight a little horny. He washed, moving ever closer to a point of taking care of his horniness himself and then he stopped. He figured that he never knew what tomorrow might bring.

In a flash, he was done and felt clean; all temptation had been washed away as the water slowly slipped down the drain. He wiped away the steam from the glass of an old clock that hung on the bathroom wall. He noticed that he had actually taken ten minutes for his shower instead of two, but he relished the feeling of relief as the shower had eased some of his tension.

In his mind, he tried to comprehend why someone like Xavier would commit such a crazy crime. Although his heart told him that the man he knew could never have done such a thing, the detective inside of him knew that when drugs were involved, anything was possible.

He even rubbed his hand over his small gunshot wound above his bicep as he thought about the little old lady who had shot him trying to protect her marijuana.

X barked again as if on cue as the phone began to ring. Wrapping the towel around his small waist, he trotted next to his bed and answered the phone.

"Speak," he said, as if talking into a mike the same way he had answered at work while shifting through a flood of calls.

There was silence on the other end, and then the voice of a woman came on. He knew her voice too well, because he had heard it at least once a week, every week for most of his adult life.

"Hello, Mom," he said, trying to apologize for the way he answered.

Like him, she jumped straight to the point, and asked, "Baby, have you been watching the news?"

He wanted to say, "What do you think, Sherlock?" but he knew that was out of the question. The last time he had smart-mouthed her, he heard crying and then she refused to return his phone calls.

"Yes, ma'am, I'm watching it now."

No matter how old he got, he knew and would always try to give her all the respect he could muster. She had raised him as a single mom working two jobs until he was able to support himself. His father died when he was young and so she was all he had—the very rock of his life.

There was a pause and then she asked, "What do you think about what they're saying about him?"

It was a simple question, but it dug deep enough to make him speak.

He replied with a question of his own, but he knew it only delayed the inevitable.

"What do you mean, what do I think? I've seen this type of thing before," he answered in a nonchalant way.

"What do you think of it?"

Neither one of them gave an answer, but continued to have the conversation as though it would eventually answer itself.

"Yea, but he was your hero. Don't tell me you've forgotten him already, especially after all he did for you."

She hit him with a fact that he wasn't ready to face yet. His life was a mess; he was divorced and couldn't see his kid; he'd been suspended from work without pay, and was nearly broke. Now the man whom he had looked up to, and whom had helped mold his life in a long-forgotten past was locked up in some townhouse with a hostage. He could now no longer classify him as a hero.

"He's no hero of mine," Charles said.

His mother seemed surprised by the coldness in his voice but continued bringing up long-forgotten memories from his past.

"You used to collect all his football cards, and you even wore his jersey number in high school. You wore that jersey so much that it started to fall apart before the end of the school year."

Charles hated that she was right, and he wanted to go back to the cold, hard, unfeeling cop attitude—the attitude that made him a good cop in hard situations.

She continued, "Remember when you were on the verge of dropping out of school?"

Charles felt the embarrassment of almost quitting, something that he promised himself that he would never do again. A deep sting burned inside of him as he was forced to relive his past. He was not proud of his failures, under-achievement, and nearly dropping out was one of them.

"You used to write letters to Xavier. He returned a few of them and sent you that book that helped get you back on track." She paused, and then murmured, "Something about vision."

It hit him and now he remembered the book he had read in the morning, before everything that had happened—the book, *Power of Vision* had been sent to him by his hero, Xavier.

Charles was not a superstitious man, but the fact that he had awakened early this morning and had read that book sent a shiver up his spine. Like true synchronicity, it was something his mom would have said that God was speaking to him.

Charles wanted to chalk it up to coincidence—nothing more and nothing less. He defiantly wouldn't let his mother know that he had read the book that morning, because he knew it would mean an additional thirty minutes of quoting the Bible, praising God, and telling him what he needed to do.

Instead, Charles just chose to tell her, "Mom, I'm not a cop anymore, and there's nothing I can do. As much as I would like to feel sorry for him, I have seen way too many good people go bad for one reason or another. You know as well as I do that we all walk that fine line between good and evil, and he may have just crossed over to the other side."

His mother was silent for awhile, but then she said, "There are still heroes left in the world, and you're one of them. I think you're making a mistake about Xavier, and I don't know why. Call it instinct or the Holy Spirit speaking to me, but I feel like he is not what everyone is portraying on TV."

He wanted to tell her to look at facts, and that the TV doesn't lie, but he knew he didn't even believe that himself. A news reporter had told the world that he was an overzealous cop when he had killed that kid, and that was a lie. Maybe, just maybe, the news from the TV reporter was lying about Xavier.

Chapter 7

Xavier glared at Le as the noise of the police car sirens stopped. Judging by the scuffling sounds outside, there were more than a few officers with their pistols pointed at the front door.

"What the hell have you gotten me into?" he asked Le, thinking how this could possibly soil his reputation.

Le stood only a few feet away now but she cowered next to the couch. Xavier's head began to throb as he tried to figure out what was going on and what he should do next.

Obviously, he'd obey their orders, but he reminded himself that he had to be cautious. He'd seen way too many clips of black men who had been shot full of holes for something that someone thought was a gun, only to turn out to be a cell phone or a wallet.

"This is the police. We have the place surrounded. Open the door slowly and let the woman go," the voice shouted as though the doors were paper thin.

Xavier made a move towards Le to lead her towards the door, but then she started to scream.

"It's okay. It's okay," he said, putting his hands up as if in a nondefensive manner. "I won't hurt you."

Each step he took towards her brought on a more intense scream until he finally stopped altogether and backed away.

The thunderous sound of a helicopter moved in and drowned out any noise they could make. Then through the blackness of the night sky, a spotlight searched through every crack and crevice of the house.

Xavier decided that regardless of his chances of getting shot, if she weren't willing to come out, then he would go first. Either way, he reasoned that it was some sort of wild mistake and it would soon be cleared up.

"Okay, how do they do this in the movies?" Xavier thought to himself. He wanted to get it right so the press clippings wouldn't read "Shot by accident." He figured that he would come out with his hands up. Then once he told them his story, everything would be all right, although deep down inside he knew that sometimes things didn't always go as planned.

Walking towards the door, Le, who was all of five-foot-two and about 110 pounds, moved with a swiftness that surprised him. She tried to block him from going to the door. Fear showed in her eyes as she spoke in Korean. Although Xavier didn't speak the language, he figured she was trying to say, "Please don't go through that door. Please don't!"

Grabbing her like a child by her shoulders and arms, he lifted her off the ground and placed her to his right side, which cleared his path to the door. She responded by moving like a pit bull on attack and grabbed at his leg. He tried shaking her loose, but she held on with a fierceness that would have impressed any pro scout.

Xavier thought of going outside with her still clinging to his leg but decided against it. Whatever mistaken idea they had would only be made worse with him having an Asian lady attached to his leg.

He grabbed her again; only this time a little bit firmer than he had realized and threw her to his side. She stumbled for a few moments, as if moving in slow motion, but Xavier clearly saw that she was headed for the only object that could cause her any harm.

"Shit!" Xavier yelled, reacting as a linebacker would.

He turned and tried to catch her, or at least knock her out of harm's way. His mind had already timed the space in between the TV and it falling onto her head and how much ground he had to cover to avert the accident. Five seconds was all he figured he had and knowing what his body could do, he figured he only needed four.

Moving at a speed that had been his paycheck for several years in the past, he took a giant step towards her, but then as he placed his other leg on the ground, the injury that had ended his career reclaimed its rightful place.

He stumbled and almost fell. He could only watch as Le fell backwards into the stand that held the TV, and the TV landed on top of her head with a thick thud and then rolled onto her lap. With outstretched hands, he screamed as he saw her eyes roll to the back of her head and then her eyelids fluttered and closed.

The day seemed to have gone from bad to worse, but he rationalized that he hadn't done anything wrong. He heard a policeman yelling something, but his mind was focused on the safety of the woman outstretched on the floor in front of him.

Rushing to her side, ignoring the pain that throbbed in his left knee, he moved the TV off her lap and held her gently in his arms. He wanted to move her but noticed blood slowly oozing from the top of her head. He had to act fast. He wasn't a killer, but regardless of the trouble he was in, she was in worse shape and needed immediate medical attention.

Xavier gently moved away, and then rushed to the front door. He opened it, and he quickly placed his hands above his head and interlocked his fingers. Blinding lights hit his face as he took his first step. He nearly tripped on the welcome mat as he stepped onto the porch.

He tried to holler that Le was hurt, but his voice was drowned out by the thunderous beat of the helicopters, more approaching police sirens, and the growing crowd of spectators.

Squinting from the extreme brightness of the lights, he saw shadows moving into position in front of him. Each shadow had arms outstretched, no doubt pointing a gun trained to shoot if he put up any resistance.

As if choreographed by a military expert, he was jumped from the side by three, then four, and then eight men, each trying to get a piece of him. His normal reaction would have been to swing back and protect himself, but he knew better. He just tried to protect his fall as much as possible. He landed face first on the hard concrete pavement.

As he laid face down on the ground, while being kicked and pushed, he heard one of the officers yell, "I hope you die, you black son-of-a-bitch. I hope you die."

Chapter 8

Harold thought about his life and the life he had had with Miriam. She had been everything to him. As she lay passed out on the floor in front of him, his heart began to sink. Maybe this was another one of her episodes, but maybe not. He quickly ran into the kitchen and located a towel. He dampened it and ran back to attend to his wife. Placing the cloth on her swollen forehead, he began to talk to her.

"I love you, dear. I love you."

She stirred a bit but then remained motionless with her eyes closed. They had fought before but not like this. He tried to think back to what had brought this on and then his anger began to stir. Now he remembered. He touched her head but his facial expression was a combination of a snarl and deep sorrow. He'd had this feeling before.

Earlier that evening they both had been sitting at the table. A pile of bills was stacked neatly in front of them. Harold took the first one and looked at the front. It was from American Express and it was addressed to him. However, he knew all too well that he wasn't the one who had used the card. Slowly opening the bill, he looked at his wife as if giving her a last chance to come clean.

"Tell me now and I won't get mad," he said half-jokingly, but his tone of voice was built on a foundation of truth.

Miriam only looked at him lovingly and smiled. Her look gave little comfort to Harold because they had been in this situation before. He opened the bill, and to his surprise, the balance was only $1,000.00. He sighed knowing that he would really have to put in some overtime to pay it off, but still he expected much worse.

She smiled at him like a little angel knowing that she had done well. He leaned over and kissed her as if it were a reward. This went on until there were only three bills left. This process was something their counselor had told them to do and was intended to keep Miriam in check with her spending habits. They both agreed to it and for the last few months, everything had been going well. Now they both smiled and looked at each other with a love that was mixed with pride and joy.

The next bill was for gas. After opening it, Harold saw that there was no drop or increase in its cost. Miriam looked down at the next bill, and her once pleasant smile became that of fear. She thought she had gotten rid of the bill that was now before her. She swallowed hard as he looked at her and then opened it.

The bill was past due and this was the third time it had been sent out. Harold looked at the numbers and his face became red with anger. He tried to control the desire to reach over and slap her when she took the initiative and lashed out at him.

"Why are you looking at me that way?" she asked. "I had to use that card to buy some things. You barely give me any money, and that's not what you promised me when we got married."

Harold had been holding back all his life. He feared his wife would leave him although lately he had been standing up to her.

"We've been through this over and over again. I can't afford to keep paying off these bills. Look at this," he said, pointing to the piece of paper, "none of this stuff is needed, and yet you keep buying. Why?"

He held the piece of paper in front of her face. Miriam sat quiet, looking guilty. By her non reply, she said everything. She had a problem and didn't know how to handle it. Shopping was her drug of choice and it was spinning out of control.

Harold went down the list, and said, "I don't even know where this stuff is, but you've got to take it back."

Miriam started to cry and then she became angry. She looked at him with cold, hate-filled eyes. The voices in her head kept telling her that this man, the man she had married, was trying to take away the only thing in life that gave her pleasure. She couldn't let that happen. Not now, not ever. She knew how to hurt him, and if anything, she would get a chance to inflict the small amount of pain that he was trying to inflict on her.

"I wouldn't have this problem if I was with..." her words trailed off as she felt herself flying off her chair.

Harold slapped her across the face. His body shook violently as he stood before her.

"Don't ever, ever mention that name in my house," Harold yelled.

Miriam got up surprisingly quick as if this was something that she was used to hearing.

"What, because you're not a man like him?" she said tauntingly.

Harold raised his hand again to swing at her, but she stood her ground, unflinching.

"Go ahead and hit me again. See if I don't call the police. Do it one more time, Harold. Just do it one more time, and you know what that means."

Harold's eyes widened, but instead of rage, there was fear. He was frightened, and she knew she had him.

He began to scream at her and felt his body tense up into an unstrung rage. Yet he was covered with a thicker layer of hurt—the type that could dig so low that it would rip your heart out from your chest as the Inca warriors did to their victims when they sacrificed to their gods.

Harold felt himself screaming but didn't even hear his own words. It was as if his spirit had floated out of his body.

He just watched the two of them go back and forth yelling at each other. At times like this, he hated her, but he hated the thought even more of losing her. She was his and no one else would have her, ever again.

Now as she lay in his arm, with her head bruised, he repeated, "I love you," in between his sobbing and tears.

Miriam blinked as his tears moistened her face. Then she heard him beginning to moan. Opening her eyes, she tried to focus on the image in front of her. It was Harold but all the anger and rage she once had for him was gone. She was just happy to see him again.

She whispered, "I'm sorry."

He put his finger gently against her lips as if to stop her from talking.

"Don't worry, dear. Buy what you want. I'll find a way to pay for it. I love you."

She smiled and then closed her eyes again. Inhaling deeply, she told Harold to kiss her. Gently, he leaned over and placed his lips on hers. He wondered if his passion could be transferred through his kiss so she would feel his love.

She sighed, smiled, and said, "I'm sorry, and I love you, too. Take me now, Harold. I'm yours."

Their anger had once again turned into passion. Although they were bruised emotionally and physically, they made love.

Chapter 9

Charles watched as they took Xavier away in handcuffs. Although the cameras were on the policemen, they still got a few punches and jabs in. No one would make a cry of police brutality after what it was assumed he had just done. It made Charles wonder what other crimes he had committed.

Although retired, Xavier still looked as though he could play football. He stood six-foot-two, and dwarfed the two shorter policemen who had led him to the car. His shoulders were still wide and muscular, which gave way to a thick forbearing neck. The only difference between his playing days and now was his lack of hair, which in some ways made him seem more dignified than when he had played.

He didn't walk like normal prisoners with their shoulders hunched and their heads hung low, as if trying to escape the onslaught of lookers. Xavier held his head high as if he were a man who had been wrongly accused of a crime and was waiting to be proven innocent.

Charles wasn't sure what to believe. How guilty could a person be? It was his Hummer. There was no doubt about that. It had twenty-six inch chrome rims, and the vanity license plate read, "x-life1." The news crew, in just a short amount of time, had already done their research. His case was as good as closed. X life 1, Charles thought to himself; how about X life to death?

Angela Stark jumped in with a quick news flash. She had already become a fixture in everyone's home who was watching News 7. Now she spoke as if she were a close friend.

"The woman…" she said, leaning forward towards the camera, as if she were telling you information that no one else had, "the woman was found unconscious on the floor of her townhouse. It's not known if she was sexually assaulted, but she's being rushed to the hospital right now."

There seemed to be a look of pity in her eyes, but it was well hidden by her professionalism. Perhaps she had once been a fan and now it was painful to report on someone she had looked up to.

"There appeared to have been some sort of a struggle in the house," she explained.

She then described the size difference between the two people—the towering black man in the house tormenting the small Asian woman. That vivid image probably popped into everyone's mind. She may as well have said that Godzilla attacked another innocent village and destroyed everything in its path.

A song by Queen sprung into Charles's mind as he finished dressing, "Another One Bites the Dust."

Charles thought for a moment and debated if he should veg-out in front of the TV for the rest of the night. Soaking up information, however, did him little good. However, he reasoned that he should try to make something out of an already ruined evening.

Out of nowhere, he felt an overwhelming desire to call his son just to say hello. Although he wasn't really part of his son's everyday life, he wanted to be.

Right now seeing his hero being led away in handcuffs gave Charles the feeling that it was an image of himself and his role as a father—no longer the hero and shackled in his own inefficiencies.

Looking at his watch, he decided to give his son a call. There was a two-hour time difference and if he was lucky, he just might catch him before he went to bed.

The phone rang several times and a man's voice answered.

"Hello," he said in a gruff voice.

Charles really didn't want to talk to the guy who had answered the phone, but he bit his lip and said, "May I speak with Steve?"

Charles felt like a child asking if little Stevie could come out and play.

"Who's this?" the voice asked in a rather unpleasant tone.

Charles knew that he had to introduce himself to the man who was now fathering his son. Charles took a deep breath and closed his eyes before speaking.

"It's Charles," he said.

Brian, his son's new father, didn't hesitate to say, "He's not here. What do you need?"

Charles wanted to say, "It's none of your business," but instead, he replied, "Just tell him I called."

Brian dismissed him as though he were only a passing thought, by saying, "I'll relay the message."

Then he hung up the phone.

Charles, shaking with anger, terminated the connection. He felt so livid, like he wanted to hit or shoot something. He had too much free time on his hands right now and his mind keep shooting images of beating up Brian. The only thing that would appease him would be to take a long drive to spend some quality time with his son. But Charles needed to find out if he was still on the force or not.

Charles looked around the room, and then felt the helpless pangs of being alone. He sighed and then breathed in and out several times until he could regain his emotional balance. The only thing that brought him comfort these days was his dog, X. Then, like serendipity, or some sort of canine super sense, X walked up to him and began nudging his leg.

It had been a long time, longer than Charles could remember, but he felt a burning in his chest and then the moistness of water in his eyes. He never liked it when he saw other men do it, but alone, with no one but his dog, he lost control and began to cry. It was strange when he heard himself sobbing. He hated the feeling that he was losing control, but it happened.

That night, as his hero was being led away, Charles knew that his own life had been destroyed. Now, with not being able to talk to his son, he let out what perhaps had been bottled up in him for many years.

Like most men, his cry lasted only for a moment, and then he snapped back to his normal hard self. Willing his mind to fight against any self-pity, he wondered why he had broken down in the first place. One thing his mom had always taught him was that you could do one of two things—ignore the problem and hope that it would just go away, or do something about it and quit crying.

Charles made up in his mind that he was going to do something about it. Tomorrow morning he would go down to the station and dig around a little to get some information on Xavier. He would also make contact with his son and plan a trip to go out and visit. The last thing, which in reality was the first, was that he would stop his stupid dog from humping his leg.

Chapter 10

Xavier felt spit come sliding across his face as the officers led him toward the unmarked police car. He wasn't sure why there was so much commotion, or why they appeared to hate him. Surely, he reasoned, it was just a misunderstanding. He hadn't done anything wrong, and the Asian lady, Le, was an accident. That wasn't his fault.

He felt confident that once he got on the stand and the facts were revealed, that he'd be released. He'd have to use his charm to help him navigate through this nightmare.

One of the police officers took him by the top on his head and pushed him down into the open back door of the police car. There wasn't a lot of room, and Xavier's swollen knee made it difficult for him to fit into the small, tight space.

He tried to tell them that it was too tight or that his body was too big to fit in the back seat. They probably couldn't care less, which was evident by the inhumane way they treated him. He was nothing more than a sardine being squeezed into a small tin can.

Several camera lights flashed in front of him and gave him temporary blindness. His mouth felt abnormally dry, and his heart began to race out of control. He hadn't experienced these feelings before, but he figured with everything that was happening, it must be a normal reaction.

One of the police officers jumped in the front seat and then his buddy slid into the driver's seat. Xavier made a mental note that each one had punched him in the side as they took him to the car. The driver was short, small-boned, and had reddish-brown hair and a mustache. He turned and looked at Xavier.

"You big, dumb idiot. You athletes think that you can just do whatever you want and then get away with murder. Ha! They've got your butt this time, and you're going to fry."

Xavier looked at him long and hard. It was not a stare-down but a curious look deep inside the face of a man who could hate him so much. He couldn't understand why he would be clumped into the same group as all the other athletes. He'd never done anything wrong to anyone. He always tried to do good in return for the privilege of playing in the NFL. Why people had such hatred toward him was certainly puzzling.

The officer's partner put his hand on the shoulder of his buddy. He didn't look back at Xavier but only said that not all of them were bad. Maybe he wasn't referring to Xavier directly, but at least someone saw the good that most of them did.

Xavier wanted to say something but decided that being quiet and asking only choice questions would get him answers and not opinions as to what was going on.

"What's going on? I did nothing wrong," he said, not being able to take his own advice. He tried to use his most charming voice.

Red, the name Xavier gave the police officer driving the car, turned to him even though he was driving. Red gave him a look that said if this had been the sixties, they would have taken a drive off-path and beat the mess out of him.

The other officer, with brown hair, brown eyes, and a nondescript face, said, "The best thing you can do is to shut up until your lawyer's present."

"I didn't do anything," Xavier said, defending himself.

He was now starting to feel woozy again. He thought that perhaps it was another after-effect from the attempted robbery he assumed had happened.

"So you think killing two people and injuring one is nothing?" Red asked sarcastically.

Xavier leaned back in his seat, eyes wide, and not sure if he had heard the question correctly.

"Kill…" he said slowly, as if just by forcing the words out of his mouth were a painful action.

Both cops turned around, which made him ponder what had just been said. Xavier couldn't remember what happened during the block of time that was missing in his mind.

He closed his eyes and tried focusing his well-trained brain to go back to an earlier time in the day. What happened, he wondered, during the time of those missing hours? He inhaled deeply and tried to relax.

He remembered being at home and then everything after that was a blank. A feeling of dread loomed within him as though he was in a haunted house and at any moment, something would jump out and take his life. He couldn't shake the images of colors and time flying by. He just couldn't grasp what was happening. He wanted to pound his head against the steel cage that separated him from the officers in the front seat, but he resigned to just wait.

Closing his eyes, he said a quick prayer for Le. Whatever her problem was, she was hurt, and he didn't want anything to happen to her. A sharp pain shot up through his knee and quickly brought him back to reality. His leg was killing him and he needed to stretch. He tried to lean to the side while putting his legs up against the dark plastic panel, but with his hands cuffed behind his back, he couldn't find a position that was comfortable.

The officers looked over their shoulders and one of them yelled, "Cut it out!"

Xavier tried to obey because he didn't want any more trouble, but what was he supposed to do when his knee was swelling up and he could feel the fluids rushing into the joints? He was in so much pain that he could barely stand it.

"How much longer?" Xavier asked, feeling his leg going numb.

As sick as it sounds, he thought, I wish it would go numb. Then the pain would go away. Xavier began biting his lip and praying for anything to dull the throbbing ache that he had to endure. Then the thought hit him that maybe he had killed someone along with their family. Their loss would be greater than any pain he would have to endure. He made up his mind to pray for them, and like some weird sect of Christianity, he would endure the pain as a symbol of his sincerity.

What he could remember was Le and the look of fear in her eyes. He wasn't sure what it meant, but it stuck with him. Out of her own innocence, she had helped him, and now she was headed to the hospital with unknown injuries.

"What about the woman, Le?" Xavier said, breaking his prayer.

He had to know if she was okay.

Red didn't even take the time to look back, as he snarled a response, "You'd better hope she's okay. Good lord, man, you're ten times her size. What in the hell were you thinking?"

This time Xavier detected, along with the anger, a hint of regret. Maybe he had things wrong, and instead of him being the hated black man, he was a fallen hero who destroyed the image of someone who really cared.

"I'm sorry," Xavier said, lowering his head.

Unfortunately, his apology went unanswered. Both officers looked straight ahead and said nothing else for the rest of the ride.

Chapter 11

The reporter, Angela, looked into the television cameras and tossed out tidbits of little known facts about Xavier's life. Charles, whose night had already been ruined by the failed attempt to reach out to his son, planned to rest, as despair and depression took over. A cold beer in one hand and the remote in the other was his sign of surrender. It wasn't that he would give up, but that this battle would have to be fought another day. Now he only wanted to look into someone else's misery and hope that in doing so, his life wouldn't seem so bad.

The sight of seeing Xavier being led away in handcuffs was something that he'd grown accustomed to seeing. A black man being led away in handcuffs was nothing new. What he didn't like was that a superstar had been accused of a crime. To young black kids, the scene of another black man going down was an image they had to deal with every day. But Xavier was a good role model, at least compared to others who seemed to ignore their status.

Charles began to recite a long list of self-defacing items from his life just to make himself feel even worse.

"Hell, I arrested half those men, and put half those images on TV. Viewers think black people are supposed to be put in jail, and now here's another one," he yammered.

He felt even more regretful that he might lose his job—not because he wasn't good at what he did, but because he had shot someone who had money and wasn't black.

As he flipped through the channels, he used the remote as a weapon. It seemed that every reporter, from every major network was talking about Xavier's latest breaking news. Geraldo was going to do a quick one hour special on the destruction of black athletes. Charles laughed but not at the fact that the piece wasn't true. He laughed because Geraldo looked directly into the camera as someone who felt compassion and hurt, but he knew that he was an actor giving a new performance, like someone auditioning for a play.

Charles figured that most reporters were all good actors and cared more about the story than the actual people involved. Deep down he wondered what type of person Xavier really was and how he could do what he had done.

The phone rang and Charles sighed. He dreaded the thought that it might be his mother again, but he wasn't going to hide from her or anyone else. As much as she preached, she was normally right and always had a good sense about people and events. She had helped him solve many of his cases by allowing him to bounce ideas off her. In return, she would use common sense or motherly logic. Although he could have gotten into a lot of trouble doing that sort of thing early in his career, it was a known fact that he had solved a lot of cases, and it was in large part to her credit.

The phone rang twice before he picked it up. No number had been displayed on the caller ID, which normally meant that it was a telemarketer. When no one answered, they would hang up. After the fourth ring, his answering machine came on and told the caller that he wasn't home, but if it was an emergency or a pretty lady, to please leave a name and number and he would call back. Most people found the message delightful, but not all, especially his ex-wife.

"Hello," the female voice said in a smooth, silky, soft tone. "I hope I'm one of the pretty people."

Charles knew exactly who it was. The woman on the other end was Alice Brice. She had always been a good friend of the family, but once he got divorced, she had become more. Their relationship was an on-again off-again affair, but deep down, they both knew they cared for each other.

Mostly, Charles blamed himself for keeping the relationship at a distance and felt that somewhere inside the recesses of his mind, he still had a chance with his ex-wife. Then again, maybe it was his fear of falling in love again only to have his heart ripped from him one more time.

Charles hesitated and then said, "Hello!"

"Is this my boo?" she asked in a loving way.

"I don't feel like your boo today."

He never fully understood why she had given him that nickname but it always gave him a feeling of comfort. That name was somehow a part of their chemistry. If she ever called him something else, it would be a sure sign that their relationship might be over.

"What's wrong, boo? Why so glum?"

Charles replied and didn't try to hide his disappointment, "Have you seen the news tonight?"

"Sorry, baby, didn't get a chance to catch it. What's going on?" she asked in a nonchalant manner as if news was not at the top of her list of important things.

She asked him jokingly if the president had been shot or if someone was trying to nuke America, but he wasn't in the mood for her games.

"Xavier was arrested today for murder," he blurted into the phone, as if almost demanding that she be more aware of current events.

There was a pause as if she had to think of who he was talking about.

In a soft, timid voice, she asked, "Xavier who?"

Charles nearly flipped at her response.

"Xavier! Xavier! Xavier!" he repeated as if believing his words would cause her to remember.

Alice remained quiet once more and then she asked, "Do you mean that ex-football player you used to talk about all the time?"

Rolling his eyes and shaking his head, he said, "Yes, that's the one."

There was a pause on her side as she waited for more info on Xavier. At the same time, Charles waited for her to remember who **the great Xavier** was. After a few minutes of dead air space, Charles, although a bit angry, began reciting his feelings about Xavier, his career, and their relationship.

"That's right, boo," she said, remembering and almost laughing like he was some sort of child talking about a god who once wore a Washington Redskin's helmet.

Charles ignored her and told her all that he knew.

"You need some company to make you feel all better," she said, as if totally ignoring everything that he had said.

Her comment was one of those read-between-the-lines sort of things. Charles thought about it for a moment, but a moment was all it took. He was alone and she was a good-looking woman. She had medium brown skin, a small waist, thick hips, and a full-size chest. She was pretty, very pretty. Yea, he felt like being a baby tonight, and he figured she would be his babysitter.

Chapter 12

Candlelight, a chilled bottle of wine and lotions to rub on the body, all of which Charles figured he didn't need to get Alice in the mood…well, except maybe the body lotion would be the icing on the cake.

There was knock on the door and Charles was ready to answer. With everything that had happened, he hoped that she would be a happy ending to a dismal day. Jumping over his small couch, Charles found new energy that only an hour before had been dormant.

"Who is it?" he said, now becoming playful.

"You know darn well who this is. Open this door, boo," Alice said playing along.

Charles responded by opening the door. He was breathless seeing the beautiful woman who now stood before him. She was dressed simple, which in his mind was all she needed to do. She wore a plain white T-shirt and a pair of faded blue jeans that gripped tightly but not too tight—just enough to let your mind take over and imagine the rest.

Charles smiled as he noticed the curves of her hips and how the oversized black belt contrasted with her smooth silk brown skin. He gazed at her for a moment and forgot all his troubles. Then he smiled. She rolled her eyes and pushed him aside as if to tell him to quit eyeballing her and act like a gentleman.

Charles grabbed her by the arm, which stopped her seductive saunter into his house. He pulled her to his side and began kissing her on the mouth.

She fervently returned his kisses and could feel his lips pressed against hers. She moaned for a moment and then caught herself.

"Slow down, cowboy," she said pushing him away while at the same time catching her breath. "Ever hear of trying to romance a girl before you make moves on her?"

Charles smiled, knowing that he knew her more than she thought. He moved to the side and revealed a freshly cleaned house. A table was set with candles, and a bottle of chilled wine was waiting to be poured. She sniffed the air.

"It smells like someone's been cooking again," she said playfully.

Charles smiled, soaking in the praise. Cooking was his hobby and throwing something together in thirty minutes was easy enough for him. He winked at her, took her by the arm, and led her towards the table.

"Where's my baby at?" Alice said, trying not to give Charles too much attention.

She gave a whistle and then heard the patter of little feet as X ran towards her. He jumped onto her lap as she leaned over to pet him. She even went so far as to kiss him on the lips, which wasn't Charles's biggest thrill, but he knew Alice was a dog lover.

"That's my good boy. That's my good boy," she said as X rolled over on his back, exposing himself and showing that he was excited.

Charles looked at Alice and gave a hinting smile, which was seen but ignored.

Go to your room, X," Charles said, pointing toward the little space that X called home.

Ever obedient even though he loved Alice, X wagged his tail and then went back to his spot.

"What's up with that?" Alice asked, looking at Charles.

She was enjoying playing with X and although she was ready to eat, she still wanted to spend some time with her favorite mutt. Charles led her to a chair, which he pulled out for her. She smiled and looked at the seat as if soaking up the royal treatment.

"For you, my lady, a meal fit for a queen," he said with a mixture of a French and English accent.

Alice understood men and the need to try to impress, so she played along.

"All right, baby, what you got for me?"

Charles smiled and jogged into the kitchen. He opened up the oven and an aroma wafted throughout the small house. Her stomach growled and X barked.

From the kitchen, Charles called out playfully, "I hope you're hungry, because I made steaks from a secret family recipe that will make your mouth water and your body quake."

Alice smiled and said, "Like most men, you probably talk a good game, but I doubt if you can deliver."

Out of all the qualities she liked about Charles, her favorite was that he loved a challenge and would never back away from a fight. Maybe that's what made him such a good detective or maybe that was what got him divorced. Whatever the reason, she figured she could scrap with the best of them and he had better deliver.

Charles walked to the table and held two plates with steaks smothered in some sort of dark sauce. She could smell a hint of red wine, garlic, and thyme, but there were several ingredients in the aroma that she couldn't identify. He complemented the meal with roasted garlic potatoes, fresh asparagus cooked in olive oil, mushrooms, and small white onions. It was finished with old-fashioned cornbread—not the kind you get out of the box, but the kind that felt heavy and tasted sweet. The cornbread recipe was a leftover from his Southern upbringing. No matter what the meal was, if it didn't have cornbread, it wasn't complete.

Alice smiled at him as he sat down and prepared to dig in. He looked at her and then clasped his hands together to say a quick prayer. Alice knew that the prayer was a product of his mother's upbringing, and even when she wasn't around, she was always around.

Like any good chef, Charles poured the appropriate wine and then waited for her to taste his creation. Alice, in a playful mood, decided that she was going to mess with his mind. Even if it was good, she was going to act as though it was not. She figured that it would knock the cockiness out of his smug look.

A slice of the knife revealed the steak was as tender as butter, and then as she placed it in her mouth, she moaned at the explosion of flavors that followed. So much for her mind games, she thought. One taste and she had forgotten all about trying to make him feel bad.

Charles smiled and figured that the steak was the appetizer and that he would be the main course. In his mind, he figured she hadn't seen anything yet.

Chapter 13

Harold awoke before Miriam did, and he stared intently at her face. He noticed the small curvature of her chin, the way her lips moved silently in her sleep and the large bruise on her forehead. She was his masterpiece, he thought, but now she was ruining it.

In the darkness, he felt his face tighten into a snarl, and his breath quickened while he contemplated their relationship. She was his first love, and the only woman he had ever been with, as strange as that sounded. They had met in college, although she really didn't give him the time of day when they first laid eyes on each other.

He was the classic computer nerd while she was a cheerleader. Everyone loved her, and she loved everyone. He knew of her reputation but didn't care. To him, she was an angel who had lost her way and he wanted to rescue her. In his mind, she was something to possess, and even before they said their I do's, she had become his prize.

Harold silently slipped out of the bed and moved quietly into the bathroom. The years of inactivity led to large bulges around his waist. He remembered how he had looked in his younger years, and refused to stare at himself in the mirror because he knew it was just a trick invented by the world to discourage people.

Harold felt that mirrors could not tell what was in people's hearts, or what was in their minds. Regardless of how things appeared on the outside, they were almost without a doubt different on the inside.

He heard his wife stir in the bedroom, but he knew she would be asleep for awhile. The bump on her head would be part of the reason, but he also felt confident that he had taken care of business, making love to her for at least an hour or so. He sometimes amazed himself as to how much control he had. It was something he had worked on all his life. He mastered control in the classroom and also in the bedroom.

Finishing up in the bathroom, he headed toward the living room to turn on the TV and catch the morning news. However, he couldn't resist giving a backwards glance at his naked body in the mirror.

"Yep, looking good," he said in almost a whisper.

The cool leather couch felt inviting against his body as he sat with his legs spread, revealing his manhood. The silver remote in his hand clicked as he smiled seeing the breaking news that flashed across the screen. The story was about Xavier getting arrested. Harold tried to hold back his excitement but a small chuckle escaped from his mouth.

The news lady, Angela Stark, went through the list of offensives Xavier had committed as she readied the audience for more. Harold smiled again and sat straight up in the chair. He felt himself getting an erection as he watched Xavier's face, not knowing what had happened to him or why.

Deep down he wanted to run into the bedroom, wake his wife up, and force her to look at the screen, but that could wait. She would see it in due time and then the look on her face would be priceless.

Harold quickly pressed the record button on his TiVo wanting to savor the moment forever. He flipped the channels trying to find out more information as to what had happened. Some reporters stated that the Asian woman was in the hospital in a coma or in critical condition. One network said that she was possibly near death. Others said that she was in bad shape.

"Xavier, you naughty boy," Harold smiled.

He flipped to a different channel and saw that a reporter was interviewing one of Xavier's former teammates. Although Harold was sure the reporter could have found someone to say good things about Xavier, this female reporter didn't. Harold made a mental note that everyone has enemies.

A former teammate, Drew Brown, faced the camera as the reporter asked questions.

"You played with Xavier, right?"

Drew nodded as if he was still too cool to speak.

"So what did you think of him when you played with him, and are you still close buddies?"

"Well," Drew said, now smiling and revealing a beautiful set of white teeth, "on the field, he was a mean mother…"

He stopped just short of finishing the sentence.

Harold thought of the old Isaac Hayes song and said out loud, "He was a mean mother shut your mouth."

Drew continued, "Anyhow, he was a bad boy on the field, but I could never understand how a person who could be that bad on the field could all of a sudden become such a goodie-goodie guy off the field."

"Did you ever witness any wild or unusual off-the-field behavior?" the reporter shot back, frustrated that he did everything but answer her question.

Drew paused and then said, "I never witnessed it firsthand, but I heard that one time Xavier shoved a woman to the ground for trying to get his autograph."

There was silence as they both looked into the camera.

Harold couldn't help it this time. He began to laugh out loud, as everything was unfolding in front of him. He couldn't have planned things better if he had tried. Xavier was in some serious trouble and this was just the beginning.

Miriam, apparently hearing his laughter, stirred in her bedroom. At first, she thought she was dreaming but soon realized it was not a dream. The pounding in her head and tiredness in her body made her wish she was still sleep, but she heard it again. Harold was laughing, which was something he had never done in all their years of marriage.

Miriam forced herself to the edge of the bed, and raked her hair back as she winced in pain. She tried to recall the night and all that had happened. Then she remembered running into the wall. She figured that maybe it had knocked some sense into her. She thought for a crazy moment that she should call the police on Harold and get him in trouble, but she decided against it.

He was her meal ticket, and in a strange way, she did love him, but not like he thought. It was more like a love of convenience or a love born of fear. Either way, he would have to do for the time being until she found someone better. Plopping back down onto the pillow, she dreamt of her ex-boyfriend, Xavier, from way back when.

Chapter 14

Charles awoke the next morning with Alice by his side. Their night, as he expected, was a night of passion and fun, but as he lay in the bed next to her, he realized that he was back to where he had started from. He still felt the emptiness of not having his son and the rage from another man raising him. On top of all that, he felt a little guilty using the woman next to him as some sort of pressure release button. He heard his mom's voice nagging at him in his head, and although he tried to block it out, it was strong and forbearing.

"Sex is not the way, baby. If you've got a problem, you've got two choices. Take care of it or do nothing at all. You can't ride the fence."

Alice stirred and then sat up.

"What time is it?" she said, still half asleep.

Even with her hair a mess and sleep around her eyes, she was still beautiful. Charles wondered if she would get tired of him and leave him for another man just like his ex.

"Hello," she said, snapping her fingers in front of his face. "Earth to Charles. Are you still there?"

It took a moment but her voice registered with him. He quickly returned her question with a smile and a kiss. She pushed him away calling a flag for morning breath.

"What did you put in my food, boo? Got me drunk, took advantage of me, and now you want a kiss?"

Charles laughed.

"That's why it's a secret family recipe," he replied. "By the way, it's 9:30."

Alice jumped out of bed realizing that she had slept in later than she planned.

"You're going to have to marry me if you keep this up," she said, half-joking, half-serious.

Charles noticed that line; that simple statement had been coming out more frequently. He had been divorced for two years and dating Alice for a year-and-a-half. Marriage was the last thing on his mind, but he knew that what he was doing was wrong.

"Living in sin," his mother would say shaking a disapproving head.

He asked Alice, "What's the rush?"

Instinctively, she said, "Some of us have to go to work."

It was an innocent statement but one that stung, nevertheless.

"Oh, I didn't mean…" her words fell short as if she had realized that he had no place to go and that all that he had worked for might be over.

The more she tried to dig herself out of the hole, the deeper she got. Finally, Charles gave her a kiss on the cheek and put her out of her misery.

"You're right," he said. "Just because I don't have a job, doesn't mean I can't work. I'm going to check around a little on the Xavier case. See what pops up."

Alice gave him a "You're my hero" look, and then she hurried out of the house.

X, with his tongue wagging, ran into the room after being patient all night. He was looking for his breakfast or perhaps an early morning run. Charles let him outside to do his business but then brought him back in. Food he would get, but the run would have to wait until later. Charles wanted to see what was happening to his hero.

After showering and getting dressed, Charles called an old buddy of his—a man named James who had been on the force ten years but still looked as though he was a rookie. James answered the phone. Charles convinced him to meet at the local donut shop for a few minutes so that they could talk about Xavier and he agreed. Although it was not James's case, he was the one to go to for information.

Besides getting information, Charles enjoyed talking with James and welcomed the fact that he could at least feel like a cop by being in the know.

James arrived first and found a seat in the back next to the window. He still liked to sit with his back to the wall, a leftover thought from watching too many Mafia movies as a child. He ordered his normal black cup of coffee and figured glazed donuts had to accompany his drink.

Charles showed up a few minutes later and waved to his old friend. They both greeted each other with a hearty handshake and smile. Charles looked at the donuts and coffee and told the waitress that he would have the same. Old habits were hard to break.

"So, how have you been?" James asked, truly concerned about his friend's well-being.

Charles gave the standard answer and hit straight to the point, "So, what's going on with Xavier?"

"Your boy is in some serious trouble."

"He's not my boy," Charles replied defensively.

James only took a brief glance at him while reading between the lines.

"Anyhow, they got him on vehicular manslaughter, attempted murder, kidnapping, assault, and whatever else they could think of. They're going to try to put him away for a long time."

"It looks bad," Charles said, not really talking to James but speaking more to himself.

"The fact is that he said he didn't remember anything," James continued. "He said he blanked out. We took some blood and should have the results back sometime in the next few days. No one wants this to be another O.J. case."

Charles didn't like what he heard but expected what he got. He asked about the Asian lady.

James shook his head again, and said, "Something's up with that chick. Her name is Le. You know that, right?"

Charles shook his head agreeing.

"Don't really know about her. She's still in serious condition, but somehow she must have some connection. We're getting pressure from a lot of different places to make this case go away quick. Like I said, your boy is in trouble."

Charles took a deep breath. It was hard for him to look at the bright side of things, but he figured he still might do a little snooping about. After pumping his friend for as much information as possible and eating a few more donuts, he decided to go see if he could dig up some more info from other sources.

James's final warning came quickly when he said, "Don't get too close. That case is pretty much open and shut. It was Xavier's Hummer that killed the couple. There were witnesses and they said he ran from the scene."

Like most of the people in the D.C. area, James could only shake his head and say, "Another brother messed up bad. Just stay away."

Chapter 15

Xavier sat alone in his jail cell. He thought of a few people to call, but at the moment, he had to deal with his own personal demons. He had never been in this type of trouble before, and from everything he heard, he was guilty.

He held his head back and began banging it lightly against the wall trying to focus. His life's story now played repeatedly in his head as he mentally punished himself for all the wrongs he had ever done in life.

You have the right to remain silent; you have the right to an attorney. Those words always sounded cool on TV, but now he had to deal with them for himself. Who would be his attorney? He didn't know anyone at the moment, but he had heard enough horror stories about the court-appointed ones to know he needed to get one.

The truth of the matter was that Xavier was broke; he had lost most of his money due to bad investments and was in serious debt. He was surviving just enough to keep his cover, but if anyone did enough digging, they would find out the truth. Now with his problem, the truth would soon be exposed.

He went through a list of people to call who could help him on the outside and the list was very short. Very few people popped into his mind. He was living as somewhat of a star, which didn't give him a lot of trust in people. Very few got past the title of just being called an associate. He also parted ways with his agent a long time ago, and now he only put his trust in a buddy from church.

A few men in the cells next to him began to yell out his name.

"Xavier, man, you in trouble. Hey, welcome to my world."

There was laughter and then, "Look, nigga, I'll protect you, but you know it gonna cost ya. You know how we do it in here."

Xavier tried to ignore what he heard but deep down he was scared. He figured he could fight if he had to, but he worried how long he would have to. The one thing he made up in his mind was that he was not going to be anyone's punk up in prison. "They're just going to have to rape a dead body," he thought to himself, while making a proclamation in his mind.

Xavier had lived a full life. Like most of the athletes, he grew up living a hard life. He got into trouble when he was young but never enough to go to prison. Football was the only thing that saved him and helped him focus his anger.

He didn't know his dad and his mother had died when he was young. Playing for the local YMCA kept him out of trouble enough to get him a high school diploma and a scholarship to college. From there, his life changed and he became a star. Now the star was being held in a jail cell dressed in a bright orange uniform.

The footsteps of a guard echoed down the hallway as he approached Xavier's cell. The guard was slightly plump but had a stern face for a white man. He stopped in front of his cell. Xavier tried to throw him a smile but was now learning that smiles meant nothing. He was no longer a person but a non-person, and non-persons didn't smile.

"Your lawyer is here," the guard said, looking him dead in the eyes.

It was not a look searching for the truth but a look of condemnation.

After placing the shackles on his hands and feet, Xavier was led away to a holding cell. There he saw a black man, standing about six feet tall, and weighing about 180. He was bald, and he also brandished a fairly large belly that hung over his thin frame. It made him seem like he would tip forward at any moment if he had one more big dinner. He held out his hand to Xavier and introduced himself.

"Eric Richards."

Xavier started to reach his hand out, but was held back by the shackles. Eric pointed to a lone table near the center of the room.

He asked the guard, "Can his cuffs be removed?"

Once it was done, Eric asked to be alone with his client. The guard left the room, still showing no emotion, but he was mumbling something under his breath.

Eric went straight to the point.

"I know you don't know me, but it really doesn't matter right now. I'm doing this out of a debt I owe your friend, Frank, but to be honest, if it wasn't because of that, I wouldn't be here."

Frank was his buddy from church and one of the few people who knew Xavier's real situation. Frank had been helping Xavier work on getting out of debt and had been like a father figure to him. Now he was saving him again.

Xavier sighed deep. Hearing that bit of info didn't give him much confidence.

Eric continued, "Let me be straight up with you. I need to ask you a few questions, and you need to be as honest with me as possible. Are you on some type of drugs?"

Xavier yelled, "No!" almost before Eric could finish his sentence.

He went on, "Xavier, do you have any history of health problems or do they run in your family?"

Xavier calmly replied, "No."

When Xavier said no, he saw Eric's shoulders slump. There was silence in the room and then Eric spoke.

"Look, I'm sure that you know there's an airtight case against you. You killed those two people and injured another. The only way we can get you off is to claim temporary insanity, or say that it was based on some medical condition. Either way…" he paused, and then leaned closer to Xavier. "Either way, you're screwed. The best advice I can give you is that you cop a plea and pray that the judge is a fan. They're looking at six years. Or, we might be able to get you a shorter time for vehicular manslaughter, which would be even shorter if you get out for good behavior."

Xavier's eyes nearly popped out of his head. He figured that he was looking at some serious time, but hearing it made his heart race. His eyes began to water and he fought back the tears. He hadn't cried since he was a child, but an uncontrollable urge found its way to the surface.

Eric had seen it before—grown men crying like little babies once they had to face facts, but he hadn't expected this from Xavier.

"I know it's a hard pill to swallow, but right now, crying ain't going to do you any good. You've got a choice to make. Either way, I'll be there for you, but do us both a favor. Just do the time. Who knows? You might get out before you get too old."

Chapter 16

Charles drove around in his old dark blue Ford Taurus trying to figure out who he could talk to that would know which prosecutor would be on the case. Several people owed him favors. The challenge was knowing who he could trust, and who'd be willing to take a risk to reveal the information.

Charles picked up his cell phone, dialed a number, and then set the sound controls to speakerphone.

When the call connected, a female voice said, "Hello."

"Hey, this is Charles. How're you doing?" he said, knowing that his voice would be recognizable.

"Better than you, I hear. What ya need?" the woman said.

Charles went straight to the point and asked, "Who's trying the Xavier case?"

There was a pause on the other end of the line.

"Why're you trying to put me in a spot? You know I shouldn't tell you. Besides, why do you need to know? Last I heard you were off the force."

The woman, Shelly, was not trying to sound harsh but that was just the way she talked. It was no wonder that she was still single after twenty years on the force. Charles couldn't recall ever hearing about her going on a date. Perhaps that's why they were friends. Charles didn't judge her, and she didn't judge him.

Charles replied boldly, "You're correct. I'll give you that. I just need to know. Let's leave it at that."

There was silence again and then the woman said, "A lady by the name of Carlita Jones. Do you know her?"

"I do, but not that well. It might be tough getting any information out of her. Thanks. I owe you one," Charles said, while disconnecting the call.

"Okay," Charles said out loud. "That one's out. I guess I'll have to find another way."

In his mind, he began plotting out other courses. Just then his phone rang. Annoyed, he looked at the display and saw that it was a long distance number. He quickly pushed the on button.

"Hello?"

"Hey, daddy," his son said.

"Hey, son," he replied, shocked that he was actually speaking to him.

Then like a prison phone call, a voice on the other end said, "Time's up."

His child's voice faded away as he said, "I love you."

The voice of Deloris, Charles's ex-wife, bellowed into his ear, "Steve told me you called asking for *my* son," she said. "Why are you trying to disrupt my family?" she asked, sounding frustrated.

Charles could only say, "I miss my son."

Although Deloris had been the one who had ended their marriage, the judge awarded her full custody of their kid. Charles was fully aware of the fact that he didn't always stay within the law while trying to solve cases, and he knew it hurt him with his son as much as it also made him a good detective.

Once Deloris was awarded full custody of their son, she left the city where they had lived. Now he found himself having to beg to talk to his own son. Reactively, Charles moved his hand to where he used to hold his gun. The more he thought about the conversation, the angrier he became.

"Look, he's my son, and if I feel like calling him, I will damn well call him."

Deloris stayed quiet, and Charles hated that. His anxiety heightened, and he pressed harder on the gas pedal. His speed accelerated well over the limit and he began weaving in and out of the lanes of traffic, endangering not only himself but all the other drivers, too. To him, it felt like nothing else existed.

Deloris breathed a heavy sigh into the phone, and said, "Look, we agreed you could talk to him on Fridays and on the weekend. Stay with the plan, please. He loves you, but like I said, I have a new family now. If you love him, you'll allow him to have some consistency in his life."

Charles nearly hit the car in front of him. He swerved to the left, riding the embankment for several feet until he finally came to a stop. He inhaled deeply and tried to control himself.

"Look," he said slowly, allowing the words to ease out in a way that might sound as if he was in control, instead of yelling, which is what he wanted to do. "I was watching the news and something just made me want to say hello to my son. Is that a crime?"

Deloris said, "You heard your son's voice. Now don't call again until Friday."

The phone clicked in his ear as she abruptly ended the call.

Charles's hand was shaking as he tried to regain his composure. He knew that he was going nowhere with the conversation and he should just have let it go, at least for now. At that moment, he wanted so bad to hop on a plane, and fly out to talk to her face to face, but he knew it wouldn't do any good. In fact, it could jeopardize his right to visit his son. Anyhow, he couldn't leave the state while his case was still pending. Again, it felt like his life was on hold, and he couldn't do a thing about it, but wait.

A motorist driving by must have felt that Charles was too close to the curve and flicked him the finger. Although they had taken away his gun, he was still able to drive his unmarked car, and he was in no mood for jerks.

He placed his siren on the front of the car and took off after the driver. At least he would take his frustration out on someone.

The driver slowed down and pulled over as Charles came up behind him in his car. He let the guy sit there for a full minute. He could see the guy looking at him in his rear view mirror, with eyes that were wide with terror. Then slowly, Charles eased his car alongside the guy and rolled down his window.

Charles glared at him and snarled for him to not ever make that mistake again while simultaneously he shot the finger back in return. That retaliation made him feel a little better as he sped away laughing.

Now he had work to do. First on his agenda was to go to Xavier's house. Charles looked down at a piece of paper where he had written Xavier's address. He drove in that direction, thinking how amazing it was that the Internet could provide almost any type of information he needed. He had an aerial shot of Xavier's house, the address, and directions on how to get there.

The drive was about an hour from his home, but it may as well have been another planet. The closer he came to Xavier's home, the more expensive the homes got. Charles was amazed that some of the homes looked like small hotels that he had stayed at over the years. Some of them were locked away in gated communities, while others were covered by trees and forest. It was hard to tell where one property stopped and another began. Charles shook his head wondering what he would do if he had that much money.

He looked down at the directions again and then made a right turn. He came to a street that wound around into what looked like woods. He couldn't tell how many homes may have been in the area, but judging by the satellite report he got from the Internet, there were only a few and each sat on at least ten acres.

As he drove up the hidden road towards the home, he noticed the first one was hidden deep in the midst of the trees. It looked like a mini castle that had been hidden from time and protected by soldiers. It was made up of wood and branches. He continued on for what seemed like several minutes, and then the road veered right for a few more minutes. Finally, he drove onto a long curving driveway that went up to the house and curved back to the road again.

The home belonged to Xavier, and it was as awesome as the way he played. Charles looked around and tried to figure out where to park. He decided that the best spot was near the detached garage. Xavier had never been married so he figured he would be safe parking there.

If he had to sneak in, it would be close enough for a quick getaway. To be on the safe side, he decided to ring the doorbell. He just wanted to make sure no one was there.

Chapter 17

Miriam drifted back to the time before her marriage to Harold—a time when she was free-loving and in college. She was one of the most popular women on the campus, and she knew it. Everyone wanted a piece of her and over time, a few gained that privilege.

Her grades were okay, but for her, college was more of a place to party and have fun. Most people thought it was automatic that the cheerleader should date the star of the football team, but that's not how she and Xavier had met.

Xavier, although a beast on the football field, was a quiet man who never really dated. There were no rumors of him being gay; just that he was a shy guy. Miriam was one of only a handful who ever got to him. She had purposely waited for him to go to the library, and then she played the damsel in distress scenario.

His big problem was that he was a gentleman and she knew it. She dropped her books in front of him, and as if on cue, he went out of his way to help. She was smart and had studied him before she made her move. She knew that he liked women who were shapely but who didn't overly expose themselves. She dressed appropriately and could tell by his quick glances that he approved.

Miriam's plan was to sleep with him, plain and simple. She didn't want a relationship. All she wanted was the challenge of sleeping with the star athlete. The fact that he was black and she was white gave her even more confidence that she could do what she set out to do.

She noticed that his hands were sweaty, which was a good sign for her. Sweaty hands after helping her with the books meant that he had no aversion to hooking up with a white girl; it indicated that he was nervous.

Quickly, she began to spring her trap, and within a week, she invited him over to her house. He stood before her as a well-built muscular black man, with dark intense eyes that focused into the depth of a person's soul.

She smiled to herself thinking about how he would look naked. She had the image of him implanted in her mind—a dark black stallion, powerful and strong. Tonight was going to be her night, and tomorrow she would laugh. He would be just another person she had added to her list of conquests.

She made her move toward him and he stopped. His eyes widened but not in anticipation of lust; he wore the look of fear. She couldn't believe it, but Xavier was afraid.

"Maybe I shouldn't be here," he said.

Miriam bit her lip trying not to laugh. He was starting to shake as she took him by the hand and led him toward the kitchen. She poured two glasses of wine—one for him and one for her. He put his hands up to protest and she nearly laughed again. He didn't even drink. She was beginning to wonder if this was going to be harder than she had imagined.

Xavier said, "I should leave."

Instead of showing him the door, Miriam took her opportunity and became the aggressor. She grabbed him by the arms and moved in tightly toward his body. She wrapped his arms around her. Then she pressed her lips against his, gently at first, and then more passionately. She could feel his heart beating fiercely under his shirt. The more she kissed him, the more she wanted him.

Xavier began to kiss back; his lips pressing against hers. He moved his hands gently against her sides as she moaned in response to his touch. Leaning her head back, he began to kiss her neck. He moved his way down to her heaving chest and then he stopped.

She had to catch her breath, having been caught up in the moment that she thought she had control over.

"What's wrong, baby?" she said. "You can have me and no one needs to know."

His massive hands tenderly grabbed her by the arms, and then he moved her away from him.

"I can't," he said and turned to leave.

Miriam stood there in somewhat of a daze. He was actually turning her down. Now it was a matter of pride for her. She was going to get her prey and nothing was going to stop her.

Xavier's penetrating stare peered deep into her eyes. It was as if he were searching for information in her soul. He wanted to know why she had chosen him and what she was attempting to prove. To him, it was so obvious that she was on a mission for something.

He remained silent for at least two minutes, and then he said, "You're worth more than what you're trying to do here."

The statement was simple, but it shook the very soul of Miriam. Although she was popular, no one had ever spoken to her like they really cared. Most of the men knew the game and played it well. Their talk was cheap—only lies to get what they wanted.

To Miriam, it felt like they were actors in a feature film, and this wasn't happening in real life.

Xavier told her, "I want to take it slow and maybe get to know you."

The very thought of not getting what she wanted started to enrage her.

"Is something wrong? Do you have a disease?"

"No."

"Are you gay?"

"No."

"Do you have trouble getting it up?"

Xavier answered her in an abrupt tone, "That's not a very lady-like question. My only reason for not having sex with you is that I want to respect you."

With that, he turned and walked out the door. She didn't follow.

For the next few months, they saw each other frequently, but all they did was talk. She was sure that no one would have believed her if she had told them the truth, but she didn't care. For the first time in her life, she was truly happy, even without sex.

Their dates consisted of talking, walking, and laughing, which was something she rarely took time to do. Everything was perfect, but her desire to control him was greater than her desire to love him.

One night she invited him back to her place under the pretense of cooking him dinner. She decided to put a little something extra in his meal, and before the night was over, she had him.

He lost control after being drugged, and they made love the whole night. It was more than she could have ever imagined; everything she had ever wanted.

When he awoke and realized what had happened, he left, knowing that he had been a victim of date rape.

Chapter 18

Years later, after Miriam had married Harold, the nightmares of her escapades with Xavier continued to haunt her. She could see the hurt in Xavier's eyes, and it was more than Miriam had expected. She knew that what she had done was wrong, but in spite of how everything had turned out, she still admired Xavier's passion and techniques.

Early one morning Miriam began having another one of her dreams. She was lying in bed with Xavier and he was silent, staring at the ceiling. She smiled and leaned her head into his massive shoulder, but to her surprise, he moved away. He shook his head like a wounded puppy and crept out of the bed.

Looking over his shoulder, he whispered to her, "What have you done to me?"

In the dream, Miriam tried to play innocent, but after a few moments, she got disgusted that she had to defend herself to the 250-pound football player.

"Look, don't play the innocent guy," she said. "You slept with me and had a damn good time doing it. Don't act like you didn't like it. Consider yourself lucky."

Xavier became angry and grabbed her by the shoulders.

"I promised my grandmother that I would wait until I was married. I promised," he yelled, and then he threw Miriam to the ground.

That's the part of the dream when Miriam woke up. She had had that same dream at least once a month, and she always woke up at the same moment. But today was different.

Harold was standing over her and shaking her awake. She blinked and allowed her eyes to adjust to the light. That's when she saw his face. He smiled at her like a child who had just gotten away with doing something wrong.

"Time to get up, sleepy head," he said.

Her head was throbbing, but she was alert enough to figure out that something was going on. As Harold gently moved her into an upright sitting position on the bed, he kissed her on the cheek.

"You were talking in your sleep," he said, as his eyes gave off a sense of concern. "I just wanted to know if you needed anything."

He seemed to be in a great mood, and the only reason she could conjure up was that he was elated because of their lovemaking session.

He smiled again and then turned to leave. It was strange, but she had grown used to his unusual habits. Miriam struggled to get out of bed, but her head ached. Slowly she put her feet on the floor and as if skating, she shuffled the short distance to her closet. She put on an old pair of jeans and a shirt and looked at herself in the full-length mirror.

"Ugh," she sighed.

Time had beaten her up and, somewhere deep inside, she felt that everything that had happened to her in life was somehow God paying her back for the evil that she had done.

As she sauntered towards the living room, she heard sounds coming from the TV. She figured Harold was in there, and she didn't really care what he was doing. Then suddenly, something an announcer said on TV caught her attention. She wasn't sure, but she thought she heard Xavier's name, and then she heard Harold laugh from the bottom of his belly. Then he laughed again.

Miriam walked into the room and saw her husband sitting on the couch. He had a drink in his hand and a bowl of popcorn in his lap. She thought that maybe he was watching a movie, but then she noticed that he was watching a news story.

The reporter mentioned something about a woman name Le, and how she was now listed in stable condition, but that she would be able to speak to the police in the next few hours. She then went on to say that they still didn't know much more about Le but her staff was working on the story.

Miriam wondered why Harold found this to be so funny, but she stayed out of sight because she didn't want to speak with him. She continued to listen hoping for more information. As the reporter talked, she understood why he was laughing. The reporter said that Xavier was still in jail, and that the judge hadn't yet set an amount for bail.

As she quietly inched her way into the living room to get a glimpse of the TV screen, Miriam nearly fell against the wall seeing a picture of Xavier. He looked the same, but the cameraman hadn't taken a flattering shot.

Harold sat watching the screen and chuckled each time they mentioned more damaging information about Xavier. She knew Harold hated Xavier although they had never met in person. Harold was the guy who filled the void that Xavier had left in her life. He had become her knight in shining armor.

She hadn't wanted the college crowd anymore and had quit school. From there, her life was heading downhill until she met him. There was no real attraction on her part, but he was kind. He was a piece of Xavier that she held onto, even though he was almost the exact opposite. She didn't mention she knew Xavier until after she and Harold were married. To this day, Harold doesn't know the full story. All he knows is that Miriam dated Xavier and that he left her.

Chapter 19

Charles tapped on the door of Xavier's home. He figured no one would be there since Xavier was in jail, but he decided to play it safe before he broke the law and entered. To his surprise, the door opened and before him stood a short, elderly black man who appeared to be in his mid-50s.

He gave Charles a quick once-over and then asked, "What do you want?"

"My name is Charles. I'm a detective."

Charles hoped that his introduction would be enough to gain some trust to allow him to enter.

With a smile on his face, the old man extended his hand towards Charles and said, "I'm Frank, a friend of Xavier's. We know each other through church. I'm watching over his home while he's locked up."

Charles forced a smile and returned the handshake.

"What can I help you with, son?" Frank asked, still smiling as though he were talking to an old friend.

Charles thought for a moment about lying but something inside of him told him to tell the truth. He had always relied on his instincts, and there was something easy about the guy who stood before him. He was almost like a father or a good friend, someone that you could trust.

"To be honest with you, Frank, I'm no longer a detective or at least not one with a badge. I just wanted to see what I could do to help."

There was a long silence and then the old man's shoulders went limp and he smiled.

"I've been praying for you," Frank said, with a peaceful look about him.

Charles knew of religion, and although he was not a firm believer, he had seen miracles in his life. Knowing how much his mom believed in it seemed to make Frank's statement not quite so shocking.

Frank moved to the side of the doorway and gestured with his hand for Charles to enter the house.

"That's it?" Charles replied questioningly. "You're just going to let me in even though you don't know me?"

Frank looked at Charles, and then in a bold voice, he proclaimed, "Like I said, I've been praying for you, and I know that God sent you here."

With a humble-looking grin, Charles entered Xavier's home, and said, "Okay, I'll accept that."

Frank smiled warmly, and then, with his feet firmly planted in the front hallway, he said with a disgusted voice, "Several reporters have come here and tried to get in. Some even tried to sneak in through the back of the house."

Charles shifted his stance and focused his gaze on what the old man was saying.

"I nearly had to come to blows with one of them."

In his mind, Charles pictured this small guy chasing off a renegade reporter and he nearly laughed at the image. It wasn't that he thought it was impossible, but that he could see it was possible. Frank appeared to still have a lot of fight in him.

"The house is just the way I found it when I got here," Frank said, as he led Charles from the home's entrance into a huge open foyer.

Charles stopped and looked in amazement at the massive size of the home. Frank observed Charles's reaction and then led him to a sitting area that was located to the right.

Two brown oversized chairs welcomed both men as Frank extended his hand and signaled for Charles to sit.

"So you've been here the whole time?" Charles asked, trying to start a conversation.

Frank nodded and then he studied Charles with an intense stare, as if trying to look into his soul. It made Charles feel slightly uncomfortable. When Frank leaned closer to Charles, as if to tell him a secret, Charles didn't know if he should move back or stay put.

Then Frank whispered, "Most people think he killed those people. All the evidence says he did, but there's got to be another reason for what happened, you know?"

Charles nodded in agreement, but he said nothing, sensing that the old man had more to say.

"We fight a spiritual battle. The devil is out to get us all the time. Xavier doesn't drink or do drugs, and he's in good health," Frank said in a frustrated tone.

"I know," Charles replied.

"Look, Charles, I don't know why you came here today, but maybe God is working through you."

Charles moved uncomfortably in his chair.

"Nothing to be nervous about, boy," Frank said. "Just do your job, and God will take care of the rest."

Charles thought about what the old man said, and then he began to wonder himself. Xavier's case revolved around a car wreck that killed two people. There was really no reason for Charles to be at his house, but somehow it all made sense.

After a few more minutes of talking, Charles asked, "Do you mind if I have a look around?"

Frank gestured with wide open arms, and said, "Look all you want. I'll be sitting right here."

Charles got up, not sure what he was looking for, but he began his search. He walked into the kitchen and stood for a moment. He tried to imagine Xavier's daily routines, and what he might have been doing on the day of the killings. Everything seemed so clean and neat. He wondered if Xavier had a maid service, or if it was his nature to be tidy.

He walked slowly around the massive house figuring that it must be at least 10,000 square feet. Every room was decorated with the highest quality furnishings, and although Charles was no interior designer, he knew expensive when he saw it.

After making his rounds, he was a little disappointed. Nothing seemed to be out of place.

As he returned to the first floor sitting room, Frank asked, "Did you find anything?"

All Charles could do was shake his head no.

"Thank you, Frank, for letting me come in the house and look around."

Frank handed him a card, and said, "Call me if you think of anything that might help."

Charles almost felt like what he did was a big waste of time. He was not sure what he expected and was disappointed at how quickly everything went. He wanted more substance from what just happened. It was like buying some cheap ice cream only to find out that it was mostly air and fluff, lacking in flavor.

As Charles got back into his car, he flicked on the radio. More news on Xavier's case stated that the Asian woman, Le, was now able to speak. She gave a statement to the police. She said that Xavier tried to rape her.

Chapter 20

Charles's mind swirled as he thought of the implications of what he had just heard. Xavier's case was becoming more and more weird. He knew that it was in every man to have a dark side, but he hoped that wasn't the case with Xavier.

Charles turned the radio off even though he knew better. Information was the key to solving cases, but he didn't want to hear anymore. He drove around for awhile trying to think things through.

Maybe the man he was trying to help didn't need or deserve his help. Maybe his hero wasn't really a very good person. The more he thought about it, the more it troubled him. However, something that Frank said stuck in his mind—God sent him and Frank had been praying for him.

Charles sighed and decided to call his mom. These were the times when she always came in handy and would give him advice. Sometimes she'd stay quiet long enough to let him figure things out for himself.

"Hello, Mom," he said, holding the phone close to his ear. "I need to talk."

There was a little silence on the other end, and then his mom said, "It's about time. I've been waiting for your call and wondered if you were okay."

Charles laughed, and felt his tension melting away.

"Mom, have you heard what they've been saying about Xavier?"

"I've heard all the news reports," she replied quietly.

Charles imagined her with her hand over her eyes while she thought and prayed at the same time.

"Do you think he did all that?" she asked.

Her response, from Charles's perspective, was that she got straight to the point and dug right into the heart of the situation.

Charles thought about it for a moment, weighing facts against what his gut was telling him.

Before he could speak, he heard his mom's sincere but demanding voice, "You've got to make up your mind one way or another, son," she said. "You're already on thin ice from your other case. You've got a lot at stake, but the worse thing is to go into this halfway and mess up not only your life but the life of someone else."

"Okay, Mom. I believe he's innocent."

"Good," she said. "That's what I figured. Now tell me what you know so far."

Charles went on to relay the information but felt as though he wasn't giving her much.

After a few minutes, she told Charles, "I've seen many men change in their lifetime."

Charles knew he had to uncover more facts about Xavier, and to get to the truth, he needed to speak with him in person.

Charles appreciated his mother in many ways. Not only was she his parent; she was his best friend. He made no excuses about being a mother's boy. He knew that she had much more wisdom than he had. Besides, he was secure in showing how much he loved his mother, and it didn't diminish the fact that he was a man and confident in who he was.

As she spoke, Charles's mind reeled with ideas. He figured that he could do a quick scan of the police records and public information available on the Internet, in case something turned up that would help him understand events in Xavier's past.

His mother switched their conversation away from Xavier by asking, "How are you doing, son?"

It was one of those conversations that he knew always followed most of their telephone discussions, although he didn't mind it today. In fact, he usually welcomed her abruptness and ability to jump right into another unrelated conversation.

He felt comfortable opening up to his mother, and she made him feel safe, regardless of the seriousness of the situation.

"I'm okay, Mom. Just taking everything one day at a time."

"What about Alice?"

"I like her, Mom. We probably should get married, but I've already done that and it didn't work out. Staying single is the plan for right now."

True to her form, his mother tossed him some of her wisdom, "Sometimes, Charles, we make mistakes, but your marriage wasn't the mistake. It was the people. God's been working on you, and I think you know that. A mistake is only a mistake if you don't learn."

He normally would debate her on the issue, and sometimes he enjoyed the dialogue, but today wasn't the day.

He said, "Okay," and hoped that his quick response would suffice until another time.

"Funny thing you should mention God," Charles said. "I was just at Xavier's house, and a man named Frank, who was watching the place, said that he'd been praying for me. He said he knew that God would send someone, and that's when I showed up."

"Praise God," were the first words that came out of her mouth, even before he could finish the story.

He felt like saying, "Go ahead, steal my thunder. Whatever," but he held his tongue out of respect. He didn't need to smart-mouth his mother.

"I've always believed that you were an angel on this earth," she said, like a proud mom.

"Mom, I'm no angel," Charles wailed, thinking about all his past sins.

"Baby, you misunderstood. I call you an angel not because of your goodness, but because of the good that you do for other people. We're all sinners."

Charles could have sworn that his mother had been a preacher but never told him about it.

The phone buzzed, which indicated that another caller was trying to reach him. It was a number that he didn't recognize.

"Mom, I've got another call. I'll talk to you later."

Clicking over to the incoming call, he said, "Hello?"

The man on the other line spoke as if he knew Charles.

"Charles, this is Eric. I'm a lawyer. I'll be brief. What was your relationship with Xavier?"

Charles wasn't sure why he was being questioned, but surmised that Frank must have told someone about his visit to the house. Charles played it cool, knowing that if he took enough time, people usually answered questions for him and then some.

"No relationship; just hate to see a brother go down that way."

A long silence followed, and then Eric said, "I'm Xavier's lawyer, and although I don't understand the reasoning, Xavier wants to see you."

Charles didn't believe what he had just heard and said, "Eric, would you repeat what you just said, please?"

"Xavier told me that he wants to talk with you. He mentioned something about a dream, and that's when your name came up. He thought it was some type of sign and that somehow you needed to be involved. He's refusing to talk to anyone but you. I really don't understand all this, but be that as it may, he wants to talk to you. I got your number from the police department and so here I am calling you because of a dream."

Charles saw images of a puzzle floating together in his mind. He wasn't sure of the full scope of things, but he knew that if he followed his instincts, he'd eventually have the complete picture.

Chapter 21

Le sat up in her hospital bed and looked frightened—not sure what was going on. She had never been in an American hospital and didn't like the one she was in now. It smelled funny to her and reminded her of a scent of death. She blinked to allow her eyes to adjust to the lights that filtered in from the opened white sterile blinds that covered the window.

Gasping slightly, she realized that she was not alone in the room. An Asian middle-aged man sat across from her and glared intently into her eyes. She pulled the blanket that surrounded her waist higher to her chest.

She knew who he was, and she didn't like him. He had spoken to her before and had not been pleasant. He was the one who told her to tell the police that Xavier tried to rape her. He was her only relative in America, and he refused to allow her to talk to the police until he planted the words in her mouth to give as a statement.

"Glad to see you're awake," he said, nodding slightly towards her.

She winced in pain but not because of the injury. She didn't want him in her hospital room. She began to speak to him in Korean, and told him that he should leave.

He answered in her native tongue, "You know I can't leave right now. You might say something stupid."

He didn't smile as he spoke to her.

She closed her eyes and reflected on her life. She had never wanted to be in such a position and deeply regretted the trouble she had caused. She regretted her past and dug deep to find the courage to speak again.

"I will not lie," she said. "He didn't try to rape me."

The man got up slowly from the bedside chair. He almost seemed mechanical in his approach as he walked over to Le. He picked her hand up and put it into his.

"He *did* try to rape you, and it would be a shame to see your family suffer because of your disobedience."

Le's shoulders sunk as she took in what he had just said. She peered into his dark black eyes and saw no hint of mercy, just revenge and blackmail.

"Now if you please, repeat the story," he said.

She lowered her head, and in that instant, he briskly grabbed the bottom of her chin and lifted it up until she looked straight into his eyes.

Le spoke in broken English, "He came over, and I let him in. He tried to have sex with me. I say no and he hit me."

The man with the dark eyes smiled and whispered, "That's all you need to say. If they ask you why you let him in, you tell them that he looked like he was in some sort of trouble and you were raised to help people in trouble. Xavier is a bad man. You're lucky nothing more happened."

Le was frightened; she knew that she was getting herself deeper and deeper in trouble. She worried about her family but also worried about the man who stood in front of her. Earlier that day, he had produced a picture of her family. It was easy for him to do because he was a distant cousin, but there was no doubt in her mind that he felt no blood ties and would not hesitate to kill them all.

He told her that at any moment they could all be dead, and he'd make it look like an accident. He had told her where they lived and recited each of their names.

Le turned to look away, but he kept his grip on her bottom chin.

"It's unfortunate that all this had to happen. Senator Stevens doesn't like trouble and this has become a real mess. We're cleaning up things, but in the meantime, we can't afford to have you messing this up. Do you understand?"

Le didn't understand his reasoning, but what she did understand was Senator Stevens's name. She had met him on a trip that he had arranged for her and her family to be brought to America. It was Senator Stevens who had given them a home in America. The agreement was that Le would be his private concubine for awhile, and then they would be given citizenship.

Although she initially had resisted the offer and the plan, the temptation of the money that she could give her family and the chance to live a better life in America made her give in. Ironically, that same wonderful life of hers in America could now be coming to an end.

She wondered how her people would look at her if she ever returned to her country. Even though she had lived the life of a kept woman with the sole purpose of providing a better life for her family, the way she did it wouldn't be viewed with honor.

A humming noise interrupted the silence in the room, which caused the Asian man to pick up his phone. He listened for awhile, and then a smile came across his face.

After pushing the off button, he turned to Le and gloated, "Good news, Le. If things go well, we won't have to worry about Mr. Xavier anymore."

Le looked puzzled but knew that even though she didn't understand, she could tell the news really wasn't good or in her favor.

"Xavier didn't rape me," she said forcefully.

The man looked at her, and his face became red with anger. He moved in closely like an eagle swiftly swooping down on its prey.

"Don't ever let me hear you say those words again," he said.

He picked up his phone and punched a bunch of numbers. Then he spoke into the phone.

"I need you to make an example of her. Let her know that we're not playing."

Le's eyes became wide with fear as she knew he wasn't joking. She didn't know who he was talking to, but she couldn't take the chance that someone in her family would get hurt.

"Stop!" she screamed, while trying to pull the tube and needle out of her arm.

The Asian man smiled and then returned to the phone, saying, "Delay that order. I think she'll cooperate now."

He ended the call and stared at her with an unfair smirk on his face.

"I don't like making threats. Don't make me do it again. Just obey me and everything will go as planned, and your family will be spared."

He moved her head up and down to force a reply. She wanted to cry but resisted the urge. She knew it would only give him some type of sick pleasure, and he didn't deserve it.

A nurse walked into the room and he quickly changed his tone and demeanor.

"It's okay, dear," he said in a soft, syrupy voice. "He won't harm you again. He's locked up and he's going to stay there a very long time."

He faked a two-arm embrace with Le, and she wanted to smack him. But to the nurse, his act was probably quite convincing. Le was amazed at the speed of how he had made the transition from gangster to mercy worker.

The nurse cocked her head sympathetically and moved in like a loving mother.

"Everything will be okay, Ms. Le. It's good that you have your family here to take care of you."

Le looked at both of their faces and faked a smile. She knew she had to play the game and play it well, or else her family would die.

The nurse looked at the man whom Le called Jimmy and said, "We have counselors available if you feel they might help her."

Jimmy smiled and bowed to her.

"Thank you for your kindness. For now, Le's okay."

After the nurse checked Le's vitals, she gave her a smile, followed by a hug. Then she walked out of the room and closed the door.

Like the wave of a magician's wand, Jimmy returned to his normal evil form.

"Great performance," he sneered, and continued as if it was business as usual.

He returned to the bedside chair and sat down with a plop. Then he glanced at the door, and leaned in closer so only Le could hear him speak.

"When they ask you about the phone call to the police, tell them that you had convinced Xavier to turn himself in. Tell them that you convinced Xavier that you were a Christian and that Jesus loves him. Tell them that he got on the phone and gave the information, but then he changed his mind and hung up."

Le looked down at the floor. Her facial expression was filled with sadness and remorse.

"Repeat what I just told you," he said.

Le recited his words as if she were reading them off a cue card.

Jimmy slammed his fist onto the mattress, and said in a loud whisper, "Like you mean it. Say it with feeling!"

As if Le had been a seasoned actor all her life, she spoke her lines with believability. She didn't want more of Jimmy's coaching.

Jimmy smiled, and praised her, "Great job! I knew you could do it, cousin."

Chapter 22

Xavier sat alone in his jail cell. The alone part he was used to, and in fact, he welcomed it. He didn't want to make friends or have to fight anyone. He didn't even want to discuss his playing days. In fact, he didn't want to see anyone. It was all he could do just to deal with the situation he was in.

He'd been alone most of his life and even though he was famous, he never truly had friends. Friendship with others wasn't at the top of his high priority list, which probably explained why he never really allowed anyone into the inner circle of his life.

Even in church he felt alone. During his more pensive moments, he thought maybe it was him, but he knew deep in his heart that that wasn't the reason. The pastor had made comments about him playing, and he had told Xavier that people would follow him. Xavier wasn't sure if that was a prophetic word, or if he was just like everyone else—the world would use him, and when they didn't need him anymore, they'd throw him out.

It wasn't until he had met Frank that he finally revealed something personal about himself, yet he only tossed out guarded snippets, a few at a time. Frank was older than him, and Xavier enjoyed hearing his wisdom, but he knew that not all old men were wise.

Nevertheless, because of his wisdom, Frank, too, was often treated like an outcast. He'd look a man in the eyes and tell him what was on his mind. There was no pretense and no flattery. It was uncanny how he would reveal bits and pieces of information that a person tried to hide as they walked around with a simple smile on their face.

Xavier's stomach began to rumble. He felt hungry and sick at the same time. His bowels cried out to relieve themselves, but looking at the cell made him clench his fists and compress his body all the more. He knew that in prison there was no room for shyness, but the thought of pulling down his pants and sitting on the small metal toilet gave him a fortitude to keep everything pressed down inside. It was a mind game he was playing. He tried to believe that he'd soon be set free and could live in the private comfort of his house again, complete with a rotating fan and a can of air freshener close by.

He looked around his cell at the four walls. He was forced to entertain the thought that he'd possibly never see the outside world again. He wondered what he would miss the most. He realized that he'd been taking too many things for granted, and if he were given another chance, he would embrace his life differently.

He thought of ice cream. Yes, it was ice cream for some strange reason. But it couldn't be just any ice cream; it would have to be Haagen-Dazs butter pecan. It seemed shallow that he would only think of ice cream and not a loved one somewhere. In reality, he had no one that he wanted to rush back home to see and pull into his hug. There were no dying souls that he had to reach—only ice cream.

He promised himself that when he got out of prison that he'd make some major changes in his life. He'd return to the way he used to be— trusting and craving more than ice cream.

Football, it seemed, had always been a way for Xavier to communicate. When he was angry, he could say to the world, "Look, I'm angry." Then during the next game, he could knock the opposing player as hard as he could, and it would make him feel better. When he followed through with such behavior, he would get paid large sums of money, which made him only enjoy hitting that much more.

If he needed to communicate loneliness, he'd play a great game and then go to the local club where he would have his choice of whatever fantasy his heart desired. He could flirt with women in front of their husbands and be thanked for taking the time to talk to them. At first it was a thrill, but too much of the same dish becomes boring and only started to emphasize his loneliness.

To Xavier, people were like vultures encircling his camp and waiting to prey on the unknowing. No matter how good they appeared on the outside, their words spoke bigger truths of the evil thoughts they held inside. It was like he owed them more than just Sunday morning entertainment. Sometimes it felt like they wanted his entire life.

It seemed that no matter how many good deeds he did, people always acted like they had a right to speak to him and intrude on his privacy. They just did whatever they wanted to do to him, and for that he should be grateful. Ha! For every night of ill-begotten sex, he had to wonder who would come back to try to entrap him, or if they merely endured in hopes of claiming his fortune and fame.

The saddest part of his life occurred when he had to face that hopeless moment of retirement and the feeling of abandonment that came with it. Sure, he still had some diehard fans, but they wouldn't go out of their way to see him. Although he appreciated them, very few got past the wall that he put up in front of himself.

Xavier realized that he wasn't going to be treated like a hero anymore. He wondered, "Where do heroes go when they're forgotten and new heroes come to replace them?"

Now as he sat in his cell, he looked down at his feet. He no longer wore his favorite Nike tennis shoes. He wore black flip flops. Everything in one way or another was secured so that he could not kill himself, although he surmised that if he tried hard enough, he could find a way.

The cot which he laid back on was hard and uninviting. He longed for his old bed that supported his back and comforted his legs. No longer a man, he felt caged and like a victim that no one cared about. He understood why prison could destroy a man's soul, or it creates so much anger that without warning it could be released on any unsuspecting person.

He told himself that he would not become an animal, and that he would not stay in the metal box. Yet deep down inside, he knew he would. All day long kaleidoscope-type images flashed in his mind—except that instead of seeing various colors, he saw scenes of himself that he truly didn't understand.

In one scene, he was driving. In another scene, he saw smoke from a car crash. Then he thought he could smell blood after he saw the car crash. As his thoughts continued to show him more scenes, it was becoming stronger and stronger in his gut feelings that he was guilty. It seemed obvious to him that he did kill those two people. He fearfully wondered if he deserved to stay in prison.

With the pity party now moving into maximum potential, Xavier lowered his head between his hands, and rubbed his bald head. Evil thoughts were trying to penetrate his reality. He imagined that the public opinion would be that he was supposed to have been a guiding light to bring hope to others, but instead, all he brought was pain and sorrow.

Breaking out of his hopeless attitude, a nearby prisoner angrily yelled, "Xavier! Hey, brother, why'd you mess up? There's enough brothers in here without a chance in life, and you go and blow all the gifts that were handed to you."

Xavier felt enraged and shouted, "Look, I don't know you. I don't care about you. Just mind your own business."

Xavier's self-pity would either continue to seep into his soul or it would transform him due to his anger. That was the most impromptu response he could muster, because he knew that words weren't his best weapon.

Anger begets anger, and in this case, it came as rapid fire shooting back at Xavier with the force of a deadly bullet.

"You think because you're a big fucking football player that I can't kick your black ass. Don't let these bars give you a false sense of safety," the nearby prisoner hollered.

Xavier shot back, "Just remember that behind these bars, you can't run if it doesn't go the way you planned."

Xavier didn't know who the person was. He only got a glimpse of him while being led into his cell, but he vowed that if given the chance, he would do everything in his power to put the man in the next cell in his place.

Chapter 23

Above the sound of laughter from his cellmates, Xavier heard footsteps coming down the hallway. He knew he had gotten the best of the person on the other side of his cell, but he knew there'd be retribution. Cowering in the corner, however, wasn't the answer.

Xavier knew from experience that small men often had a small man complex, which meant that they wanted to fight the biggest man they could find, just to prove themselves. A lot of the smaller guys he knew were very good fighters, but most people always seemed to forget that big guys were good fighters, too. Maybe if he made an example of the guy in the next cell, he could ward off any trouble in the future.

The guard stopped in front of Xavier's cell, apparently oblivious to the yells and screams.

He looked at Xavier, and said, "You have a visitor."

Xavier smiled, and was glad to have an opportunity to get out of his prison cell. He wasn't sure who his visitor might be, but he sure hoped it was Frank.

The guard unlocked Xavier's cell and the two of them walked down the hall past the other prisoners. Xavier made it a point to focus his eyes straight ahead. He didn't want to see them, and he didn't want them to see any insecurity that might be reflected in his own eyes.

The lights that surrounded him as he walked gave him a brief flashback of an old game. But in reality, he hated to admit that he was getting used to the routine of being led in and out of various rooms. As he entered the meeting room, he looked around for his old friend but didn't see him. That was disappointing.

The good news was that he recognized Eric, his lawyer, who was accompanied by another man, who Xavier could only assume was Charles. He had befriended Charles a long time ago, when they were both younger. However, even though he hadn't stayed in contact with him, he knew of him and often kept press clippings of cases that Charles had solved. For Xavier, Charles might be his only hope of ever getting out of prison.

Eric seemed annoyed that Xavier wanted to speak to someone other than himself, but nevertheless, the three men took their seats. Xavier extended his hand to Charles and it was returned with a firm handshake.

Xavier knew that if he had had a son, he would have wanted him to be just like Charles, although they weren't that many years apart. They both looked at each other for a moment, and then it was Charles who spoke first.

"I'm not sure why you asked me to be here, but I'm here."

Xavier smiled even though it wasn't appropriate, and then he said, "I'm glad you came." His voice held back a strangling feeling that crept up around his throat. "I didn't know if you would."

Charles remained quiet, but he looked squarely into Xavier's eyes. It was as if he was searching for something—a clue—that would restore his belief that Xavier was really his hero.

Charles reminded him, "I'm not your lawyer, and I'm not sure if anybody or anything will help you at this moment."

Xavier stared intently into Charles's eyes. Then Xavier leaned back and smiled.

"Actually," he said softly, "you're the only one who popped into my mind. I apologize if this was a bother to you."

Charles felt almost foolish at Xavier's politeness. However, not one to be blown over by kindness, he went straight for the jugular and asked, "Did you kill that couple?"

Xavier lowered his head and then to everyone's surprise, he said, "I believe I did."

His lawyer jumped up and confronted Xavier, "Stop talking. I don't want you saying anything else that might incriminate you. Do you understand?"

Charles put his hand up to stop Eric from moving or speaking.

"Let him speak," said Charles.

Xavier continued, "I don't remember much of that day. It's mostly a blank. But from what everyone has said, and the bits and pieces that I do remember, I think I did kill them."

It looked like Charles and Eric were sitting there in shock trying not to show it.

"Did you try to rape that woman?" asked Charles.

This time Xavier shot back quickly and with confidence.

With his voice raised several notches, he stated, "I swear on my mother's grave that I've done nothing wrong."

Xavier quickly listed all the events as he remembered them happening. As Charles listened to Xavier, and watched his body language, he didn't need Xavier hooked up to a lie detector machine to tell him that Xavier was telling the truth. The odd part, however, was that he had just contradicted his prior statement of confession.

Eric arose from his chair and pointed a finger at Xavier, saying, "I told you to be quiet."

Xavier and Charles stared at him.

Charles tried to slow things down so they could start from the beginning.

"Try to remember that day up until the time when you couldn't remember anymore."

Xavier closed his eyes, and tried with all of his might to think of all the details that had happened that day. He felt annoyed that Eric hadn't even bothered to ask him these simple questions.

Xavier began, "That morning at my house, I remember getting up, watching the news for a bit, checking the mail, signing some autographs, and writing a letter. Then I recall going out to get something to eat. After that, everything's fuzzy until I was at Le's house. But Charles, I didn't rape her."

Charles turned to Eric, and asked, "Did they get a blood test from Xavier?"

Eric's look told him no. Eric sighed and his eyes reflected a look of noncommittal. Charles, however, didn't believe in giving up. He continued asking Xavier more and more questions which he hoped would fill in the blanks. He knew from experience that even though something was not obvious on the outside of a person or shown through an expression, that with deeper inspection, he could uncover the truth.

"Xavier, tell me about your day again. Where did you eat? Who was sitting next to you? Who did you sign the autographs for? Did someone buy you a drink, or did someone give you a drink? Was your drink out of sight for a long or short period of time? I'd also like a list from you of your friends and possible enemies."

Eric stood up and started to protest, "This is my case. He is my client, and I don't want you to take him away from me and undo all the work I've already done."

Charles replied, "Your case is now more than a simple hit-and-run accident. Xavier needs all the help he can get."

Eric sat back down in his chair, but he created enough noise doing so, that it was as if he wanted to make sure that everyone knew he was not happy. Xavier and Charles didn't react to Eric's tantrum.

Xavier wanted to do something that he hadn't done with anyone except Frank—he had to be completely honest about everything. Vulnerable or not, he needed to become transparent. All he could hope was that Charles would believe him.

"The truth is that I'm broke, and I'm on the verge of filing for bankruptcy."

Xavier glanced at Eric, which Charles knew explained why he had been assigned such an inefficient and uncaring lawyer.

"I've been trying to sell my house for almost a year, but there haven't been any takers. The market's not like it used to be, and unfortunately, my type of home is in the price range where anyone with money could build their own dream house. They wouldn't need to buy mine."

Charles didn't know whether to play a violin or to show contempt for what he had just heard. It was the same old story—black athlete makes money, doesn't know what to do with it, and now he's broke. His only comfort was in knowing that wealthy white people had the same story, and had lost their money, too.

Xavier began to tell Charles and Eric about his lack of trust for people and how it had led him to trust the wrong people and make bad investments. Charles didn't care so much about the money unless it had something to do with the case.

After explaining his finances or at least justifying things in his own mind, Xavier began talking about his relationships. He listed the women he had been with, but to Charles's and Eric's surprise, there hadn't been many—maybe only twenty, which wasn't what anyone would expect from an all-star pro athlete.

Charles's evaluation of Xavier was that he was a normal man with a lot of faults, but he wasn't a man who'd intentionally hurt someone.

"How did most of your relationships end?"

"They ended fine. You can ask any of them."

Charles took down the names and phone numbers that Xavier gave him. Charles found it amazing, however, that Xavier had remained in contact with all of them and that they were still friends. Although Charles felt extremely frustrated, his many years of experience had taught him to be patient. He decided to change gears.

"Tell me about the day of the event."

A slight frown appeared on Xavier's forehead as he began to say, "I remember going out to eat lunch and then it all went blank. I know there must have been more but sometimes I wonder if maybe I took too many hits in the head. My days sometimes seem like a blur to me anyhow.

Charles was frustrated that Xavier's lawyer didn't ask more questions. Maybe this was medical. There had been a lot of news lately about athletes and the damages that concussions had caused. He should have had a physical or at the very least, had his blood work done. Charles made the suggestion to Eric as Eric looked insulted by Charles's remarks.

At that moment, the guard entered the room, and said, "Visiting time is over."

Xavier and Charles looked at each other, gave each other an unseen handshake, and departed. Eric looked around the room wondering what had just happened.

Chapter 24

A kernel of corn fell to the floor as Harold continued to enjoy his popcorn. He knew that it wasn't the time to be eating such a snack, but he always enjoyed doing so while watching a good movie. To him, watching Xavier on TV was the best thing he had ever seen.

He stiffened as he felt Miriam's presence behind him. Now he would have to temper his joy and change it into something else. He had always been good at acting, and didn't have to think twice about making things up in the spur of the moment.

Turning slightly to his right, he acted surprised to see Miriam. He sat straighter in the chair and tried to cover up his nakedness. Walking around fully exposed wasn't anything new for him or Miriam, but out of respect for the situation, he felt it wasn't proper.

He placed a towel over his lap, and said, "I was waiting until you woke up before I jumped in the shower. I didn't want to wake you."

Miriam straightened up and rubbed her eyes as though she were wiping sleep from the corners. They both were acting, fooling no one but themselves. Yet, they still had to play the game.

"I can't believe what I just saw on TV," he said.

"What were you watching?" she asked.

"A news report; someone viciously murdered two older people who were out sightseeing. Then he tried to rape another woman."

Harold's words contained colorful adjectives to add to the climatic finality.

"The murderer's name is Xavier."

In her mind, Miriam could never picture Xavier ever hurting anyone. She reacted in the way that a mother or lover would if they had just found out the bad news about a loved one. She braced herself against the wall as if she had just been visited by a ghost.

"Xavier?" she said, with a slight pause in her voice.

She felt convinced that her response wouldn't give off the wrong impression. Harold leapt up from his chair, wrapped the towel around himself and ran to her side. He held her tightly in his arms and gently squeezed her.

"I know," he said to her, "I know."

Miriam wasn't sure what he was talking about, but she pushed him away gently.

"I'm okay," she said, not really wanting him to touch her.

Harold faked being hurt but gave her the space that she needed.

"I know about you and him in college," he said, rehashing what she had already told him.

Miriam shook her head, and said, "College was such a long time ago, and everything between us ended. I have no bitter feelings toward him."

Harold looked at her and put both his hands on her shoulders.

"I know about him and you in college."

The way he said it puzzled and disgusted her.

Feeling the need to defend herself, in a loud whisper, she said, "I've told you, I'm over him."

Harold shook his head as though he were talking to a child.

"No," he said gruffly, "I know what you told me, but I also know the truth."

Miriam was curious, even more so because he left the end of his statement hanging. She wasn't sure what he meant by the truth. Was it the truth as she knew it, or the truth as he knew it in his imaginary world? She looked at him, puzzled, and allowed her gaze to examine him.

"What do you mean 'the truth?'" she finally said after too many moments of silence became uncomfortable for her.

Harold looked at her, concerned. Then he hugged her, and said, "I know that Xavier attacked you in college."

Miriam was shocked at his statement. She had told Harold that she and Xavier had broken up, but not that he had attacked her. The truth had been the other way around, and now she wondered how Harold had come up with such a statement.

"He didn't," she began saying.

Just then, Harold put his hand against her mouth and stopped her from speaking.

"After you told me that you and Xavier had broken up, I did a little investigation of my own. I couldn't believe that Xavier would let such a beautiful angel walk out of his life. Something else had to have happened. Knowing the reputation that athletes have, I was just curious to know if there was more to the story. At first, no one would tell me anything, but then your old college roommate spilled the beans one night."

Miriam looked at him in horror. The look was real, no acting needed. Her roommate, a young woman named Phoebe, had been her friend and partner in crime. They would pretend that they were the dynamic duo seeking and capturing their prey, which, of course, were men.

She was the only one whom Miriam had told about Xavier and how she wanted to get him. In fact, she had even made a bet with her. After the breakup, and in order to save face, she told her that Xavier had attacked her. But she begged her roommate to keep quiet about it. Miriam thought that Phoebe had kept her promise. When Phoebe died a year later in a car accident, Miriam thought her secret was safe forever.

Miriam glared at Harold. Was he testing her to see how she'd react, or did he really know the truth? The believability of her next statement, she decided, would depend on her playing on the side of caution.

"I never told you that he attacked me," she said, trying to mix in a sense of fear along with concern, "and Phoebe died years ago."

Harold acknowledged her by saying, "You're correct, but what you didn't know, was that we met for a brief time before she died. She was concerned for you. She wanted to make sure that I was the right person for you. She even pried into my life, but after doing so, she knew that I had your best interests at heart. She told me what happened between you and Xavier, and she made me promise that I would take care of you."

Miriam's body showed signs of the tension leaving her as she listened intently to Harold.

He leaned in closer, and said, "I kept my word, and like an angel sent only for you, Phoebe was taken back to heaven when her work was done."

Harold made his words sound so poetic, but they dripped with evil. Miriam could only think of her roommate and the memories of their past. Part of her was angry for betraying the truth, but the other part longed for the closeness they had once shared.

Harold brought her back out of her dream state, and said, "You have to do something about this."

Miriam wasn't sure what he was talking about, but then she noticed that he was pointing at the TV. Her eyes widened to the horror of what he was apparently contemplating. Perhaps she was reading him incorrectly, but she hoped it wasn't so. There was no way in her heart that she wanted to go to the police with her story.

Chapter 25

"I will *not* go to the police," Miriam said, stamping her foot.

Harold looked disappointed, and mumbled, "I'm sorry, but I guess I jumped the gun."

She didn't want to ask what he meant. In fact, she'd rather not know, but she could tell by the glint in his eyes that he wanted her to know. She gave in and asked for clarification.

"Do you want to tell me what you meant by that?"

"I called that reporter, you know, that black lady on TV. I called her while you were sleeping. I told her what Xavier did to you."

"You did what?" Miriam shot back.

Now she was angry, and she wasn't going to play the game anymore. Even if Xavier had attacked her, she felt what her husband was asking her to do was totally wrong. He had no right to tell anyone her story without her consent. Now she was caught in a web of lies.

Taking a deep breath, she began, "Harold, you're going to call that news woman and tell her that you made a big mistake. Then you're going to promise me that you'll honor my wishes about not talking to anyone about Xavier."

Harold looked hurt, but it was all an act. He knew she wouldn't like what he did. He figured that she would protest, but he also figured that what he was doing would be for her own good.

He tried to touch her, but she moved away. He told himself that she probably would act like that until she saw the light. He loved her and she was his angel, but she was dirty. Her purity had been soiled by someone who took what she was not willing to offer. He had to make things right and the time was now.

To him, Xavier was an animal who should be kept in jail for the rest of his life.

Suddenly, Miriam screamed, "Why?"

She felt like she was losing control and her wave of emotions surged forward.

Harold felt compassion for his wife. He imagined that she had to carry the pain and shame around for all those years just because of Xavier and what he had done to her.

Miriam screamed at Harold again, but he ignored her. He looked at his wife, moved in close for an embrace, and held her tight. He wanted to say that he was sorry but fought the need to apologize for doing what he thought was right.

To him, Xavier was evil. He could understand his wife's hesitancy, however, because he was the one dredging up all these painful memories that she had to deal with.

Harold assumed that once she spoke to the police, and once the filth was exposed, she would feel clean again. Then in some magnificent way, their marriage would be better than ever.

Miriam started to cry and Harold felt as though she was having a breakthrough. He convinced himself that he was doing the right thing. No matter what she said, they would have to see this through to the end. Just at that moment, as he held her even closer, the doorbell rang.

Miriam looked up in surprise.

"Is it the news people?" she questioned. "I feel like the walls are closing in around me."

Her heart began to beat rapidly as moist droplets of tears forced their way down her cheeks.

Harold took hold of Miriam's hand and the two of them walked to the door. Even though she tugged at his restraint, he didn't let go of her. She wasn't going to run away this time.

For a brief second, he was about to get cold feet, but his gut told him he was doing the right thing. The doorbell rang again just seconds before he opened the door. Harold recognized Angela from the news channel, and she stood alone at the door.

She smiled at them.

From Angela's perspective, she wasn't sure what to make of this couple. The woman looked as though she had recently been beaten up with that reddish bump on her head, while the man had a look of craziness in his eyes.

She had agreed to meet them alone as the man who called had requested. She figured that this risk she was taking might turn out to be the story of a lifetime.

Harold provided information about Miriam and the connection to Xavier that seemed easy enough for Angela to check up on, which she had done the moment after she hung up talking to him. She found the connection to be true, and everything he had said about Miriam was credible, also. Then she did research on Harold and found that he had done time in prison for drug charges, but his record was nothing serious.

To be on the safe side, she had one of her co-workers park down the street and out of view. The agreement was that if she didn't call or return in thirty minutes, then they would come to her rescue.

Still holding onto Miriam, Harold extended his free hand towards Angela. Reluctantly, Angela shook his hand. Miriam appeared to stop struggling, and Harold let her stand off to the side, but not without noticing her cold and uncaring stare.

Miriam didn't want to be in this spot right now, but she also didn't want to appear crazy in front of the news reporter. Her dignity, at this moment in time, was worth more than her hatred towards Harold.

Angela said, "Hi, I'm Angela."

She wasn't sure if she should move forward or not.

At that moment, Harold nodded his head towards a small brown chair, which seemed awkwardly miniature, like a child's chair, compared to the rest of the furniture in the room. This didn't make Angela feel comfortable at all.

"Have a seat," Harold said.

Once seated, she decided to get as many questions out of the way in as short a time as possible. She wanted to be ready to leave in less than fifteen minutes. Inhaling deeply, she took on the demeanor of a news reporter.

"Hello, Miriam," she said, introducing herself.

She spoke as if Harold wasn't in the room, and as if it was just two women confiding in each other.

"I know this may be difficult for you, and I can't even imagine what you've been living through all these years."

She glanced towards Harold.

"Xavier needs to be stopped before he hurts someone again. You can help end your own nightmare."

Miriam crossed her arms around her breast defiantly, and snapped, "You're wasting your time. I have nothing to say."

Angela looked at her, shocked, and not sure where to go next. She contemplated trying to convince Miriam to talk but then decided against it. The fact that she felt uncomfortable around Harold helped her make her next decision. She stood up and extended her hand to Miriam.

Harold's eyes nearly popped out of his head. He couldn't believe what was going on. He went to stop Angela's hand, but she withdrew it.

She didn't really want to talk to him, and she definitely didn't want him touching her.

Harold felt like his world was falling apart. He thought he had everything figured out, and now all of his plans were being destroyed.

His shock quickly turned into anger and he wanted to slap his wife, but he knew we couldn't do it in front of Angela. He tried to refocus so that his fear wouldn't be felt by the two women. He forced a pleasant smile.

"Angela," Harold remarked, "thank you for taking the time to come here. I'm sorry it didn't work out."

As he escorted her to the open door, Angela's look showed concern for Miriam's safety. As she stood on the porch, she inhaled deeply and hurried down the walkway toward the street. She shook her head, not really sure what had just happened. She knew that she'd stay on the story, but she was determined to stay far away from Harold.

Chapter 26

A smell permeated the air, and it was both familiar and sickening to Xavier. To his amazement, it was his fear. For some reason, he was scared. He couldn't shake the feeling that something was happening around him, but he couldn't place it. Several men yelled at him as the guards walked him back to his cell.

The guard who had been his normal tour guide wasn't accompanying him this time. This new guy was even quieter than the first. His jaw seemed large for his square face and no doubt he would be able to take a punch if a quarrel arose. Xavier tried to joke with him, but he didn't laugh. The only sound that could be heard was the clanging of his keys and the occasional taunt from other inmates.

Xavier tried to shake the thoughts that ravaged his mind, but he couldn't. There was no reason for him to be frightened. Besides, he was capable of handling himself in any situation, and he knew that his buddy, Frank, was trying to raise the money to get him out. He was convinced that he'd be out soon. Unfortunately, the judge had set bail at a large amount and, as of now he couldn't even come up with the 15 percent to give to a bail bondsman. At least his lawyer had done something right by getting the judge to even set bail.

The prosecutor wanted bail denied and stated that Xavier had fled the scene of a crime and posed a flight threat. However, Eric reminded the judge that Xavier was the one who had called the police, not Le. He also shot back at the judge that a man was still innocent until proven guilty.

Xavier stopped in front of his cell expecting the door to open, but it remained shut. The guard grabbed him by the arm and led him to the next cell that was full of inmates awaiting trial.

The guard belligerently said, "Celebrity time is over. It's time for you to be in prison."

Quiet filled the air and no one moved. They stared at Xavier. He wanted to protest, but decided against it. He'd never been in prison before, but he figured street credibility was important. The worst thing he could do would be to come in crying and complaining like a baby.

Holding his head up high, and throwing his shoulders back, he tried to appear as large as possible. His size was much larger than some, but there were a couple inmates who even made him look small. He could only imagine what crimes they had committed.

Walking inside the cell, he signaled a greeting with a slight movement of his jaw. Then he looked for an open space to stand. He saw an opening between two smaller guys near the wall, and he figured that was good enough. At least his back would be against the wall and he would have full view of anyone who might try to move toward him.

One man, a smaller black guy with several tattoos on his arm and a large scar on the left side of his face, moved several paces towards Xavier. Even from a distance, he could see the guy's rotten teeth and imagined how bad his breath smelled. His bald head shined in the light of the room, and when he walked, he leaned to one side. Xavier couldn't detect a deformity, but perhaps the man had one leg shorter than the other or maybe he had scoliosis of the spine.

He walked up to Xavier and stopped inches away from his face. His eyes were deadly cold and uncaring, no doubt from being a victim as a child of unloving parents.

Xavier tried to return his stare, matching the coldness in his eyes. For a moment they looked at each other until he spoke. His words were slow and almost painful but straight to the point.

"You kill those people and try to rape that girl?"

Xavier tried to respond in the same cold tone that it was given.

"No!" he said. "Not my style."

The young man wiped his mouth with his hand as if he were contemplating some great mystery of the world.

He spoke, "Yea, that's what I told 'em."

Everyone in the room broke out in laughter.

Xavier wasn't quite sure what to make of things. Maybe the guy was telling the truth, but maybe not. The young man extended his hand to shake Xavier's. In the back of his mind, Xavier was thinking about Frank, wishing that somehow he would magically appear and say that his bail had been made and that he was free to go.

He returned the handshake—almost doing it the white way—thumb to thumb, and handcuff to handcuff, as opposed to shaking like a brother, leaning forward hugging each other with the free arm as you grasped the other.

The young man introduced himself as Thrice. Xavier felt a sense of relief feeling that if names were introduced, he must have passed the test. The images of what he thought prisoners would be like were both reinforced and destroyed at the same time.

Several of the men came over in a friendly manner and shook Xavier's hand. Other men named their stats and told him how they rooted for the opposing team. In response, Xavier easily tossed out remarks that filled the cell with laughter. The friction of the previous moments was gone.

The feeling was unusual for Xavier. He wanted to ask each man what he was in prison for. He wondered if they would all say that they were innocent or if they would admit to specific crimes. Most of the men seemed likeable, but he made a mental note to wash his hands when he got the chance.

Thrice had been staring at Xavier from the corner of the cell. His dark eyes seemed to take in information, as a hunter would size up his prey. Xavier wondered if he had committed any of the crimes that appeared tattooed on his arms. Maybe that was what he did with his victims before he began his attack on them. Stare, watch, contemplate and then strike, that's how he imagined a killer would do it.

After a few more minutes of silence, Thrice came over to Xavier, and said, "Hey, man. What's it like to be famous?"

He had a look in his eyes that gave a hint of the curiosity of a child. Xavier was on guard. An uneasy feeling came over him as he gazed into the man's eyes. Swallowing hard, he told Thrice a little story.

"Life as a celebrity is pretty much what you see on TV, but you still have to put your time and effort into the game. Nobody gives you anything. You have to earn it."

Thrice nodded his head in appreciation and said, "I understand."

He went on to explain to Xavier how he used to play ball when he was little and that he was pretty good. The coaches didn't like him, he said, and his dad would beat him. His mom was on crack, and he didn't have money to really amount to anything.

Xavier thought about everything that Thrice said.

"You can make anything you want out of yourself, even from here if you just believe."

Although Xavier knew what he said was true, he also knew that it was almost impossible to win certain battles. Xavier shook his head and felt sorry for Thrice. Out of an act of compassion, he put his hand on Thrice's shoulder like a longtime friend would do to offer comfort. Thrice moved his shoulder away.

With his dark, cold eyes, he said, "Oh, by the way, I'm supposed to kill you."

Chapter 27

Xavier's eyes widened. He wasn't quite sure if he had heard Thrice correctly. When he looked at him, he saw the same dark, empty stare that had previously covered his face. Death was not something Xavier was afraid of, but hearing those words from someone he had just joked with a moment earlier threw him for a loop.

Not in his normal voice, but in a soft, almost childlike whisper, he said, "You were *supposed* to kill me?"

Thrice didn't blink as he repeated his statement. Then he leaned in closer to Xavier, and said, "I could if I wanted to. It could have happened a long time ago."

Xavier felt a pointed object probing his side. He looked down and saw a metal shank that if placed at the right spot, could have ended his life quickly.

Words seemed to slither out of Thrice's mouth, but his thick almost swollen lips didn't move.

"When you're in prison and someone wants you dead, you won't last very long."

As Xavier began to protest, he felt the shank move deeper into his skin. Sizing Thrice up, he figured that given enough room, he could easily take him to the ground. However, considering his current situation and position, Thrice would probably make sure he'd be dead, or at least he'd create a puncture wound near Xavier's lungs.

Thrice moved his body closer, and mumbled, "I don't want you dead, but if I don't kill you, someone else will, or maybe they'll kill me for not doing my job."

In a way, Xavier felt sorry for this young man. There was something about him, a sense of hopelessness that made him feel that he had no choice in life. It was like all he could do was to play the role of the puppet. Someone else pulled the strings.

"Hit me," Thrice said.

Xavier wrinkled his brow as if to ask why, but then Thrice clenched his jaw and said it again.

"Hit me."

Once the message was received, it didn't have to be asked again. Xavier swung his fist and connected with the boney part of Thrice's nose. Blood immediately began to spring forward as Thrice jumped up.

Everyone in the cell moved back, giving the two men room to fight. They had no doubt seen prison fights before and knew that the impeding action could cause harm to their own bodies if they somehow got in the way, or if they mistakenly helped the wrong side.

Thrice, now upright on his feet, lunged at Xavier and shoved the shank in towards his gut. Xavier was not sure, but it seemed a half-hearted effort. Nevertheless, he wasn't going to question Thrice's actions.

Moving to the side, he caught Thrice by the arm and delivered a punch to the kidney. Thrice buckled over in pain. He bent down on one knee and cursed, as he spit blood from his face. He tried to lunge once more but missed. He nearly fell over and stabbed himself.

Someone yelled that the guard was coming. Both men stopped and looked at each other. Xavier stood his ground, ready for the next move, but to his surprise, Thrice wiped his mouth and sat back down on the seat.

Everyone else moved back in place as if nothing was happening. That left Xavier standing alone in the middle of the cell with his fists up in the air ready to fight an invisible enemy.

Two guards ran to the cell, looked at Thrice's bloodied face, and asked, "Is there a problem here?"

Thrice spit blood on the floor and said, "I fell."

The guards looked around at everyone and then at Xavier. The guard with the square jaw told his partner to grab him. They took him out of the room, which was what Xavier had been praying for. He wasn't sure what had just happened, but he was glad to be out of that cell.

The guards asked him what had gone on, but Xavier remained quiet. Everyone else kept quiet about the incident, too, and he didn't want to be the one to break some silent code.

Pulling him away, Xavier looked over his shoulder at his would-be assassin. Thrice lifted his head and gave a slight nod in his direction. It was only a slight movement that could have easily been missed if no one was paying attention, but it was enough to let Xavier know that Thrice had thrown the fight.

"Thugs and Angels" was a song that Xavier had heard a long time ago, and the very words seemed to be a reality.

"The soul of a gansta, crying out like a pranksta. Priest, trying to live his life right, but his death is the death of a man past the limelight."

Xavier could do nothing but thank God as he walked towards his freedom or at least the small amount that he would have for the moment. His life had been spared by the most unlikely person, and he wondered what was in the heart of his Savior.

Xavier was placed back in the small cell that he had been in before. Even though he had only been in there for a short time, he still felt the loneliness and hopelessness that he could only imagine how each person had felt who had sat there before him.

Lowering his head, he tried to pray, but prayer seemed so far away from him now. Two people were dead and he did it. Prayer wasn't what he wanted or needed, but he wanted to find out the truth. He wasn't sure what had happened, and he wished that if there was a God, that he would magically change back the hands of time and piece together the events of the past.

Xavier pictured Le in his mind. He couldn't believe that she had said that he tried to rape her. He wondered what he had done to deserve the bad luck that he was receiving. The fight in the other cell had left him shaken.

He inhaled deeply and tried to catch his breath. Why would someone want him dead? He knew hitting the old couple might have angered some people, and it may have even angered them enough to want him dead. What he didn't understand was who had enough pull to actually put someone in prison to have him killed?

Now all he could hope for was to get some bail money before someone else had a chance to really kill him. As if on cue, the guard walked back to his cell door and unlocked it.

In his sullen, deadpan voice, he said, "You've made bail."

Chapter 28

A red tomato—a big, bright, juicy, red tomato—was what Harold's face looked like. Veins protruded from the side of his neck, and his eyes bulged as he shook in the very place where he stood. Miriam had been scared, but she stood her ground. She wouldn't talk to the press about something that Xavier never did, but worse, she hated her husband for calling the media to their home. Normally, she would try to bully Harold, but this time, she was afraid of him.

He glared at her and watched her standing there like a statue. The more time that passed without her moving, made him angrier and more frustrated. His face grew redder by the moment.

In Miriam's mind, she hoped that he would blow a fuse and have a heart attack, but it didn't happen.

"I don't understand what's wrong with you," he shouted. "Why, after all I've done for you, would you hide the truth? Are you trying to protect him?"

He stopped fuming for a moment, and then as if figuring something out, he said, "I have to ask you, did Xavier really rape you?"

Miriam froze. She couldn't tell her husband the truth.

Harold moved in closer and his face was within inches of her face, when he said, slowly, "Did Xavier rape you?"

She could smell his anger, almost taste it. She tried to move away, but he grabbed her and pushed her against the wall. She tried to stand her ground, but he was strong, much stronger that she remembered.

He took his other hand, put it around her throat and began to choke her. She tried to fight, but the more she moved and resisted, the tighter his grip became.

The look in his eyes was like that of a wild and crazed animal. It felt like he wanted her dead, and she felt her life slipping away. She began to cry. Pain was not her concern. She just didn't want to die by the hands of her husband.

Harold clenched his teeth and snarled as Miriam's eyes began to roll to the back of her head.

A tingling sensation started at the tips of her fingers and ran up her arm. Coldness slipped over her body and caused her to want to seek warmth. This is it, she thought, as darkness covered her, giving the room a gray and black hue.

She could hear Harold's voice yelling at her in the background, almost as if he were three rooms away.

"Did you love him?" he screamed.

Before everything went black, and before her world faded into nothingness, she mouthed the words, "Yes, I did!"

Harold, seeing her body go limp, somehow managed to take control of his anger. It was the vision that he had always dreamed of but never thought he would be living out. Miriam's body dropped to the ground with a thud. She lay still as Harold prayed that she was faking it, like she had done before. But this time she didn't move.

Her lips were turning a pale blue, and when he felt for her pulse, he couldn't feel it. In seconds, he played a different scenario in his mind. He tried to bring her back, and he hoped that she would forgive him. But somewhere deep inside, he knew that he had crossed a boundary that wouldn't allow him to return. He could try to get rid of her body and say that she had left him, but after the news reporter's visit, it would be more complicated.

He paced frantically from the living room to the front hall. Then he bent over her again to check her pulse. With a faint glimmer of hope, he thought he felt several light heartbeats. Maybe she wasn't dead. Maybe she was just hanging on. He was relieved at the thought of her still being alive, but that presented a whole new set of problems.

Several moments later, her heartbeat became stronger and she came to, though weakly. Not knowing how long she had been blacked out, she saw Harold leaning over her. In her half-crazed state, she swore to herself that she would leave him or go to the police and turn him in once this was all over. Miriam's breathing was shallow. She was alive, but she also slipped back into her unconscious dreamland between life and death.

In a strange way, Harold felt more alive than he had ever felt, at least in the past few years. As sick as it sounded, choking his wife almost to the point of death somehow made him feel that he was releasing his inner demons. He rubbed her neck, and when he saw the bruises where his hands had been, including his fingerprints, his heart began to race.

As if reenacting what he had just done, he lightly gripped her neck, and placed his hands exactly as the imprints were on her neck. Again, he squeezed her neck lightly until he heard her moan. The noise and the thought of choking her again were almost too exciting for him. Nevertheless, he knew he had to control himself, or this time he would kill her.

He had to think about what to do, or more exactly, what he wanted to do. He could nurse her back to health, but then again, she didn't have a whole lot of friends, so people wouldn't miss her. The main emotional and psychological problem, however, was what he had just done to her.

If he let her live, how would he ever explain the marks around her neck? He closed his eyes and tried to think, but the feeling of his hands around her neck almost became an overwhelming obsession. With each passing minute, the desire to strangle her became more and more powerful. There was only one thing for him to do. He had to get up and walk away.

His heart jumped as he heard a knock on the door. Quickly scanning the room, he tried to look and see if anyone would be able to look in and see Miriam's body on the floor. The wooden door had no windows, and the living room shades were down, so he felt somewhat safe, at least for the moment.

If someone were really trying to get in or find out if someone was home, he imagined that after several knocks, the visitor would try to move to the side windows to at least look inside. Harold couldn't take a chance that that would happen. He had to be cautious. If he opened the door too wide, he'd undoubtedly expose a portion of Miriam's body lying on the floor. He had to make a decision. He rushed to the door and opened it just a crack.

Angela, the news reporter, smiled as she stood ready to knock again. Harold opened the door just enough to see that she was alone. However, he did note that a white van with blacked out windows and a News Channel 7 logo was parked close to the curb.

He had no time to worry about it, but still, he felt betrayed by the reporter. Now he had to be doubly careful knowing that he couldn't trust her.

Angela asked in a polite voice, "Can I talk to Miriam?"

Boldly, he stated, "Miriam's lying down. She complained of a really bad headache because of everything that's happened. In fact," he added, "she has a migraine."

To Harold, it appeared as if Angela looked concerned, but not as much as she was just being nosey. He sensed that she was after a story, and he didn't like her persistence.

Angela said, "I'm sorry for the intrusion, but I came up with several background questions about Xavier that I'd like to ask her. Sometimes I'm like a bumbling idiot and I feel like I'd forget my head if it wasn't attached."

She feigned a soft laugh, but Harold was on to her.

"Would you please tell Miriam that it will only take a minute?" Angela said, now curiously noticing the subtle thing that Harold was doing wrong.

She noticed the way he leaned his body against the door as if to conceal any vision of someone looking in. She noticed the sweat on his forehead even though earlier Angela knew they lived in an air-conditioned home. She also noticed that when his eyes scanned the surroundings, one moment he was looking at her, and then the next moment he was focusing on the van parked near the house.

Angela had also been trained to recognize when someone's body language indicated that they were lying. Harold, oddly enough, exhibited most of the patterns. In fact, he touched his face as he talked, was stiff, and his words and body seemed off-key.

Pressing the issue like any good reporter would do, she took a step forward and said, "I'll only need a moment."

Harold's arm quickly stopped her. He became slightly enraged, and spoke in a loud voice, "I've already told you that my wife is in bed with a migraine, and now I'm asking you to kindly leave."

With that, he pushed her out of the way and slammed the door.

Angela almost expected as much and would have been shocked if it hadn't ended that way. Now her senses were tingling, and she knew she had a story.

Chapter 29

Angela, the news reporter, looked over her shoulder several times before entering the white Channel 7 van. Harold watched her get into the van, and then he waited until they drove away. He knew he only had a small window of time before someone would come snooping around again, and he had to work fast.

Everything was backfiring on him, though, and it was all due to his wife. Now he was getting unwanted attention. He quickly looked around the room, frantically contemplating what to do next. His world was spinning out of control, but oddly enough, he enjoyed the feeling.

At his job, they used him to solve problems, and this wasn't any different. He stopped and took a deep breath. Then he created a mental timetable as to the length of time he would have, and how he would put everything into action.

First on his agenda was to get Miriam out of the hallway and off the floor. He didn't want to take a chance that someone would show up at his door again.

He lifted her up the way a fireman would carry a victim—draping her over his shoulders. For some reason, she felt heavier than he imagined as his knees almost buckled under her weight. He braced himself against the wall and forced his way into the bedroom.

The room, although fairly large for the size of their home, had only one central window. Harold didn't mind that because it wasn't his final destination for her. He quickly moved her into the bathroom and laid her gently in the tub. Smiling, he looked at her and thought to himself how beautiful she was; almost angelic as she laid still.

He felt her pulse again and it was getting stronger. That was even better news for him and his plan. He walked out of the room and headed towards his closet. Moving the hanging clothes to the far side of the closet rod, he reached into the back of the closet and pulled out a small metal box. He dug into his pants pocket, pulled out a set of keys, and unlocked the box. Moving swiftly, he removed everything that he needed and headed back to the bathroom.

He looked at Miriam lying in the tub, and he noticed that she was beginning to move a little. He knew he had to work fast. He opened a vial that he had retrieved from the metal container, and poured its contents into Miriam's mouth. She stirred for a moment, swallowed, coughed, and then fell back into her slumber. Harold hoped that he had done it correctly. He was pretty sure that he had given her the right amount, but he had felt rushed. He knew he wasn't in total control of himself as he wanted to be, so he just hoped for the best.

Standing over her, he plotted out his next plan of attack. Ice, he thought to himself. He needed to get some ice. He made a quick dash into the kitchen and opened the freezer compartment. Looking in the cabinets to his left, he grabbed a bowl and filled it with two handfuls of ice. Then he quickly ran back to the bedroom, but not before peeking out the window to make sure the Channel 7 van wasn't there.

Harold's heart rate rose rapidly, and he could feel the heart beats pounding against his chest. He chuckled to himself thinking that if he could really pull this off, then he must be a genius. He wanted to praise himself for what he had done already, but stopped. He remembered his father's words, "Early praise will lead to early failure." Harold had become a firm believer in his father's wisdom.

Holding a few pieces of ice in his hand, he began to rub the ice around Miriam's neck where his hands had been. He hated to see the imprints fade, but he knew that if he could somehow reduce the swelling or even the appearance of his hand prints, then everything would be in order.

Miriam was still out cold even though he was rubbing ice on her. It was as if she was dead or a shell of the woman that had once been his bride. He admitted to himself that this way seemed much more to his liking.

Harold used the ice for about twenty minutes and then stopped. He thanked God that he could no longer see any swelling or marks on her neck. He also could barely see any hand prints. He imagined that when she became conscious again, her neck would be sore, but he had planned for that excuse.

Next, he removed her clothes, and filled the tub with water. It was a risk, but he figured it would be one worth taking. He gave her a bath, and made sure that some of her hair remained in the tub. Miriam stirred some, but she still laid in her slumber as Harold dried her off and put a bathrobe on her.

Then he carefully pulled the covers back on their bed and gently laid her there to continue her slumber. When everything was cleaned up and put back into its proper place, Harold went into the other room to watch TV.

He wondered if there was anything more he could do, but it felt like he had done everything he had to do. It was out of his hands now. All he could do was wait. As he positioned himself comfortably on the couch, he wondered if he could find a news channel and perhaps learn more about Xavier. He continued to press buttons on the remote control.

"Xavier has just been released on bail," the voice on the television said.

That was it. The news reporter went on to talk about other stories. Xavier was old news now. Harold sighed. He wanted to know more. He flipped through several other channels and struggled to find more coverage on Xavier. Although he heard short snippets of news, it still wasn't enough to satisfy him.

Closing his eyes, he tried to imagine himself as the athlete and what he must be feeling right now. He tried to imagine that fear of going to prison and knowing that his reputation was ruined. It was an image that brought a smile to his face, but to his surprise, the thought of choking his wife gave him an even greater high than any news he could hear about Xavier.

No matter how hard he tried, he knew he was losing control. His body shivered with the thought of reliving the incident over and over in his mind. He could still feel her warm neck in his hands, and he relived that power raging though his body.

The greatest part of it all was the fear he had seen in her eyes and her greater-than-thou attitude slowing slipping away and disappearing into that of a fearful child searching for help.

Feeling his pulse rise in his body, he couldn't sit still anymore. He had to get up and look at her again, to see what he had done. Jumping to his feet, he power walked into the bedroom. His eyes widened and the corner of his lips curled upward into a smile as he looked at his wife. Her damp hair swirled around her face and her eyes were closed.

Even though she had put on a fair amount of weight, she was still beautiful to him. He took a step forward and then stopped. He wanted to continue walking but fought against it. The feeling of losing control was a thrill for him, but he still fought to command his body. Leaning forward, afraid to move anymore, he stretched his neck and tried to get a glimpse of her throat.

A soft pinkish color now returned to her face as she breathed in and out using deep and slow breaths. He began to match her breathing, inhaling and exhaling as she did. Closing his eyes, he imagined once more that his hands were tightly encircling her neck. Then he pushed the thought out of his mind. He knew it was something he could do. After all, this wasn't the first time that he had gotten away with a crime.

Chapter 30

After posting bail for Xavier, Frank stood in the lobby of the jail and with his hands extended, he welcomed his old friend. He always looked to Xavier as somewhat of a son, and he hated seeing him in his current situation. It was as if the illusion of being better than animals had now been stripped from him and replaced by fear.

Xavier was silent and pensive, as though confused as to what he should do or say to Frank as they walked to Frank's car.

Xavier decided to sit in the back seat.

With a curious tone in his voice, Xavier asked, "Are you okay?"

Frank looked at him through the rearview mirror, not minding his position of being the chauffeur. Even after all the troubles that Xavier's had to face, Frank thought, it's still amazing to me how my friend always thinks about others before he thinks about himself. Frank nodded and then began to drive.

The silence and heaviness of the situation made the trip feel as though it was weighed down with the weight of the world. Age-wrinkled fingers pushed the button on the radio of Frank's old 1984 Cadillac. His car was dated but still in top condition for an automobile of its age. The car was a small glimpse of the man who owned it. Although old, he was in fine condition, just like his car.

Jazz with an up-tempo beat created a light pounding sensation in both men's ears, but because of the situation, it couldn't force its way to their souls as jazz was meant to do.

It had only been a short time since Xavier had been locked up, but it seemed like forever. The beat of the music, the horns, and the piano only seemed to remind him that it was background music for a sad play. It was as if he was living a true-to-life nightmare, and he couldn't wake up from it.

The more his mind dwelt on the position he was in, the more he wanted to blame someone. Like his days in football, he wanted to exact his vengeance on the enemy in front of him, but the enemy was unseen.

"Why in the hell is this happening to me?" he said, not really sure why or how the words had come out of his mouth.

Frank looked in the rearview mirror. His gaze searched Xavier's face, not in judgment, but in compassion for the man he called his friend. Frank started to say something but decided not to. He figured that sometimes God had to speak for himself, and he only needed to get out of the way.

The drive was slow and long as each man sat in silence. Frank continued glancing back at Xavier, and in his mind, he silently prayed for guidance. Maybe like Moses, he, too, would see a burning bush.

Xavier's face brightened as they drove up the pathway to his home. There was safety in his castle, and everything in him wanted to jump out of the car, even though it was moving. Frank's car slowed to a squeaky stop. The weather was warm and pleasant, and gave no sign of the unpleasantness of the situation.

Xavier walked with a quick pace to his front door and walked inside. His mind was focused as he headed straight to his bedroom. He closed the door and looked in the mirror. He was free, but like the golden frame that surrounded the glass mirror, he saw his reflection surrounded and encased, and it made him regret that he was who he was.

Frank knew that Xavier needed to have his space, but he worried about leaving him in his current condition. Silently he prayed for him, hoping that the closed door was only to separate himself from life for a moment, and not to take his own life.

Pain shot through Xavier's skull as the man he looked at had become less than a man. All the evidence pointed to him killing the older couple, and that in itself was a hard thing for him to bear. He hadn't harmed anyone intentionally, but he did have to face the fact of what he was accused of doing. Two people would no longer enjoy each other on this earth again.

His encounter with Le was still a mystery to him, too, but he felt confident that he'd somehow be found innocent. The thing that worried him the most upon his release was the fact that someone wanted him dead.

A knock on his bedroom door made him jump. Angry at himself for being fearful again, he shook his head and walked to the door, but he didn't open it.

He didn't intend to yell, but his voice came out in a gruff grunt, "What the hell do you want?"

Frank stood on the other side of the door, shocked, but not surprised by his tone. He didn't want to reply, not yet. Not because of hurt feelings by Xavier's temporary rage, but the fact that he knew that Xavier didn't mean it. He didn't want him to suffer the indignity of having to apologize.

Xavier hated what he was becoming, but he felt angry. He wondered why God was cursing him with everything that was going on. He heard the light tap of a knock on the door again as if this time would be the right pass code and he would be allowed in.

Frank waited, and after a few more moments of silence, he relented, gave in, and walked away.

"Good," Xavier thought. "I don't need a Bible preaching old man talking to me about the word."

Xavier shook his head. Everything he said was wrong, and he knew it.

Opening the door quickly, Xavier rushed out and saw Frank as he returned to the couch. He walked over and put his hand on his buddy's shoulder.

"I'm sorry for what I said," he murmured, holding back his mixed emotions.

Frank, like usual, only looked up and smiled.

Then he said, "I called the detective, and he's on his way over."

Xavier smiled, although he didn't know why. Even though his dream had included a detective, his faith was diminishing. He rationalized that dreams were nothing more than distant thoughts.

Looking at Frank, he asked, "Is there any new information or anything that could help me?"

"I'm not sure, but the detective told me he was searching around and hopefully he would come up with something."

Xavier still felt an anguish that he only remembered from his childhood—a life of hard knocks that made him into a great football player but was smoothed over by his fame and wealth.

He wished he could close his eyes and somehow forget, but each time he opened them, he saw Frank and felt the pain of what he was accused of doing.

Chapter 31

Time had passed since Le returned home from the hospital, but she still had that lost feeling inside of her. The traumatic events remained in her memory. She reached for the tea kettle on the stove, and stared at her hand that trembled. She felt like a nervous wreck.

Just the thought of how she had lied to protect her family wasn't the difficult part. The unnerving emotions were wrought by how she was convicting an innocent man—a man who hadn't hurt her at all, and in fact, he had probably saved her life.

Even though she had never been attacked before, she knew what it felt like to have sex without love. Senator Stevens, whom she had agreed to give her body to, in exchange for him allowing her and her family to enter the country, was a situation that she regretted more with each passing day.

Yes, she was glad they were living in America, but just the thought of being a servant to him whenever he waved his hand or commanded her to do something for him, made her sick to her stomach. If it wasn't for him, she wouldn't be in all this trouble.

A male voice from the other room made her jump. She knew he was there, but he was like a ghost. His voice seemed to penetrate her soul, while his gaze followed her every move.

"I'd like some tea, also, cousin," the voice said.

Then before she could even acknowledge him, he repeated what he had just said.

She froze, feeling that each time he spoke, he took bits and pieces from her soul. To anyone who observed them, it might appear that he was her protective angel. He wouldn't allow any man even close enough to touch her, but she knew what was in his heart and soul. To her, he was the demon—the anti-Christ in her life.

As she prepared the tea, she felt his cold hands touching her shoulder. He spoke to her in a whisper, but she could feel his hot breath on the nape of her neck.

"You know, cousin," he said, "you've caused a great deal of trouble. Was it too much to ask for you not to open your door to strangers?"

Le wanted to say that she had done what was right, but she knew that the devil who stood next to her wouldn't acknowledge that there was a difference between good and evil. She was just his pawn, and nothing she could say would make any difference.

Placing his hand next to hers, he began to caress her, moving from her right side to behind her body, and making sure that he brushed up against her.

"Once this is over," he said, "I'm afraid the senator will have no use for you, but not to worry."

She stiffened, afraid to move.

"American men don't understand how to treat Korean women. But you won't have to worry about providing for yourself or your family. Once the senator tosses you aside, I'll take care of you if you'll take care of me."

Le knew what that meant for her. She knew of his charity and what he had done with other Korean women. Some worked the streets, and some worked in American massage parlors; but all of them became pleasures for others just to earn more cash for her cousin.

Le moved away and pretended to search for something in the pantry. It had become a regular routine of hers as the senator had often tried to kiss her neck, and she didn't know how to escape his advances. She knew her place with him but hated it when his lips touched hers. His thin pockets of flesh made her skin crawl, as he'd often try to pretend that what he was doing was out of love for her.

Jimmy laughed knowing that he made her uncomfortable and that was the way he liked it. For him, women were nothing more than pets, and although Le was someone else's pet, he knew he would soon have her.

Perhaps the senator would order him to kill Le, which he figured would be okay with him also. Either way, he would have his fun first and then fulfill his duty. Laughing to himself, he figured no one would be around to find out what he had done.

A knock on the door drew him out of his mild daydream and back to reality. He sighed as he thought about dealing with another reporter. The more they hung around, the more of a chance they would have of finding something. The senator didn't like mistakes.

Jimmy motioned to Le. He pointed to a chair and waited for her to sit.

"Don't say a word," he whispered, and then he put his hand next to his chest where she knew he carried a small gun.

Le did as she was told and took the tea with her as she sat in the chair next to the table. Moving as stealthily as a cat, Jimmy quietly and swiftly moved towards the door. His stride was controlled and strong, yet fluid, like a dancer. He looked back at her once more before opening the door.

The sun hit Jimmy's face, and he squinted to get a look at the man in front of him. The figure didn't resemble the reporter, but he had learned to never judge anyone by their look or their physique. The senator didn't seem like the type to go after Asian women, but his own job was a testimony to the fact that you can't judge a book by its cover.

"Can I help you?" he said in his politest voice, while bowing slightly to the man in front of him.

Charles stepped back, not sure what Jimmy was doing as he put a noticeable distance between them.

"I'm here to speak with Le," Charles said trying to sound official again.

Both men had been trained and both men sized each other up for the truth and to somehow judge the abilities and fighting skills of the other.

Jimmy asked, "Are you a reporter?"

Charles said, "I'm a detective. I just want to ask Le a few questions."

"My cousin has been through a lot already and is taking a nap, detective...," Jimmy said, letting his sentence hang, as if waiting for Charles to tell him his name.

"Charles. My name is Detective Charles. I'm sorry for disturbing you. I understand, and I know she's been through a lot."

He reached into his pocket and pulled out one of his detective cards and handed it to Jimmy, saying, "I'll try back at a later time. I only have a couple questions that I'd like to ask her."

Jimmy smiled, but already he knew that he didn't like the man in front of him.

Suddenly, the sound of breaking glass startled both men. Charles noticed that Jimmy's first move was to grab at something on his left side, which revealed a small handgun. To Charles, knowing that the man had a gun made him suspect that this wasn't just a friend of Le's who was trying to help her.

Charles moved a few steps to the right where he could glance into the next room. He saw Le picking up the glass off the floor. He started walking towards the door.

Although Jimmy was only five-foot-seven, he stood his ground. In a flash, Jimmy put his hand out and blocked Charles's attempt to enter the room.

Charles smiled and said, "It looks like Le's awake now. I'll only be a minute."

Charles attempted to move Jimmy's arm out of the way, but that's when he noticed the tight bundle of muscles in Jimmy's forearm. Jimmy didn't budge. He continued to block the doorway.

"My cousin doesn't wish to speak to anyone right now," he said, pushing Charles a little harder.

Both men glared at each other until Charles glanced towards Le. He saw fear in her eyes.

His attention was brought back to the man standing in front of him who demanded, "Show me your badge."

Chapter 32

Charles looked straight ahead knowing that he had to play the game by Jimmy's rules. He just didn't know what he would say next, since they had taken away his badge.

Jimmy stared at the business card Charles had handed him earlier. As Charles watched him, he became aware of the telephone number that was on the card. At that moment he knew that Jimmy could call the office and the game would be over.

Charles cleared his throat and tried not to show any signs that a person lying would exhibit. Opening his mouth, he prayed that the right words would come out.

"I…" he began to say, but was interrupted by the presence of Le walking towards him. "Excuse me, miss, could I have a word with you?" he shouted.

Charles looked at her face which seemed to be pained as she continued walking towards Charles. Jimmy clenched his jaw muscles and then turned towards Le. His face was red with anger.

Le looked at him with somewhat of a fearful glance, but she was determined to speak with Charles nonetheless. She marched right past Jimmy and stood directly in front of Charles.

Her face appeared sweet and simple. She held her head up while at the same time Jimmy put his hand on her shoulder. Charles held his breath in anticipation of hearing her say that Xavier was innocent.

"Please leave me alone," she said.

Charles was shocked. He tried not to show it, but her words cut through him like a knife. Whatever hope he had, was gone. Quickly, he decided to try a last-ditch effort. He wasn't quite sure, but something in her eyes told him that there was still a glimmer of hope.

Maybe her statement was a cool ruse to fool Jimmy who was now peering over her. Quickly, he moved his hand into his side pocket and palmed a card. It was a move he had practiced several times before, almost to perfection. Taking her by the hand, he placed the card in hers, but out of Jimmy's view.

"I know you've been through a lot, but if you..." Charles's words fell short.

As if on cue, Jimmy reacted by pushing Charles in the shoulder. Charles allowed his body to go numb as he absorbed most of the impact, but he could still feel the force of the blow.

Jimmy was strong and knew how to use what he had. His size betrayed his strength, and the push brought a slight throb to Charles's shoulder.

Charles lowered his head as if he had been defeated and turned to walk away. He hoped that his acting bought Le enough time to take the card and place it someplace where Jimmy wouldn't see it. The cards that he kept in his pocket contained his private numbers, and he used the cards for cases just like this one.

Several times in the past he had to stop domestic disputes, and out of fear, the woman would clam up. He would hand the husband the office card knowing that it would be trashed, but at the same time, he palmed the other card and handed it to the female. Because of such a maneuver, several women made it safely to an abuse protection center without their husbands knowing they had talked to the detective until it was too late.

His only hope was that he had read Le's face correctly. He was taking a big gamble, and if it didn't pay off, he could be in some serious trouble.

Charles slowly backed out the front door and headed towards his car. Once inside, he cautiously backed out of the driveway. Glancing at the house, he saw Jimmy standing defiantly at the window, as if to let him know that he was guarding Le and the house.

Charles gave him a military salute as a wave of goodbye, although his true desire was to extend his middle finger to let him know what he really thought. He figured that he'd have another opportunity in the future.

Jimmy closed the door and then grabbed Le by the arms. He pulled her into the center of the house. She had safely put the card away in her pants pocket, but knew there'd be a price to pay.

As expected, Jimmy pushed her to the floor, and like a cat, he quickly jumped on her. His eyes had lost their dark black color and now seemed to be replaced by slits that housed no lights.

"Please don't hurt me," Le said, hoping her begging would be enough to stop the violence that might come against her.

Jimmy raised his hand high in the air, palm facing upward to strike a blow that would do damage, but not with the force of his bare knuckles. It was a technique he had done before. Le closed her eyes in anticipation of the pain. She held her breath and waited, but the pain never came. Jimmy removed himself from straddling her.

She opened her eyes and saw him staring at her. His chest moved up and down in a vigorous motion like he had just run several sprints. This to her was more painful than the punch she would have endured.

He angrily stormed out of the room, with his words spraying a path of spit as he ratcheted his head around and hissed, "Don't *ever* disobey me again."

It wasn't much, but enough to covey a simple truth. If she disobeyed him again, she would die. Le began to shake violently and nearly lost control of her body.

"I told him to leave," she said, but she wasn't sure if getting in the last word was the right thing to do. It might've been better to remain silent.

Jimmy came from around the corner and just stared at her. Like a lost child, she felt alone and afraid. Cautiously, she moved to set herself up right. He continued to watch her, and didn't show any emotion. His anger appeared to be under control, and she thought that he was breathing normally again.

Le turned with her back facing Jimmy for a moment to adjust her outfit. When she turned back around to look at him, she jumped. He was standing within inches of her. He had made no noise, and she had no sense of him moving in the room. She couldn't understand how he could move from across the room and stand directly behind her, yet she had no sense of him being there.

He whispered in her ear, and she knew if she was to remain alive, senator or no senator, she would have to obey Jimmy.

"Fix us some tea," he said and then returned to the couch.

She no longer existed for him. Like a small bug, she knew she'd be crushed without a second thought. From that moment on, she knew she had no choice but to obey him. She also knew that somehow she had to make contact with the detective.

Chapter 33

Night came swiftly as Frank settled in at Xavier's home in preparation for being his babysitter for the night. It had been fairly quiet, with only a few reporters showing up to ask occasional questions and making idiotic statements.

Years had passed since Xavier had played his final game of football. Although Frank still thought of him as a great player, he felt somewhat disappointed at how he had overestimated Xavier's value to the world. Fame didn't serve athletes very well unless they were a mega star. Nevertheless, Xavier had been good for his team, even if he never reached the level of godhood as other players had.

A knock on the door drew him away from his comfortable spot on the couch. He assumed that it would only be another low-level reporter trying to find some dirt that the bigger crows had overlooked. He already had his standard reply ready as he opened the door.

However, he didn't have time to react as he stared down the barrel of a gun shoved into his face. All he could do was put his hands above his head. The barrel, no doubt enlarged by the proximity of the gun, pressed coldly against his forehead.

Three men stood on the porch; each wore a simple, dark black mask. The man with the gun didn't speak. He just placed his index finger perpendicular to his lips, signaling for Frank to be quiet.

Religion, if done right, is a good teacher of obedience and Frank was a good student. Although he wanted to scream, he knew that they could have killed him already.

He was pushed gently back to the couch, where he sat down like an obedient child waiting for punishment. His legs trembled as he imagined the force of a gun with such a close range exploding into his skull. The two other men moved around the house with their guns drawn, almost in military precision. The one holding the gun pointed at Frank's head must have been the lead as he pointed out directions by using sign signals.

For a moment, Frank thought back to the days of his youth and imagined himself being fast enough to take the gun from the gunman's hand. It was only a fleeting thought. He knew even at his prime, he would never have had enough speed to perform such a maneuver.

One of the two men, with slow and steady steps, headed toward Xavier's room. The other man stood with his gun pointed towards the hallway with a clear shot at anyone exiting.

Frank's gunman continued to point his gun towards him while looking over his shoulder. He appeared calm and unbothered. He nodded his head and both men vanished into Xavier's room.

In less than a minute, Xavier was escorted into the living room wearing a pair of gray jogging shorts and a T-shirt. He had a look of terror in his eyes as they made him sit in a chair across from Frank. The man holding the gun to Frank's head reached into his pocket and pulled out two pieces of paper and a pen. He pointed the pen at Xavier.

Frank looked over at the papers with only his eyes, not being close enough to see what was written. The gun was pressed close enough to his head that he feared the slightest movement would make it go off. The gunman pointed to one of the sheets of paper that had some writing on it, and then he pointed to the other sheet of paper.

His men moved in close and surrounded Xavier even tighter than before. It was if they had prepared for this moment all their lives—trained to be efficient in their duties. Xavier's eyes widened and he spoke for the first time.

"I will NOT write this note," he said belligerently, as he pushed the other paper away.

One of the men started to raise his hand as if intending to slap Xavier across the back of the neck, but he stopped in mid-air as the leader stared him down. He now pressed the gun deeper into Frank's skin, and for a quick second, Frank felt pain from the cold steel against his forehead, and he winced.

The gunman cocked the trigger. Frank thought that no matter what he might do, he'd lose this game. Who could win such a standoff when three men had guns and one didn't?

"Our Father, who art in heaven," Frank began to say.

It was the only thing that he could think of, but he was happy to know that God was still so deep in him that even in the worst situation he would call on his name.

Xavier looked up like a child searching for advice or asking for permission to speak. Frank blinked as a signal to let him know that everything would be all right, which gave Xavier some amount of comfort.

With a trembling hand, Xavier began to write. It was only a few words but enough to make the gunman relax his gun on Frank's head.

With speed that even surprised him, Frank decided to make a move. He reached for the gunman's hand and pushed the gun up towards the ceiling. A loud shot rang out as flakes of wood and plaster fell to the floor.

Xavier moved quickly and pounded one of the men in the face and the other in his lower extremities. His blows hurt them, but it would be only a moment before they recovered. Grabbing the guy nearest to him, he twisted his neck until it popped; his body fell to the floor with a thud.

The other man slowly recovered from his first punch and witnessed his friend's death. That's when he pointed his gun at Xavier. He paused for only a second and then a loud bang was heard.

Xavier closed his eyes and braced for his death, but it wasn't his death that came. The gunman in front of him dropped to the ground. His arm twitched for a moment and then he stopped moving. Xavier looked up to see Frank struggling with the remaining gunman. It was his gun that had gone off; he had killed his own partner.

Frank was holding on for dear life as the gunman tried to overpower him. It was amazing enough that Frank at his age was strong enough to force the gunman's hand towards his partner to shoot, but that he could still hold on was a miracle.

Xavier reached over to help, but once again his knee gave way and he stumbled. Frank had now lost his grip on the gunman's hand and fell back onto the couch.

A loud bang, a wisp of smoke, and Frank lay motionless. Xavier regained his stance and stared at his friend sprawled out in front of him. Blood oozed out of Frank's shirt near his chest.

In a rage, Xavier lunged at the gunman and knocked him to the ground. His weapon fell from his hand. Xavier dove for the gun and both men wrestled for it. At one moment, Xavier felt that he had control of it. He grasped the handle and moved his hand towards the trigger, but as he squeezed, nothing happened.

The masked man's eyes smiled as if he had a secret that no one else knew. He hit Xavier in the face, which caused him to stagger back for a moment.

Between the blood and the pain, Xavier couldn't understand why the gun hadn't fired. The masked man grabbed the pistol, flipped the safety lever, and now pointed the gun, once again, at Xavier. The safety had somehow been put on while they were in the midst of their struggle. Now there was nothing stopping the bullet from exiting the gun.

To make matters worse, the other gunman who Xavier had thought was dead was now starting to move. He hadn't died from a gunshot wound; he had merely been stunned. The tough, heavy material of the man's bulletproof vest quickly flashed in Xavier's mind, while at the same moment he wanted to curse God for making bulletproof vests.

Death was coming for him, just like in jail. Except this time there'd be no one there to stop it. The gunman took aim but then turned for a quick second as something distracted him.

It was Frank once again with his dying breath. It gave Xavier one last chance to be saved. He gasped loudly, seemingly to call forth his Master. A microsecond passed between the gunman's distraction and Xavier's right cross to his face. It floored the gunman.

Forcing his knee to work by his strong willpower, Xavier ran for his life. No shots in the back and no loud bang. He fled from his home and ran deep into the woods with the image of Frank's death playing in his mind.

Chapter 34

Trees and bushes assaulted Xavier's face and body as he ran for his life. He couldn't think about anything, except putting enough distance between himself and the two gunmen. His body ached, especially his knee, and every muscle screamed for him to stop, but he pushed himself and kept running.

He wasn't a Boy Scout, and he'd never learned survival skills, but running was something he had done all his life. Running in the night's darkness forced his body to relive memories of his past.

With no light to guide him, he was lost, even though he was near his property. The moon hid itself and refused to shine its nightly glow as a beacon for him to follow. Darkness brought a coolness that two lovers might find enjoyable, hidden lovingly under a blanket, but for Xavier, it was cold.

His sweat attached itself to his forehead and droplets of perspiration moved begrudgingly across his brow. He had to stop soon. He knew it, but feared that any moment the two remaining gunmen would be standing behind him waiting to finish the business they had started.

A loud pop from a branch breaking beneath his feet made him stop running. He stood frozen in place, looking around, trying to detect any movement in the darkness. He listened and slowly turned 360 degrees, looking, watching, listening, and waiting. But it seemed like he was alone and not being followed. He breathed deep and considered his options.

He was tired and his body screamed out in pain from lack of air, but he still wanted to push on. Gingerly, he completed a few long strides forward, and then his body gave in. His legs trembled and folded beneath him. He used his hands to break his fall as he hit the ground and rolled to his side.

Holding his breath, he turned, half expecting a bullet to tear through his flesh and leave him lifeless like his pal, Frank. He waited and then waited some more, but there was nothing; only the sound of his heavy, rugged breathing and an occasional chirp from a bird.

He almost hated himself for choosing to lift weights instead of keeping up his running routine. The outside of his body looked tone and fit, but he could only imagine the damage his internal organs must have endured due to his poor diet choices and lack of aerobic training.

Xavier held his head back and gazed up into the darkened sky, almost instinctively asking God why he had allowed Frank to die, but not really expecting an answer. At the moment, he was angry at himself for running away and leaving Frank there to die alone. He was a strong man and should have wrestled the gun out of the stranger's hand. But he lost, and his mistake had cost his friend his life. His soul wanted him to justify the event. Maybe it was old injuries, or perhaps the stranger had been trained to protect his gun. Xavier grasped at anything to help alleviate the guilt.

There was no peace; no feeling that everything would be okay; no thought of forgiveness; just the cold hard facts. Frank was dead and it was because of him.

The old man had given him a chance at the cost of his life, and he failed. Childhood insecurities filled him and made him want to cry out for a hug or a comforting word that would make things all better. He waited, still looking up at the dark void that would be the night sky. He struggled between his anger at God and waiting for something, anything, to make him feel better.

Xavier tried to mentally replay what happened, He wanted to be sure that this time he wouldn't blank out. He was determined that if anyone asked him what happened, he could tell them in full detail.

He was in his bed, not asleep. He wasn't even lying under the covers, but on top, with his entire body spread like an "X" over his bed. His eyes were closed as he thought about his life and where things were going. He had made his peace with Frank and had returned to his room to rest. He heard footsteps outside his closed door, but thought nothing of them. He knew Frank was in the house, and he could only assume that he was the one making the sounds.

The gunmen rushed his room, catching him off-guard. They moved quickly as they pointed the gun towards his head and then pointed a finger towards the door. Xavier had never been afraid of guns. In fact, he learned how to shoot when he was quite young. However, staring down the barrel of a loaded pistol and knowing the damage it could do, immediately put him in a submissive role under their authority. He followed their orders with the strict obedience of a football player.

Xavier wondered if he knew the gunmen and could recognize their facial features underneath the masks. He wasn't sure about his connection to them and could only imagine that it was probably related to his would-be jail execution fiasco.

A thought flashed into his mind and he winced in pain. His body began to shake as he relived his actions in slow motion. The piece of paper, he thought—the piece of paper and the words caused chills to crawl up his flesh. Images of him writing the sentences filled his soul with terror. He had written, "To whom it may concern: After all I have done, I can't live with myself any longer. Goodbye."

It was a suicide note. If he could kick himself at that very moment, he would. How could he have written those words? Fear had made him do it. He was scared and only did as he was told to do at the time. That was his excuse. He knew he was signing his own death confession, but the look in Frank's face said to follow along and everything would be all right.

His mind raced with a mixture of sorrow and self-pity. Why was someone trying to kill him, and why was he in this mess?

The sound of twigs breaking in the distance caused him to jump. His eyes strained to see who was coming. He crouched lower to the ground, not sure if he could be seen in the moonless night, but wished he could somehow magically disappear.

He waited for several moments, holding his breath as long as he could. A few more minutes and then there was nothing. Maybe his mind was playing tricks on him. Maybe it was the sound of his pounding heart.

A small animal ran past Xavier, allowing him to relax, but only a little bit. Everything about the woods was pretty much unfamiliar to him. It's not that he was just a city boy, but he never had much use for trees, plants, or insects. To him, plants and flowers were meant to brighten up a home, but not enough to go camp out in the woods to see what goes on day and night while they grew.

Heck, he could watch the Discovery channel to learn about things like that. He surely didn't need to get familiar with living in a forest to appreciate nature. Yet, he was the one who had bought his home out in the middle of nowhere to get away from his fans. Now the distance, the empty space, and the trees that seemed to be in the distance when he viewed them from his home, appeared to come alive to choke the life out of him.

Trying to gain some recognition of where he was, he paused, thinking back to the direction he had come from. He figured he must have run at least two or three miles, which would have allowed him to cover an incredible distance on foot in such a short amount of time.

West, east, he couldn't be sure which direction was which. Even if he discovered his location, he wasn't sure if he would know what to do with it. Thinking about his long drive to his house, he knew there was a home nearby, but at this moment, he had no idea where he was, or even where the other house was located.

He hated the fact that he really didn't know his neighbors. What would they think of him if he showed up breathing hard and covered with leaves, dirt, and branches? Would they help him, or would they call 9-1-1 to have him picked up?

Xavier decided that the best course of action was to keep going straight ahead. He couldn't tell where he was at, but the thought of the gun staring him down made him push himself beyond the pain of his swollen knee. Fire raced up and down his back leg. His lower back screamed for him to stop, but he vowed that he would continue, if not for himself, then for Frank.

Trees seemed to leap in front of him in the darkness, which caused him to stumble and fall to the ground several more times. His mind kept telling his body to give in, but he had trained too many years to ignore his mind.

He pushed harder to get up. Straining and favoring his left side, Xavier unexpectedly caught a glimpse of a light in the distance. It was far away, but he knew it was a light, which meant someone might be home. He just prayed that the gunmen weren't trying to follow him, and asked Frank's spirit to somehow guide him to safety

Chapter 35

Harold gazed at Miriam's sleeping form, and judging by the outside light, he must have been standing there for a couple hours. His body ached as he shifted his weight from one leg to another, and then he leaned against the wall for relief, wondering when she'd awaken.

He ignored his pain, but delighted in his pleasure of being able to stare at Miriam—she was his prize. He felt like he couldn't control himself. He waited with animal instincts arising within him for her to wake up.

Like killer whales with their seals as they would play with their prey, he wanted to relive the moment again, take advantage of his prey, and turn his rage and madness into some sort of perverted fun. Several times his heart raced with excitement when she stirred in her sleep. He couldn't wait to see how she would react when she awakened.

But during the past several hours, it was as if he were being betrayed by her. Every time she woke up, she would immediately slip back into her unconscious slumber. Time seemed to stand still, but he couldn't move from his spot. He felt that if he moved, in a strange way, the thrill of seeing her awaken would lessen his thrill of the total experience.

Miriam rolled over on her side and faced Harold. Her glistening body was almost too much for him to resist; yet, he waited patiently. Then, when he least expected it, she moaned. Then her eyes snapped open.

She stared at him. She tried to focus her gaze on him, yet everything appeared as a blur. She fought the fog that veiled her eyes, and she stared at him again, hard this time as she tried to gain control over her sight. Although her vision was blurred, she wanted to know if it was really him.

"Harold," she called out to him, "is it you?"

Harold changed positions and moved closer to her, but he said nothing. He had been waiting for this moment for hours. He looked at her, and then closed his eyes, as if living a fantasy.

She watched him. She saw that uncontrollable fixation when his pupils turned into large dark orbs. She didn't want to respond to him. She closed her eyes and pretended to slip back into her deep slumber. She allowed her body to go limp and her breathing to become rhythmic. She wanted to pretend she was still in a deep coma. If she let him know that she was beginning to awaken, he'd want to put his hands all over her body. She couldn't bear the thought of him touching her—not now and maybe not ever.

He closed his eyes and he stood in front of her, lost in a fantasy world as if paralyzed by the thoughts that consumed his mind. Miriam's throat hurt and she felt tired. So after several minutes, she gave up her ruse and forced herself to get up.

Raking her hands through her hair, she was aware that her body ached and she just felt "off." What happened, and why was he standing over her?

Harold continued to stand over her as some ancient witch doctor in a trance praying over one of its members.

She knew something was wrong, but as hard as she tried, she couldn't remember what had happened before she had awakened. She kicked off the sheets that shrouded her body, and with as little noise as possible, she tried not to arouse him from his trance as she sat up in bed.

She realized that she was naked, but she couldn't understand or remember how or why she would be that way. Then she examined every inch of her naked skin.

"What did you do to me?" she demanded as her frustration from not remembering came to a boiling point. "Did we have sex? Did you do something to me because you were so angry at Xavier?"

Harold opened his eyes and moved closer to the bed, but for what seemed like minutes, he said nothing. He gazed at her, in a sensual way, while moving closer to her.

Miriam, seeing the panther-like look in his eyes, became frightened. She pulled on the bed sheets and tried to draw them around her naked body.

But Harold was no dummy. He took his time, and allowed himself a few more visual moments, as he enjoyed the confused look on her face.

More than that, he reveled in the fact that it appeared as if his plan had worked.

Miriam pulled the sheets tighter against her body. She felt violated somehow and used. The frowning expression on Harold's face annoyed Miriam, yet she said nothing.

He asked, "What's the last thing you can remember?"

He prayed that his little plan had worked.

Miriam thought about it for a moment, but then as she tried to focus, her mind suddenly went blank. She tried to come up with an answer to his question.

"The only thing I can remember is when I was talking to a news reporter," she replied.

Harold tried to hide his smile but inside he was jumping for joy. Things had worked out better than he had planned. All he needed to do now was fill in the rest of his plan.

"After the reporter left, you said that you wanted to take a shower; something about you feeling dirty about the whole situation," he said.

Harold couldn't wait to see how well he could turn into the actor he imagined himself to be.

"I thought you were dead," he said. "I found you in the shower passed out, nearly drowning. I didn't know what to do."

Miriam leaned back and squinted her eyes at him. She could feel her forehead wrinkling as she stared at him in disbelief.

He continued with his charade, and said, "You were leaning over the tub in an awkward position with your neck over the edge of the tub. When I went to grab you, you began fighting me. I grabbed your neck and head while trying to pull you out from under the shower. I guess the stress of the day and the fall you must have taken from the shower almost killed you."

He figured this would explain away any remaining bruises.

Tears began to flow from his eyes as he moved closer to give her a hug. Miriam believed that he was lying but couldn't prove anything either way. Her body became an empty vessel as she allowed him to hug her.

He whispered over and over in her ear, "I was so frightened at the thought of losing you."

Miriam closed her eyes and allowed his body to press hard against her. She wanted to die. She didn't want to live this type of life anymore.

Harold put his hand on her shoulder and pushed her away gently. Then he looked her in the eye and said, "You need to see a doctor."

He knew it was a gamble on his part, but he knew that she had a fear of doctors and would only go if he forced her to do it. The bottom line was that it would make him seem like he had nothing to hide.

Miriam shook her head violently, and hollered, "I'm fine. I don't need a doctor."

Harold pretended that he hadn't heard her as he tried to convince her that he had feared for her life. He yammered on that a hospital would be the best place for her, yet she resisted.

Vaguely, she remembered him asking if she needed anything. Yet all she could remember was that she had wanted her memory to return so she would get back to normal.

Time flew by for her and now she stood in front of her husband. His eyes seemed loving but she knew they were only empty pits—no compassion, and definitely, no love.

Harold fought the urge to smile, and to reach up and grab her neck again. He began to shake slightly, and closed his eyes. He knew he had to resist reliving his dream, but he was losing the battle.

He watched as his hands moved stealthily around the base of Miriam's neck. He saw a look of fear in her eyes, but it excited him all the more. At that moment, he knew from deep down inside himself that he had to regain control of this situation. He couldn't afford to mess up his plan with his lack of discipline.

Smoothly and naturally, Harold adjusted his hands into the position of a loving husband's massage on the nape of her neck. Gently, he kissed her cheek. Looking at her, he examined her body and made sure there were no marks on her neck. Once satisfied, he walked out of the room.

Miriam couldn't remember what had gone on, but she could have sworn that she had heard him laughing as he turned to leave.

Chapter 36

Le felt like a mouse that was waiting for a hungry cat to pounce on her. Jimmy surveyed her every move, and smiled as she walked. It was as if he was enjoying knowing that he caused high levels of anxiety to explode within her. The thought of him touching her made her stomach turn, but she had to stay focused. It would be only a matter of time before he didn't care what the senator said and would decide to do with her whatever he wanted.

His eyes, like a mirror to his soul, were black, dark, and cold. She feared for her life, and she had only one strategy for escaping this nightmare. Moving quickly in the kitchen, she wanted to ensure that everything was normal. He was watching her and she knew his eyes were keen. She placed a large black teapot on the stove and waited until the water boiled.

"I'd like some tea now," he demanded.

She knew that she needed to be subservient to him. She also knew that if she wasn't quick, he'd become angry, and she feared his anger. Moving to the cabinets, she looked through all her herbs. Some were for tea, some for healing, and some for sleeping.

To the untrained eye, they would look the same, but she knew which ones to use. Taking two cups, she mixed the tea with the sleeping herbs. It was a gamble, but if she could get him to drink enough, she would be free.

Jimmy spoke from the other room; his voice was calm, but demanding.

"What are you doing?" he asked, aware that it was taking her longer than usual to brew a pot of tea.

Le tried to think like he would think; her reply would be important.

With her back to the door, she said, "I'm making the tea, and I know how particular you are, so I wanted to do it right."

There was silence, and then as if by magic, she felt his breath on the back of her neck.

"When I ask for tea, it had better be quick. Get used to it."

His words were meant to scare her and they did. She was frightened and immediately had doubts about her plan.

Turning, she stood face to face with him. He looked at her and didn't smile. In fact, Le thought, he showed no emotions—just raw, controlled hate.

"I'll take that from you," he said as he took the cup out of her hand.

It wasn't the cup she wanted to give him, but because she was determined to outsmart him, she had placed the sleeping herbs into both teacups. Jimmy looked at her and then the cup. His eyes wandered over, past, and through her body.

He studied her for a moment and then asked, "Where's your cup?"

Le quickly turned and lifted up the second cup of tea that she had made.

Jimmy laughed and then said, "Woman, I'm not stupid. You're Korean, and Korean women are tricky." He laughed again, and then his mood changed abruptly, as he snarled, "I don't trust Korean women."

Le's heart began to pound hard and fast as she tried not to show fear in her eyes, but she was scared. Perhaps he wouldn't drink the tea. Maybe he'd force her to drink the tea that was in her cup, proving his point. She just didn't want him to hurt her, but she knew he could.

Jimmy laughed again and then took the cup that she had poured.

"We drink together," he said.

Le didn't blink. All she could do was stare at him and hope that he hadn't seen past her facade. She lifted her cup and they both drank. Le tried to drink her tea as fast as she could—a gulp and a swallow and she was done. Even as the water passed over her lips and burned her tongue, it was worth it to get away from the man who stood in front of her.

Jimmy took small sips and licked his lips slowly as if indicating his plans for her later. She wanted to get away from him, and made an attempt to leave the room, but he stopped her.

"Slow down," he admonished. "Enjoy the flavor."

Her stomach turned as his suggestion had a sexual undertone, but she had to play the part. She pretended there was more tea in her cup as she took short sips of air.

He smiled at her and whispered, "Perhaps I will not kill you."

Then he chugged the rest of his tea.

Jimmy led her into the living room and sat her on the couch. He began to stroke her hair as he talked to her. She tried to close her eyes, but he continued to speak and move closer. Le prayed that the herbs would kick in soon. She hated him being so close to her, but she knew she couldn't escape his caresses.

Suddenly, Jimmy stopped talking. He put his hand on her leg. She wanted to pull away but bit her lip instead. Expecting the worst, she closed her eyes, inhaled, and waited, but nothing happened.

Afraid to open her eyes, she waited again until she heard the heavy breathing and the sound she had longed to hear—Jimmy snoring. Sound asleep, his head and shoulder slumped limply against her body.

Le breathed a sigh a relief and pushed him off of her. Although she had also put the sleeping herbs in her own teacup, she had been smart enough to drink something earlier that counteracted the effects.

Running away was something she had thought about, but she decided to stick to the plan. She reached into her pocket and pulled out a piece of paper that had a number written on it. The number was for the detective.

Chapter 37

Xavier wanted to jump for joy at the sight of the light in the distance, but he calmed himself. Going to strange houses had gotten him into trouble before, and he didn't want to make the same mistake twice.

He had never really taken the time to speak with his neighbors, and he doubted they even knew who he was. He also thought about the fact that he was a large black man, with branches, dirt, and twigs all over his body. If a neighbor saw him walking up their driveway late at night and even if their security lights would illuminate his approach, he surely didn't want someone to grab their firearm and blow his head off just because they felt threatened. But he had to take the risk of asking for help.

The wind blew across his face and his body ached. The light in the distance encouraged him to move forward, if nothing else, for Frank's sake. He wanted to honor the memory of a man who had been more than a friend to him. He had been like a father.

The lights, like heaven itself, were becoming brighter as he approached the immensely large estate. A dog barked, and the sound made Xavier jump. He stopped walking and listened for another sound.

The dog barked again, and he knew he wasn't dealing with a small-sized dog. He hoped the animal was tethered, and he also hoped that the gunmen weren't responsible for the dog being there. However, while he was lost in his thoughts thinking about the size of the animal, another dog came barreling towards him as if engaged in a game of distract and destroy. In his tired and aching body state, the inevitable made him sick to his stomach. He was in no mood to get chewed on by dogs.

Xavier ran in a zigzag pattern towards the house. He wasn't sure why he did that, but maybe it was his football training that instinctively kicked in. Better safe than sorry, he thought.

Suddenly he heard two barking dogs behind him. Their barks and growls were loud and angry. Xavier tried to figure out their proximity to him. Whoever lived in the house couldn't afford to let them run loose, but he determined that they had probably been trained to protect their turf.

With the front door in full view, Xavier began an all-out sprint. Just as he approached, he realized that while the dogs were free they were also enclosed behind a strong metal fence.

The large, deep mahogany door had a beautiful swan glass imprint on it that dwarfed even Xavier, who was a large-statured man. He felt insignificant next to it as he imagined that it was precisely the owner's intent.

He leaned on the doorbell continuously, but no one answered. Although relieved that the dogs were encased, he needed to get some help. He knew somehow, someone had to be there if only to feed the dogs, yet several tries later, no one answered.

The barking dogs were going crazy and Xavier was now faced with a decision he didn't want to make. He could continue his stealth run in the darkness, looking for a place to hide, or he could attempt a break-in just to use the phone.

He hated to commit a crime again, so soon after being released from prison, but in his mind, he had no choice. If he waited any longer, the gunmen would kill him. In his distress, he thought about Frank's death and now his own soul cried out for justice.

Xavier wasn't sure if he could jimmy the door open, but he knew that this was one time when his strength was an asset. His hands trembled as he reached for the knob. To his surprise, the door was unlocked. He walked inside and quickly scanned the area as he closed the door behind him. His mind raced but more than anything, he felt guilty for all that he was doing, but not guilty enough to turn back.

Out of the darkness, Xavier heard an old man's voice calling out, "Hello?"

It startled him, especially because he thought no one was home. He turned and thought about running out the door, but his legs wouldn't carry him. He felt frozen in place.

"Great!" he murmured.

"Hello?" the voice screamed out again. "I've got a gun."

Xavier immediately put his hands above his head to show that he had already surrendered.

"Who's there?" the voice demanded.

"Xavier. I'm your neighbor, and I need to use your phone."

There was silence for a moment, and then from a far corner of the room, a man became visible. From the distance, he appeared to be in his sixties and still in fairly good shape. He had thinning gray hair, wore glasses, and had a taut jaw. A large dog stood next to him in eerie silence.

Xavier wondered why the dog didn't bark, but it really didn't matter. From the look of the dog's snarl and big teeth, he knew that the animal was ready to kill on command.

"You broke into my home to use a phone? That's a funny way to introduce yourself, neighbor," the old man said.

Xavier still kept his hands in the air fearing that any wrong move might lead to the dog being released or him being shot. The old man moved slowly towards Xavier. The dog continued to bear his teeth, but walked stride-for-stride alongside his master.

Xavier understood why the other two dogs were in the yard. They were probably the man's warning system, because the dog inside the house appeared to be the muscle.

"You're that athlete who's been on the news lately, aren't you?" the old man asked while pointing a boney finger at Xavier.

"Yes," Xavier replied, in a humble tone.

By now, Xavier's arms were starting to feel the exhaustion of the day, but fear gave him the extra will to keep them up in the air.

The old man didn't bother to introduce himself but got straight to the point.

"I should let this dog tear you into shreds, but I won't," he paused, "'cause I used to be one of your fans!"

Chapter 38

Xavier wasn't sure what to do next. The old man still had the dog and just because he was a fan, didn't mean that he couldn't become dog meat.

"You can put your arms down," the old man instructed him. "As long as I'm the one with the dog, I have nothing to worry about."

Xavier lowered his hands slowly, fearing that at any moment the dog could go crazy and his master wouldn't be able to handle him.

"I don't have a gun," Xavier assured the old man.

There was a chuckle. The old man was laughing at his comment.

"I assure you," the old man said, "if you did have a gun or even tried to reach for it, not only would my dogs devour you, but I'd pump a few bullets into you just for the heck of it."

The old man showed him the pistol he had referred to earlier.

Xavier swallowed hard.

"Come in, son," the old man said, "but walk slowly and don't raise your voice."

Xavier could hardly believe what was going on. All he knew was that he urgently needed to get to a phone.

"I need to use your phone, sir. Please, it's an emergency."

The old man seemed oblivious of anything that Xavier said. He rambled on about nothing of importance while he moved closer to Xavier.

"You know, son, I've really enjoyed the way you played ball. I tell you, you played with a lot of heart. That's something that is missing nowadays."

Xavier stood still, listening to the compliments he had heard so often in his past.

Now the old man was within a few feet of him, and said, "We've been neighbors for years now, but I've never met you. I do value my privacy as I'm sure you do."

Xavier hated to interrupt him but he needed to get to a phone.

"Sir," he began to say, but was interrupted once more by the old man.

"I'm sorry. I didn't introduce myself. My name is Senator Stevens, but you can call me Steve."

The name meant little to Xavier other than the fact that he was stopping Xavier from making his call.

The old man continued, "Son, do you believe in fate?"

Xavier didn't understand what he was talking about, but shook his head in acknowledgment.

The senator went on, "Good, because I believe in fate, also. Take you, for instance. Never in all my years would I have expected you to show up on my doorstep."

Xavier was starting to wonder what the senator was talking about. To him, he sounded crazy. In fact, he looked crazy standing there holding a gun with an attack dog next to him.

Without warning, the senator changed subjects.

"My property, and the land all around here, is surrounded by cameras," he said, chuckling. "When I told you that I wasn't worried about you, I really wasn't. I had been watching you. I've got you on film, breaking into my house."

Xavier's jaw dropped, and he sighed deeply.

"Too bad about you and Le," he said out of nowhere. "I guess it was fate that this would be the only chance I would ever get to meet my neighbor."

The name Le seemed familiar to Xavier and then it hit him. Le was the Korean woman he supposedly attacked.

"You know, son, you have a bad habit of blacking out. You really should give up that drug habit of yours."

The senator slowly lifted his arms so that his gun was pointed towards Xavier's chest.

Xavier retaliated with an angry tone, and said, "What are you talking about? I don't do drugs."

The senator laughed, and replied, "You will by the end of the day."

His statement puzzled Xavier. It seemed to be coming out of nowhere. Xavier wondered if maybe the senator was suffering from some sort of age disease, like dementia or Alzheimer's.

"Maybe that's why they got rid of you. You don't listen well. Anyhow, it doesn't matter. I have you on film breaking into my house," he said.

Xavier glared at the old man, but said nothing.

"I jumped up, frightened, and I shot you. That sounds about right."

The senator was talking crazy, and Xavier couldn't believe what he was hearing.

The senator smiled, saying, "Guess what's going to happen now?"

Xavier was getting mad. He raised his voice and yelled, "I don't care!"

The large dog barked.

The senator said, "I warned you, Xavier, not to raise your voice. I'm not sure if I'm strong enough to hold this dog back, because he really does want to attack you."

Xavier put his hand back in the air as if to signal that he understood. He silently waited for the senator to speak.

"Son, do you remember the letter you wrote before your buddy was shot?"

Xavier didn't care anymore. Dog or no dog, he was going to kick the old man's ass. His heart was pounding from anger and the death of his friend. Then it dawned on him. How did the old man know about the house and what he'd written?

A smile spread across the old man's face.

"I see you remember. That's good!"

Xavier started to think about what he had been forced to write. It was a suicide note, and with the death of Frank, there were no witnesses to the truth.

The senator coughed and then straightened himself up.

"I've already called the police. They're on their way. They'll think you were on drugs, that you tried to kill yourself, but instead you killed your friend. Then you came to my house, broke in, looking for money."

Xavier rolled his eyes. Of all the houses in the neighborhood, he had to choose this one.

"Oh, right," the senator said, "I forgot. Then I shot you."

A loud blast from the chamber of the old man's gun filled the quiet night air. Xavier's body flew backwards and then he dropped to the floor from the force of a single bullet.

Chapter 39

Charles drove away from Le's home with a sense of hope that somehow he was going to get some answers. His hope also slipped into a prayer that Le would find a way to call him, and that she'd be okay.

He picked up his phone and dialed his mother's number. He figured it was time to give her an update.

In response to her son's report, she said, "Keep doing what you're doing. I feel like something big is going to happen."

"Thanks, Mom. That's exactly what I needed to hear."

He knew that he relied on her to give him a word of encouragement, praise, or swift kick in the butt. Today's words of wisdom, however, gave him space to do his work.

Driving around, Charles allowed his mind to wander. He imagined fighting with Jimmy, Le's cousin, or whoever he was, and that brought a smile to his face. Jimmy seemed like he would be a worthy adversary, but Charles believed he could take him.

Charles was by no means a bad fighter, but he knew how to learn from his failures and could adjust to most situations. Now what he needed to do more than anything was to just drive and enjoy this quiet time. Being on the force for so long had taught him the value of this.

The sun began to set as darkness rolled in from the horizon. Charles checked his phone to make sure he still had a signal. He didn't realize he had driven so far from his home, and it took him nearly two hours to get back.

As he pulled in the driveway, he remembered that he had not seen his dog all day. He wondered if dogs really cared about their masters. He knew X did, but still, he wondered if all dogs had the same level of love that people did.

His question was answered as he walked to the front door, pulled out his keys, and heard X barking. When Charles opened the door, X whined, jumped up and down and rolled onto his back for Charles to pet him.

Charles looked at X's bowl and saw that there was food still left, so it wasn't food that made him miss his master, but love. Charles quickly changed into jogging shorts and figured that he'd spend a little time jogging outside with his buddy.

It was a warm night, which meant that he could only jog for a few miles before X wore out, but figured he'd take his cell phone just in case he got a call. He also brought along X's favorite ball. After the run he'd throw the ball, X would fetch it and drop it at his feet. It was a game they often played even when both master and dog were tired.

As Charles moved midway between his run, he paused for a moment to let X do his business. He thought about his marriage and wondered if he had been like X, willing to sacrifice out of love, if he'd still be married. X looked at Charles and began to lick his bare leg. His warm saliva and rough tongue were the marks of loving expressions from X.

Charles returned the favor by petting X behind the ears, which was his favorite spot. Both man and beast looked at the darkness ahead of them and continued jogging.

Not much time had passed when suddenly Charles's phone rang. It was his buddy from the police force. Charles didn't like the sound of his hushed tone as he began to speak.

"Have you been watching the news?"

Charles stopped jogging and threw the ball for X to retrieve. He knew that anytime a conversation starts off with, "Have you watched the news," that it wasn't a good sign.

"What's going on?"

His day had been long and he was in no mood to waste time.

"Xavier's been shot. He's nearly dead," the voice on the other end said.

Although Charles had stopped running, his heart began racing as if he were involved in a marathon. When X returned, it was as if he intuitively sensed his master's anxiety. He moved in close to him and stood at attention.

"What? Where? When?" Charles demanded.

"Xavier's in the hospital, barely hanging on to his life. The doctors don't think he'll make it through the night," the officer said in a low tone.

Charles closed his eyes. He didn't want to hear anymore news about Xavier. This was too much to bear. The night air seemed cooler, almost freezing, and the darkness became claustrophobic. Charles ran back to his house. His goal was to make it to the hospital before Xavier died. He had to see him in person to promise him that he would try to clear his name. One way or another, he'd get there.

The jog home went faster than he expected. X could barely keep up. He was panting and at one point he almost sat down in protest. Charles hated treating his best friend that way, but in his mind, he had promised that no matter what, he would see this through with Xavier. He'd find a way to make it up to his dog later.

He had no time to shower, and he figured that people would have to deal with his smell. Xavier was more important to him at the moment. X whined a bit as he saw his master leave, but it was something he had grown accustomed to.

After a few moments, he headed to his usual corner. Charles left a quick message for Alice to let her know that his schedule might be all over the place and asked if she could check in on X every once in awhile.

Tonight was one more example of all the things that he had put his family through, including the countless hours they spent on the force. He put his car in reverse and tried to get rid of the raging thoughts that filled his mind.

The road seemed to disappear as Charles raced to the hospital. En route, he received another call. His informant told him about the suicide letter that Xavier had written. He also mentioned that they found some drugs on him. That was another blow to the circumstances, but still, somehow, he knew what he felt.

He still believed that Xavier, against his own will, was caught up in some crazy scheme. Even though he couldn't put his finger on it, he knew deep inside that Xavier was innocent.

Chapter 40

Charles arrived at the hospital, which had now become a mad house. Xavier took over the top spot in the news again. He was being accused of killing Frank and was also being charged with the attempted murder of the senator.

Even if Charles wanted to, there was no way he was going to be able to see Xavier. He tried to use every connection he could think of, but even if he was still on the force, getting in to see Xavier would be nearly impossible.

Charles searched for answers but he was like the hundreds of others who were looking for something to grab onto. Everything seemed to be going out of control. The thought of Xavier trying to attack a senator was beyond crazy. It was just plain stupid, even if he was on drugs. Who would do something like that when they were already in trouble?

The big news stations pulled out their top people to cover the story. Given that Xavier was an ex-football player who previously had a good reputation, only fueled the fire for reporters to dig up more dirt about him.

Charles rubbed his head and wondered what to do next. Things weren't looking good for Xavier. Not granting a dying man his peace seemed utterly unfair, but being treated fairly had never been part of his life.

Charles felt the touch of a hand on his shoulder. It was the news lady that he'd seen on TV before and may have spoken to at one time or another about a case. He recognized her face but couldn't remember her name.

Extending her hand, she smiled and introduced herself as she obviously knew him.

"Angela," she announced.

Charles nodded in response but he didn't shake her hand. He didn't feel like talking to her especially since she was a reporter.

Angela retracted her hand, and gave him a look as if he had deeply insulted her.

"I know you don't care too much for reporters, especially the way they attacked you after your shooting incident."

That information hit Charles the wrong way, but now he remembered her. He pointed his finger at Angela's face and said, "Get the hell away from me."

Angela smiled, knowing she had his attention now.

She asked, "Why are you here at the hospital?"

She knew that he was off the force and wondered why he had shown up.

Charles turned to walk away. Angela followed. She continued to talk as if anything he said or did wouldn't bother her. Charles stopped and looked at her for a moment, nearly snarling.

"Look, I'm not in the mood to mess around."

Angela put her hand on his chest and snapped, "Listen, I assume you're involved somehow in Xavier's case, even though you're not on the force. Am I right?"

Charles was trying to think of the best way of getting rid of Angela without making too much commotion.

Angela continued, "Look, I've got information that could help you."

Charles stopped walking. He turned around and stared at her.

"What do you know?" he asked, with a sense of hope in his heart.

"Have you ever heard of Harold and Miriam Fisher?"

Charles shook his head no.

She then began to tell him the story of how Harold had called her and told her that his wife had been raped by Xavier. Charles didn't like what he was hearing. He didn't want to believe his rollercoaster emotions would end with the fact that Xavier could be a serial rapist, also.

Angela saw the look in his eyes and couldn't help using the dramatic pause to build up more suspense. She continued. She told him about all the events that had happened at Harold's house, and she told him about Miriam's denial. That's when she started to do her own investigation, she told Charles.

"Apparently, Miriam has a fairly clean record, but she had dated Xavier for awhile when she was in college."

Charles looked surprised, but he wasn't impressed. Xavier was a good-looking athlete, and Charles was sure that he had dated several women. An unknown Caucasian woman didn't surprise him.

Angela continued to tell Charles how weird Miriam and Harold were, but especially Harold. She said that she found out something interesting about Miriam's roommate, Phoebe Swan. It seemed that she died in a car accident while she was attending college. They thought she must've been drunk by the way she'd been driving, but they found no alcohol in her system.

Now Charles was getting interested. The story sounded a lot like Xavier's story. Angela continued smiling because she knew she had more to reveal.

"The case was put to rest as an accident, but what I found really interesting was that Harold, Miriam's husband, had been accused of manufacturing drugs several years later. When he was busted, they found heroin and several other drugs."

Angela moved in closer to Charles for a more dramatic effect.

"And get this; he also had a small supply of Ketamine and other drugs."

Charles looked confused with the information she had just provided. He understood what the drug was but didn't understand how it all blended together.

Angela continued, "Ketamine can make you forget everything that happened over the past five or six hours. It's known as a date rape drug. Harold did a little time in jail, but the charges were eventually thrown out."

Angela was getting excited now, and she began to speak in a fast rhythmic pace.

"Phoebe, Miriam's roommate died, as I mentioned, but during the autopsy, they never tested her for Ketamine in her system."

Charles's eyes widened. He knew there was a thin connection, but it would be nothing that would hold up in court or even draw any attention.

Charles asked, "Angela, why are you telling me this?"

"The authorities probably wouldn't buy this trivial information, because I couldn't prove it. But, I know that you're the type of person who thinks outside the box. I've covered several other cases that involved you, and I believe that you got a raw deal."

Angela hesitated a moment, and then she quietly said, "I'm also a fan of Xavier's."

She opened her purse, looked inside, and pulled out a slip of paper. She handed it to Charles and said, "Their address."

Charles accepted the piece of paper, glanced at it, and then jammed it into his pocket.

Angela said, "I've taken things as far as I can right now. I can't do much more alone. I could use your help."

Charles nodded to indicate he understood.

She added, "If this amounts to anything, I want a complete exclusive."

Once a reporter, always a reporter, Charles thought. The good thing was that it gave him hope again.

Chapter 41

Harold asked himself over and over again what he could have done to be so blessed. He didn't believe in God but felt that something or someone was smiling down on him.

He had just finished watching the news when he heard the story of Xavier being shot and in a state of near death. He figured he couldn't have written a better book than what had happened. Once Xavier was gone, he would have his wife all to himself. He figured she would see him for the hero that he was. Harold had always pictured himself as a knight in shining armor, and this would be more proof that she was in need of a hero.

It had been several hours since Harold had checked in on Miriam. He only briefly wondered what his wife was doing. She had been in their bedroom since he left her there, but he figured that she would be safe by herself.

There were only brief intermissions of noise, but Harold couldn't bring himself to go back in there and see her. The temptation could have proved to be too great for him, and he might have laughed in her face or inched his way towards her throat again.

He figured he would sleep on the couch for the night and allow her to rest fully. Tomorrow morning he would tell her about Xavier being shot. By then, he would have regained control over himself.

The door to the bedroom slowly opened, and he wondered if tonight was going to keep getting better. His mind conjured up the thought of Miriam coming to reward her big daddy. A smile came across his face as he pictured himself making love to her.

His dreams, however, were rudely changed into a nightmare when he saw Miriam fully dressed with a suitcase in her hand. Harold's eyes began to blink in disbelief, and he wondered if maybe this was some sort of evil trick.

He couldn't understand why she would be dressed and why she would have a suitcase in her hand. In his mind, everything had worked out perfectly. She should be happy and ready to throw herself into his arms.

Miriam stopped a few feet shy of the bedroom door. She wore a look of fear in her eyes. A solitary teardrop found its way down her right cheek. Inhaling deeply, she licked her lips.

"Harold," she said, "I'm leaving you."

Harold's heart began to pump hard and fast. He stumbled. His breathing was erratic and purposeful. Miriam sat her bag on the ground but kept her distance.

Her voice was still raspy as she repeated, "Harold, I'm leaving you. I can't be tricked into falling for your games anymore. I'm done!"

Harold raised himself up on one knee and stared at her, dumbfounded. His eyes bulged with disbelief but there was no denying what she had just said. He stood to his feet and took a step towards her. She took a step back. She raised her hand as if in a threatening attempt to stop him from coming closer to her.

Clearing her throat, she said, "I know what you did, Harold!"

Harold had done a lot of things in his life and wasn't sure which one she was talking about. He had to let her continue.

"I saw the stuff you used on me," she wailed.

Harold thought back for a moment, and then he hated himself. He remembered that he hadn't put the drugs away in his excitement of feeling that he had gotten away with something.

"Miriam, I…"

"Stop talking, Harold. It bothered me that I couldn't remember anything that happened in the last few hours until I saw the drugs that you must have used on me. I'm still not sure what happened, but I know that I would not have taken a shower, and I vaguely remember your hands around my throat. You tried to choke me, Harold, didn't you? Tell me I'm lying!"

Anger was now replacing the fear that he had been previously feeling.

"You have the audacity to think that you could leave me? Really? After all I've done for you? Miriam, honey, you're being irrational."

Harold took a few more steps towards her, but then noticed that she held something in her hand. He stopped and stared at her. She must have been searching in the closet and retrieved the gun, he thought, that he had kept there in case of an emergency.

With arms outstretched, Miriam cradled the gun between both hands and pointed. She cocked the weapon and aimed at Harold's chest.

"I said I'm leaving you. Please don't try to stop me, or I'll use this."

Harold spit on the floor, and hollered, "You ungrateful whore! I've done so many things for you. I've sacrificed for you. And I've lived with your coldness and accusations for all these years. You never had problems spending my money, did you?"

Miriam didn't budge an inch. She stood with her feet firmly planted, while keeping the gun pointed at him.

She swallowed hard, and then with a vehement growl, she said, "Don't try to stop me! Once I leave here, I want your promise that you'll leave me alone and not call the police. I'm done! Do you hear me?"

Harold wanted to reach over and choke Miriam, but he knew he couldn't. She was a good shot. In fact, he knew how accurate she was because they used to go to the gun range to practice shooting. She amazed everyone there because with her shooting precision, she could easily administer a lethal kill. Yet, deep in his heart, Harold felt that even though she could act tough, she lacked the heart and conviction to really kill someone.

Harold moved to the side and motioned with his hand for Miriam to leave. She hesitated, shocked by his sudden understanding. Her hand began to shake as she picked up her suitcase and walked towards the front door. She gazed outside as if seeing her own freedom, and then she looked back at Harold again.

Like a poker player, Harold seemed to study her every step. Back and forth her gaze moved between the door and Harold. She rushed out fearing that if she stayed any longer, she might have to use the gun to keep him away from her.

Miriam power-walked towards the door, and her steps were brisk and strong. But somewhere between the moment of looking at Harold, and then looking at the door, he pounced on her with a deliberate attack that brought them both to the floor, just as he heard the click of the gun.

Chapter 42

Looking down at the address written on the piece of paper, Charles drove with a renewed sense of purpose. He wasn't sure what he could do, but he knew he had to do something. In his mind, he plotted out the next course of action knowing that he couldn't very well just show up at someone's house and expect them to open the door. Time was of the essence for him. If Xavier died, then at least he wanted him to know that he had died with a clean name.

The drive from the hospital took about an hour. He was happy that his schedule allowed him to respond with no time restrictions, and it also gave him time to call his mom. She picked up the phone on the first ring and jumped right to the point.

"Charles, he is *not* guilty."

It wasn't like her to jump the gun with no facts, but doing so made Charles wonder if she somehow had vital information that he didn't have.

"Charles," she said, before he could respond to her statement, "don't ask me how I know. I just do."

Deep down, Charles felt the same way, but he was a policeman. He could go on his gut instincts, but he also had to follow up with facts.

"I don't think the court will buy your gut feeling, Mom."

"Doesn't matter," she said. "I know what I know, and I know he's not guilty."

From her tone, Charles knew to leave well enough alone. He would just have to prove that she was right.

Just as he started to move the conversation into another direction, his phone beeped, which alerted him that he had another call coming in. It was a number that he'd never seen before. Not too many people had his number, and so any call he received was important until proven wrong.

"Mom, I got to go," he said.

They exchanged simple loving wishes with each other, and then he connected to the next caller.

"Hello?" he answered.

All he heard was dead air for a few seconds, and then he heard Le's frightened voice.

In broken English, she said, "I can't talk long, but I must tell you the truth. Xavier didn't try to attack me. Everything that happened that day was an accident and not his fault. He was confused and lost. He couldn't remember anything. He knocked on my door for help and wanted to use the phone. He called the police because he thought he had been mugged."

Everything that Charles heard her say was encouraging news, but quickly his thoughts turned to concern for Le's safety.

"But you, where are you? And are you safe?" he asked.

"I'm at my house. I drugged Jimmy so I could call you, but he won't be unconscious much longer. He's coming out of it right now, and I'm not sure what to do."

Charles asked, "Can you drive?"

She answered, "No."

"Do you have any relatives nearby who could help?"

Again, she answered, "No." Then in a whisper and sounding hurried, she said, "Jimmy's stirring. I have to hang up."

Charles had lots of questions for Le, and he feared for her safety.

He told her, "Hang tight. I'm coming to get you."

Fearful but with a sound of hope in her voice, she said, "Please hurry!"

Charles's heart sank. He couldn't let her down. Several more questions went through his mind, but there was no time left. He just prayed that she would survive until he got there.

Deciding to chance it, Charles asked one more question before she hung up

"Can you quickly tell me who Jimmy is and what's going on?"

"Jimmy's my cousin, and he works for Senator Stevens."

Without another word from Le, Charles heard the phone click, and he knew she had ended the call. He was shocked beyond belief when he tried to digest what she had just told him.

He tried to lay the pieces in order. Le had stated that Xavier had attacked her, but then she had changed her story. Jimmy was at her house protecting her, but he worked for Senator Stevens. The senator was the man who had shot Xavier.

Charles also tried to figure out how Harold and his wife fit into the picture. Solving these puzzles was the part of his job that he liked, but it was even more of a mission because of the players involved.

Looking at his watch, he realized that it was nearly 10:00 p.m. He was supposed to go on a late night date with Alice, but didn't have time to try to call and explain. She knew the work he was in and would have to assume that something came up.

Charles shook his head acknowledging how sporadic his life was. Once again, he promised himself that when this case was settled that he'd change his lifestyle and get into a more normal routine.

He calculated that it would take twenty minutes to get back to Le's house, but he also knew that twenty minutes in the hand of a killer could seem like forever.

Racing through red lights, Charles drove like there was no tomorrow. He wished he could somehow will himself to go faster, but at the risk of his own life, he went as fast as he could.

At 10:21 p.m., Charles slowly pulled into the driveway at Le's townhouse.

Chapter 42

Harold jumped Miriam the moment she diverted her gaze from him to the front door. He could feel her soft flesh and then the hardness of bones crushing as he swung his right fist across her face. It was a blow that he assumed a boxer would have been proud of as Miriam's body jerked and fell with a thud to the floor.

Harold stood over his wife's motionless body. Sweat dripped off his forehead. His perfect world had now been turned upside down. Everything that he had planned, along with all the maneuvers he tried had seemed to blow up in his face. Now his mind raced, but it wasn't his fear that consumed him. It was the angst of deciding what to do next, since he had gone beyond the point of no return.

The gun that had misfired remained on the floor in the corner of the room a few feet from Miriam's body. Her once firm hand that gripped onto the piece of metal was now limp. Her eyes fluttered back and forth as the redness of blood rushed to her jaw. Harold knew he couldn't explain or fake his way out of this one. It was over, and now she'd leave him for sure.

Images of her going into the arms of Xavier began to fuel his anger. He paced back and forth in a circle around her body. The more he walked, the more he imagined her and Xavier in erotic positions. The thought of her in Xavier's arms enraged him to the point where he felt as though he would explode.

The gun, although small, seemed huge now to Harold. He bent down to pick it up and then stopped himself from putting his fingerprints all over the gun. Then he thought for a moment about what he was going to do.

He inhaled deeply each time he took a breath and gained strength with each movement. A part of him said to walk away, but he was overwhelmed with rage. He felt it was time to put a stop to all things; it was time to make a statement. Harold bent over and picked up the gun. He looked at it closely and rubbed its dark black handle. It felt heavy in his hand but also light; it was death but also life to those who wielded its power properly.

Harold put the gun in the small part of his back underneath his belt. It was something he had seen in a movie, and he knew he needed both hands free. This was going to be the finale, and he figured he would do it right.

He leaned over and picked his wife up and placed her on the couch. Then he quickly marched towards the back room and opened the closet door. At the back of the closet and buried underneath a large folded moving blanket, hidden from where he had stashed the gun, was a black bag.

He pulled the bag out and opened it up. Inside were several stacks of hundred dollar bills that he had been saving since he and Miriam had gotten married. He calculated that he had saved nearly $100,000.00. He then quickly got a duffle bag and tossed some clothes inside. Time had ticked away, but Harold was still focused. Things were going to happen fast, and he needed to be in control of the situation.

Miriam stirred in the other room. She was somewhere between consciousness and lost in a world of her own. Harold was nowhere to be seen in her world—only the joy of her and Xavier. She ran into his arms and he held her tightly. He looked into her eyes and smiled. There was no sex in her dream, only the two of them holding hands looking at the sunset. She felt safe and secure. They were in love as she had told him that she had wanted to be with him forever. He smiled but said that he couldn't because she was a married woman, and it wouldn't be right.

Suddenly an onslaught of pain reeled through her heart and then across her face. She couldn't fathom why she felt such a hot pain in her face and then she understood; half her face was swollen. Miriam bit her lip while trying to hold back the tears. Sharp jolts of pain shot through her body and she began to shake into the land of the conscious.

Her one eye was swollen but she could see that the room was empty. She wasn't sure how long she was out but she could hear Harold in the other room. She figured that he must have moved her there. Her gut told her she had to escape from the house.

She looked around the room for the gun, but it was gone. Now she was beyond scared. She knew that Harold had reached the point of no return. He could storm into the room at any minute, and she knew that soon after she'd be dead.

Her suitcase was where she had left it—near the bedroom door, which was too far away to retrieve without alerting Harold. With no other options, she'd have to leave with only the clothes on her back.

Her body ached as she tried to stand up, but pain was the last thing on her mind. Shaking her head to clear her thoughts, Miriam forced herself up as quietly as possible. Her legs seemed to have a life of their own and as she tried to put one foot in front of the other, it felt like her legs were going to sleep. She tried to will them to obey her. Each step she managed to take brought her closer to the door.

Her heart began to beat stronger against her chest as she tried to search for a way out. Looking around the room, the window was her only way to escape. She wondered why he would leave her alone but knew of his cockiness. He imagined that he had thought his punch was sufficient enough to keep her out for awhile. Being left alone gave her even more of a chill as she could imagine him planning more ways to torture her.

Holding her breath, she moved in slow, timed movements trying not to make any noise. The window was locked and had not been opened in awhile. She felt her heart stop, as the lock seemed stuck.

Biting her lips, she called on some unseen god for help and as if an answer to her prayer, the lock moved, slowly at first, but then it opened.

The window was friendlier to her as it moved up with ease. She felt the cool air hit her face like the sweet caress of freedom beckoning her to come outside. Willing herself to move, she climbed through and then looked to the skies as she felt freedom.

She tried to move through the pain as she slowly hobbled across the lawn, but she didn't get far when out of the darkness she heard Harold calling her name.

Knowing he had the gun, and for sure he could outrun her, she stopped, turned, and faced him.

Harold stood not far behind her with his gun pointed in her direction. Even though she had gotten only fifteen yards away, he knew he could easily shoot her from where she stood. He didn't care if the neighbors saw him now. He was beyond caring. It was hate that fueled him now.

His hands didn't tremble. He didn't have to wait until his eyes adjusted to the night's darkness. He was sure that he could make his shot. Squinting one eye, he pulled the trigger.

Chapter 44

Jimmy moaned in his sleep. It wasn't loud but enough for Le to know that he was starting to come around. Le quickly ran to his side and laid down next to him. She put her head on his shoulder and pretended to be asleep. It was the only thing she could think of to do.

Jimmy would have known that he had been drugged, but maybe seeing her asleep next to him would confuse him enough to give her a chance. She had decided not to run away, since she had nowhere to run to, and no one would hide her. The last time she had tried to escape, he found her and threatened to kill her relatives. This time, she didn't need a reminder. All she could do was pray that Charles would arrive in time to rescue her.

Jimmy stirred once more and put his hand around her waist. The touch of his arm on her body made her skin crawl, but she had to endure. She could feel his hot breath on the nape of her neck, and even in his unconscious state, he seemed deadly and in control. Le prayed for Charles to hurry. It felt like torture having Jimmy's body touching hers. She didn't want to think about what would happen to her if Charles never got there.

Jimmy's eyes fluttered for a moment as he began waking up. He licked his parched lips, feeling the effect of the sleeping potion in his drink. Anger was not his first reaction, but he was concerned because he had let his guard down. He was a professional. Professionals weren't supposed to ever lose their control. His body felt sluggish, like a signal that he had been drugged. As his anger escalated, he knew that he had to kill Le.

The challenge would be trying to make her body disappear under the radar. He didn't need attention drawn toward the murder. He just knew that he'd have to find a non-traceable way of making her disappear after he had killed her.

Inhaling deeply, he tried to allow his body to catch up with his mind. The more he gained control, the more he began to think about the last few moments. Then, suddenly, he wondered where Le had gone. He would have to find her, but all of a sudden as he attempted to sit up straight, he felt someone lying next to him.

He forced his head to move to the side, and that's when he saw Le asleep on his arm. It wasn't the scenario he had pictured in his mind. Nevertheless, he was glad that he didn't have to go searching for her.

He nudged her, but she didn't react. Gaining more control of his body, he nudged her again, and this time she stirred. With a sleepy glance, she looked at him as if she had been drugged, too. Then she slowly regained consciousness.

Le pushed herself away from his shoulder and sat upright. She had a look of fear in her eyes. She looked at Jimmy as if he was the one who had drugged her, and maybe even violated her.

If this had been a different situation, Jimmy would have laughed out loud. But the thought of drugging a woman just to take advantage of her was crazy. If he wanted Le, he would have Le.

Le licked her lips; her time with the senator had taught her how to become a good actress. She fixed her gaze on Jimmy and asked him what happened. He reached out and grabbed her by the throat and applied pressure.

She could feel his strong fingertips around her throat, and they were suffocating her. She gasped for air and tried to speak but her voice left her. She knew how to fake a cry and this cry wouldn't be much of a problem. The ordeal enabled the tears to flow naturally.

Jimmy glared at her and relaxed his grip around her throat, just long enough to say, "What happened? What did you do to me?"

Le reached for her neck and massaged it, while purposely not looking at him.

Then she gazed into his eyes, and purred, "I don't know what happened. I've been asleep."

Jimmy didn't like her answer, but he considered the fact that she hadn't run away, which rather confused him. He looked down at his watch and realized that he'd been asleep for almost an hour. She could have done anything within that time, and yet she hadn't run away or tried to escape.

Jimmy reached for his gun to make sure it was still there. He saw fear in Le's eyes which was what he had intended. For Jimmy not being able to account for an hour was dangerous. Even when he slept, he was in control. He knew where he laid his head, when, and for how long.

He grabbed her by the arm and forcefully led her into the kitchen.

"What did you put in my drink?" he snarled.

Le quickly looked down at the tea that was still on the counter. She put her face between her hands and started to cry.

"I'm sorry, Jimmy. I gave you the wrong type of tea."

Jimmy slapped her across the face. The blow was strong and left her falling to the ground. He quickly pulled out his gun and placed it to the top of her head as she struggled to get up.

She could feel the metal against her skull. Dying wouldn't be a problem for her but knowing that an innocent man would get accused wrongly because of her lies was something she couldn't deal with.

Le rose from the floor so that she could face the gun and her would-be killer. For a few seconds, she stood; defiant in the face of death, but then she realized it was crucial for her to continue her dramatic acting performance.

"I must have been mixed up, nervous, and put in wrong tea. I am sorry," she said, and began to whimper and cry again.

She began to shake almost uncontrollably waiting for him to pull the trigger.

Jimmy looked at her. It was his call now; he could pull the trigger, but he'd have to deal with the senator. Or, he could do nothing and wait for a better time. Sooner or later, Le would have to deal with him, so he chose to wait.

He put the gun back into its holster, while trying to convince himself that maybe it was a mistake. He ran the scenario through his mind, one more time. She had been asleep, lying next to him. That could indicate that maybe she was nervous. It was plausible, but he doubted it.

With one hand, he lifted her face up and looked into her eyes. He saw fear, which is what he expected but nothing else. She was void of any other emotion.

Not wanting to be played the fool, he knew she didn't have a cell phone and wouldn't be so stupid as to use his. The only other way to communicate would have been to use the home phone. It would be a simple test, but he knew the simplest tests were the ones that often brought the most fruit. He walked over to the phone and pushed the redial number.

Le's heart skipped a beat. She didn't even consider the possibility of him pushing the redial button. If Charles answered, she knew that she'd be dead within moments. She started walking towards Jimmy, but he pulled the gun out again and pointed it at her. She froze and bowed her head.

Jimmy smiled and told himself that if the police answered the phone, he'd kill her. There'd be no question about it, and the senator would have to clean up the mess.

The phone rang, and then the voice of a woman answered. She sounded old and introduced herself as an employee of a grocery store. Jimmy hesitated for a moment, and apologized, saying that he'd dialed the wrong number. Then he hung up the phone and faced Le.

Chapter 45

Charles heard his phone ring, and after glancing at the caller I.D., he didn't recognize the number. He thought it could be Le, but knew it was from his private line. His gut instinct told him that he'd better disguise his voice just in case it wasn't her.

He answered and disguised his voice as a woman, and announced the name of a grocery store. He had always been proud of his impersonations, and this one was his finest bit of work. When he heard the voice on the other end, he knew it belonged to Jimmy, which infuriated Charles. It took everything he had to stay in character.

Charles had prepared himself for this kind of situation, since it had happened many times before. He knew that a first call would usually be from the woman who was in trouble or in need, but the second call from the same number could be tricky. If they had somehow found his card, it could mean death for the woman. So he always disguised his voice when he got a call from the same number that was from someone who was in trouble.

The fact that Jimmy called Charles's phone meant that Le was in danger. He pushed the gas pedal a little harder to try to get there quicker.

Charles estimated ten minutes before he would reach her home. He could envision Jimmy possibly shooting Le and getting rid of the body or taking her to a safer location. Either way, Charles figured that time was running out, and he had to be there before Jimmy got away.

Driving at full speed, Charles made a mental image of Jimmy and how he would take him on. Jimmy was small but seemed to be strong.

Even in their short encounter, he could tell that Jimmy had a good sense of balance.

Charles figured that Jimmy had studied martial arts or something like that, which was okay with him. It was stereotypical, but he knew that most stereotypes were based on some element of fact; Jimmy might be one of those facts.

Charles knew a lot of martial artists who relied on technique rather than learning how to adjust to street fighting. He figured that Jimmy might be one of them. Charles had about twenty pounds on him, which he thought he could also use to his advantage.

All of the lights seemed to be green, which appeared to be a good sign. Charles believed in signs, and so far, he felt that things were going in his favor—at least in his favor as far as getting to the house. He was only a block away when he pulled his car to the curb and stopped. He got out and looked for the best way to enter.

Charles crept slowly to the side of the house and then tiptoed up the stairs. He heard a noise and peered through the window. He could see the kitchen, and from there, he could see Jimmy standing in front of Le. She was standing still with her head bowed as if submitting to an adult who was shaming her.

Charles debated about ringing the doorbell, not sure if doing so would save her or put her in more jeopardy. He continued watching them until he saw a gun. It was pointed at Le's head.

Charles decided to go ahead and ring the doorbell. At least with the doorbell ringing, he figured Jimmy wouldn't shoot knowing that there could be a potential witness.

Jimmy quickly put the gun away into its holster under his jacket. His gaze turned slowly towards the door and window. Charles ducked out of sight and prepared himself for his next maneuver. He figured he would have to be quick and concise to make things work.

Jimmy opened the door prepared for danger, but he didn't have his gun exposed. Charles moved fast and hit him in the stomach, and then reached for the gun in Jimmy's holster. Jimmy's face winced in pain as the blow caught him off guard.

Charles pushed him to the floor; it was a quick military type move that drew no blood. Charles now held Jimmy's gun in his hand and pointed it at him.

Charles yelled at Le, "Get over here."

Le started to run towards them, but Jimmy said something in Korean. Le stopped.

Charles took his gaze off Jimmy for just a second so he could look at Le. That's when he heard a pop. The pop was the sound of his wrist snapping.

Jimmy was amazingly fast. He had kicked the gun from Charles's hand and now stood facing him. Just as Charles had expected, Jimmy knew some form of martial arts and was good at it.

Charles made a swing for his face and Jimmy moved to the side and quickly kicked him in the ribs. It was a hard and well-placed jab. Charles leaned to the side to stop himself from buckling over. Despite Jimmy's size, he was strong and fast.

A quick right to Charles's face sent trickles of blood down his lip. Charles understood that most good fighters knew enough to press their advantage so that their enemy couldn't recover.

Charles over-acted and believed that Jimmy would press the issue. It was a hard and painful hit, but he had been hit harder when he used to fight in the streets. Faking it, he shook his head and nearly dropped to a knee. Jimmy didn't disappoint him. He stepped closer to either hit or kick him.

Charles readied himself and then saw his opening. Jimmy lifted his leg high to kick, and Charles hit him dead between his balls. It was a forceful punch in the groin that made Jimmy's eyes roll to the back of his head.

He cuffed himself holding his private parts and then fell to the ground. Charles rose from his position and shook his head. He wasn't on the force anymore, but he kicked Jimmy an extra time in the ribs for good measure.

Chapter 46

Harold shouted Miriam's name as he squeezed the trigger, but once again the gun misfired, The gun had a habit of misfiring but two times in a row seemed odd and yet fortunate for Miriam. She didn't have time to thank some unseen force because she wasn't out of danger yet. He could run after her and if she got caught, he would do unimaginable things.

Despite the pain that he had inflicted on her, she sprinted across the lawn like a young gazelle trying to get away from a deadly hunter.

Miriam didn't look back, but what she heard even from her distance was the trigger of the gun going off. Maybe in his deranged fit of rage, he imagined shooting her over and over again. So he continued pulling the trigger, which gave Miriam a few more seconds to run farther away into the darkness.

She didn't know where she'd go, even though she didn't have time to go back for her handbag, or have any money, she didn't care. She just knew that she had to get away from him. She'd figure out the rest later. Running as fast as she could, she felt her jaw swelling up more, and her whole body was hurting so bad she could barely manage the pain.

As she got farther away from the house, she could hear Harold still calling her name. She just pleaded that she'd never have to see his face again. She didn't think she was capable of it, but she hated him. She hated the sight of him and the sound of him, but most of all, she hated that he had tried to kill her.

The blackness of night made her appear almost invisible as she blended into her surroundings. She was thankful that the moon was hidden that night.

Harold, on the other hand, ran back into the house and into the bedroom. He went to the closet to search for his other gun, a black .45 handgun that he had purchased without her knowledge. He lost himself completely, and now all control was gone. He wanted death and he wanted it now. He was a man who would be respected. Loading the gun, he ran back out to the front door.

Jumping into his car, he started his search for her. His foot hit the gas pedal with such an impact that his back tires spun until they finally gripped the road. He scanned the streets and peered into the darkness looking for Miriam. He held the gun in his hand while he drove, and his fingers trembled over the trigger as he thought about shooting his wife.

One day earlier, and this never would have happened, but now he was beyond being in control. He tried to figure out where she could be. He knew her thought patterns, or at least he thought he did.

He circled around the block hoping to catch a glimpse of her. They had no friends in the neighborhood, and he doubted that she would be smart enough to go to one of their houses. Yet, he still slowed the speed of his car just in case he saw something unusual.

Miriam ran until she felt that her lungs would nearly burst. She wanted to stop, but she also didn't want to put anyone else in danger. Harold was a crazy man now and he'd kill anyone who dared to help her. Small bugs hit her face as she headed for a section where some local stores were. If she could get there, then she could call for help. Blending in wouldn't be a problem.

A car drove past her and she jumped off the road and hid in the bushes. It wasn't him, but it just as well could have been. She'd have to be more attentive to watching out for approaching headlights. She couldn't take a chance that he'd find her that easily.

She continued to run and the store's lights were only about 100 yards away. She had hope until she heard a loud bang, and then she felt a sharp pain in her arm. She turned and saw Harold holding the gun and staring at her. Warm blood trickled down her arm and then onto the pavement below.

Harold walked closer to her and pointed the gun at her head.

"Get in the car!" he ordered.

She shook her head no, but she couldn't run. Her screams became a distant memory as the pain moved from her arm to every place in her body. She didn't want to die, so she got into his car.

Chapter 47

Charles grabbed Le's hand, and said, "I'm taking you to a safe place. We need to get out of here quick."

Le obeyed willingly and they both got in his car and sped away. For the next half hour, Le unloaded many stories about her arrival in America, her family, and her eventual torture by the senator and Jimmy. Then she told Charles what really happened that day with Xavier, and how she had been blackmailed to tell those lies about him.

Charles drove and listened to every word she said. If her stories were true, then Xavier was innocent of the crime, and the senator was a monster. He also wondered about Jimmy. He was a dangerous man and leaving him there put Le's family in jeopardy but they had no choice.

Charles tried to put the pieces together, not sure how everything fit, but he knew that he had to get Le to safety. By now he was sure that Jimmy had already gotten up from the floor and would be jabbering with the senator about his own version of what had happened. Charles was sure he wouldn't be taking the rap for inattentiveness where Le was concerned.

Senator Stevens was one of the most powerful men in Washington. He seemed to have the respect of both the Republicans and Democrats, which in these times was a rarity. Trying to prove what Le said would be difficult. Trying to prove it against the senator and his reputation might be impossible. Charles thought about the case.

Le had already accused Xavier of trying to attack her. Now she wanted to change her story, but she'd have no proof that she and the senator were linked. Charles was certain that the senator would have been smart enough not to leave any trace of his involvement. He couldn't afford to have anything lead back to him.

Then Charles thought about his own life and remembered that he wasn't on the force because of men with power not liking his results. Things were not looking good, and he needed a place to hide Le.

Charles thought about going to the police, but that was an iffy choice, considering that he didn't know how far in the senator had connections. He had already shot Xavier, and more than likely, he figured he had gotten away with it. Images of the picture-perfect senator laughing at what he was able to accomplish made Charles mad. He tried to soften his anger by telling Le that he never did like the guy and didn't vote for him. Le didn't smile or laugh. She just stared straight ahead, showing no emotion.

As Charles drove, he suddenly got an idea. It was a long shot, but he figured that it might work. Pulling into an old gas station, he was relieved to see one of the old standard pay phones still intact. He knew that calls on his cell phone could be traced, but the pay phone would be okay.

Grabbing a few quarters, he dialed Angela's number—the TV news reporter. It was her cell phone and she answered the call immediately. Charles quickly reintroduced himself and gave her a brief overview about what had recently gone on.

He told her that he needed a favor, which she almost instinctively knew when he called. For a moment, Angela was hesitant. She knew she was a good reporter and had done risky stories before, but nothing of this caliber. It not only involved her job but her private life as well.

Charles had no choice but to take a chance that maybe Angela could help. Who would think to look for Le at Angela's home? Clearly, Le could stay there until he could sort things out.

He wasn't sure but he figured that Harold and Miriam were the final pieces to the puzzle. All he had to do was put the pieces together. If he could do that, then he could clear Xavier's name and also help to free Le from her most uncomfortable predicament.

Angela was still silent on the other end after Charles made his request. He was starting to get frustrated with her, knowing that she wanted a big story, but possibly unwilling to stick her neck out to help.

He would have asked his mom or maybe even Alice, but Jimmy knew who he was, and the senator's thugs would probably go there first to look for Le. This reminded Charles that he'd do well to call both of them as soon as he could to give them an advanced warning. Great! Now everyone he knew was in danger.

When Angela began to speak, her voice sounded a bit dry and shaky, but she agreed to let Le stay with her for awhile. She emphasized the word, *awhile,* to let Charles know that this was not going to last long.

Charles understood, got her address, and quickly made a U-turn. She didn't live far from where he was calling from, and it comforted his soul to know that in a few minutes Le would be safe.

As much as Charles hated to admit it, this was the type of moment he lived for. His blood was pumping as he raced through the night. He had to fight not to go over the speed limit and draw unwanted attention to himself. A few lights, some curves, and straight streets, and he was at the address that Angela had given him on the phone.

She lived in a townhouse, and from the outside it looked similar to the one that Le had lived in. The biggest difference Charles could see from a quick observation was that this area seemed a lot older, and the years' effects had taken their toll on the dwellings.

Charles looked around before stepping out of the car. He half expected a gunshot to ring out at any moment, but the coast was all clear. He quickly ran up the steps and knocked on the door. Angela opened it. Charles looked past her for a moment and scanned the house. He had to be careful. If something happened to Le, the case would be closed, and Xavier would never be proven innocent.

Angela smiled and told him that she was alone. She also looked past him to the car to see Le sitting in the front seat. In the night's darkness, against the small light of her garage, Le appeared as a ghost. Her small frame seemed like an image as opposed to real flesh,

Charles once again asked, "Angela, are you okay with having Le stay with you for awhile?"

Angela shook her head in agreement. She tried to imagine herself in the same position, and she hoped that someone would help her the way that Charles had helped Le and Xavier.

Charles smiled and ran back to the car. He opened the door for Le and escorted her up the steps into Angela's place.

"I know you don't know her, Le, but she'll provide a safe place for you until I can figure things out. Do you understand?"

"Yes," she replied quietly. "I'm very grateful that you hurried."

Once inside Angela's home, he closed the front door and introduced the women to each other. He then moved in the house and closed the vertical window coverings.

He looked at Angela, then at Le, and said, "Now you can take your time interviewing her."

His comment apparently broke the ice, and both women smiled.

As Le and Angela stood facing each other, Charles noticed that they both were nearly the same height, but that's where the similarities stopped. Angela was a bit heavier, and in Charles's mind, prettier. Le appeared to be younger but not by much.

"I'll get you settled, Le, and I think I have some clothes that will fit you," Angela said, in a caring manner. "You're going to be all right," she said, trying to comfort her.

Le nodded.

"Ladies, I have to leave. I'll be in touch soon. Be careful, and Le, don't go answering the door when Angela's not home, okay?"

There was no smile or acknowledgment of the joke for Le, only a polite bow.

Charles climbed into his car and drove away. Harold and Miriam were next on his list.

Chapter 48

Harold looked at his wife as he drove her back home. Her face was wrought with pain as she tried to keep her hurting shoulder still. Part of Harold hated to see his wife in agony, but his sympathy was overruled by the anger that still burned inside of him.

Tension filled the car as he drove through back roads on his return trip home. He didn't think anyone had heard the gunshot, but if they had, he wanted to be long gone before the cops showed up. He had plans for Miriam and going to jail wasn't one of them.

Blood made its way from Miriam's arm onto the car seat. That angered Harold even more. He was at the stage where he looked for anything to get angry about. He just wanted to be mad. Being angry allowed him to do what he had to do. It was a filter that pushed out any feelings that he once had for his wife.

She began to close her eyes as she faded away from shock and blood loss. Harold glanced at her and continued to drive. The only thing that was important to him right now was to get home.

Pulling into his driveway, he noticed that the neighborhood was silent again. The neighbors had gotten used to their fights and responded by going back to their nightly routines. It was late and dark. Even if he and his wife did make noise, it would only appear that Miriam was drunk and that he was taking her back into the house—a routine that they had seen many times before.

His car door creaked open as he jumped out and ran to the front door of his house. He opened the door and made sure that the interior lights were out. He didn't want any of the neighbors to see what he was doing.

With the front door open and the lights out, he quickly ran to the passenger side of his car and helped Miriam get out. He placed his hand near her mouth to ensure she wouldn't scream. He had to almost drag her inside because she could barely walk. Fortunately, Miriam didn't fight him.

She had given up hope and had lost the will to live. She was sure she was going to die. She just hoped he would do it quickly.

Her legs felt heavy and the loss of blood made her tired, but she was still alive. The bullet had gone through her shoulder and didn't appear to hit any major blood vessel. Blood had already started to clump up against the matted shirt, and as long as she didn't move, the pain had become somewhat bearable. However, she knew that taking her to the hospital wouldn't be in his plans.

Harold continued to take her into the house, closing the door behind him. He carried her to the back bedroom. The light was still on in there and he could get a good look at her face. It was the face of someone who had given up, which wasn't what he wanted. He wanted her to know pain before she died. He wanted her to beg for her life, and then he would take it away.

Miriam watched him with a wallowing feeling of not caring and yet wanting to tell him to get the show on the road. But Harold continued to dawdle. He seemed to pace the room aimlessly like a crazy man trying to decide what to do next.

She wondered what was going through his mind, but that curiosity was only a casual whim, not something that troubled her. She was going to die, and he was going to do it. It was a plain and simple fact.

Harold stopped and smiled. It was as if he had just had a brainstorm. He walked purposefully toward the closet. Inside, he knelt down and lifted one of the floor boards. Then he removed something that looked like a book. He smiled and walked over to Miriam. He sat down on the bed right next to her and began to stroke her hair. She watched as he opened the book. The writing on the pages resembled Harold's handwriting.

He grinned, and said, "I'm going to read you a little story, dear, that I'm sure you will like."

He moved her into position like a father ready to read a bedtime story to his child.

He began, "Once upon a time, there was a woman named Miriam who loved to tease men. She slept with quite a few of them and had become a very, very bad girl. She even went so far as to sleep with a black man."

Harold raised his eyebrows and made facial expressions to go along with his words.

He continued, "Now even though she didn't know it, her prince was waiting. He would be the one to kill the evil black dragon who had trapped the princess with a wicked spell. The prince had to find out information from the princess's friend, and then he sent her away to live in heaven."

Miriam didn't understand what he was talking about but turned to look at him. Harold smiled. Things were starting to get good for him. He was enjoying getting inside her head.

"Yes, he gave her friend a little potion and then she crashed her car. Everyone thought she was drunk, but the prince knew better. He smiled because he got away with it."

Miriam's eyes widened as she thought back to her friend from college and how she had died. She wondered if he really had something to do with her death.

Harold lifted the page and turned it. The sound of the paper seemed to magnify as it creaked to its resting place. Miriam winced as her pain raced up and down her arm again. But her pain was not only about the injury he had inflicted upon her. She also felt the pain from understanding what Harold was telling her. He had killed her best friend.

Harold noticed her reaction, but that only brought more enjoyment to him. He continued to read.

"The big black monster tried to destroy the princess. He even had his way with her, and the princess was lost."

Harold turned her head so that she could look at his face.

He put the journal down and said, "Her prince came to her rescue and took her away from the black monster. But the princess couldn't let the black monster go. He was inside of her head and heart, stirring her emotions. At night, she would mention his name in her sleep. When she made love to the prince, she seemed to still be making love with the monster. The monster had a spell on her and the only way to get rid of the monster was to make him go away."

Miriam was suddenly more alert than ever.

"You?" she said barely able to speak. "What did you do to him?"

Harold laughed, "Oh, I did enough. At first it was hard because he really was a goody two shoes, but I finally did it."

He didn't go into detail but he started to laugh when he said, "I got that mean old monster good, and everything else was just the heavens smiling down on me."

Harold stopped, stared at Miriam, and asked "Now what should I do with the princess?"

Chapter 49

Charles drove towards the address that Angela had given him. He wasn't sure what to expect, but his gut was telling him that he could trust her. He looked at himself in the rearview mirror and saw craziness in his eyes. This kind of excitement was addictive to him, but like a junkie, it was also killing him. It had destroyed the relationship with his ex-wife and possibly his son. It nearly destroyed his career, and it appeared that it wouldn't stop until it destroyed him, also.

"This is it," he said. "I'm making a promise to myself that no matter what happens, I'm going to quit the force."

Somehow just by saying it out loud gave him a newfound outlook and attitude. He knew that he was capable of doing something else. After all, he thought, he'd majored in marketing out of college; maybe he could start his own business.

His phone vibrated against his hip, which jolted him back to reality. He wasn't expecting a call, and he hoped that it wasn't Le. The number didn't look familiar to him, but there'd been a lot of unfamiliar numbers lately. He clicked a button and connected with the caller, except at first, all he heard was dead air. Then he heard a familiar voice.

"This is Jimmy. You've made a huge mistake."

His words were sharp and cold. Charles knew the aloofness of Jimmy's voice, and it brought a chill to his soul. He certainly hadn't expected to hear from him so soon, but he knew that revenge was his number one priority, even before he uttered another word.

Immediately his thoughts were about his family's safety. He figured that Le would be safe, but his family could be in jeopardy. Charles waited to hear what was next, but there was only silence.

After a moment, Charles gave in and hollered, "Say something. You're the one who called."

Whether out of anger or fear, Charles wasn't a patient man when anyone tried to manipulate him. He hated to demand that Jimmy speak, but his voice sounded like death and the silence felt like a cold grave. He wasn't just going to sit there and not say anything.

Jimmy laughed and then asked, "Charles, do you think I'm stupid?"

Charles knew how to negotiate and played along by saying, "No, Jimmy, you're not stupid."

Charles phrased his words and was cautious about the tone of his voice so that he wouldn't sound condescending. He knew the easiest way to tick off a killer was to sound as though you were a parent speaking to a child.

Most killers had issues with their parents or memories of one or more bad incidents from their childhood. Speaking to them with disrespect would only drudge up those old thoughts and angry feelings.

Jimmy snapped back, "I am not stupid. You won the battle but battles are not fights. Do you understand what a fight is?"

He didn't wait for Charles to answer.

"A battle is something we did—two men in conflict and one walked away. A fight is to the death, to the end."

Charles didn't like the sound in Jimmy's voice.

Jimmy continued, "I have very powerful connections."

"Like Senator Stevens?"

Charles couldn't resist interrupting Jimmy. He wanted to let him know that he wasn't completely in the dark. He also wanted Jimmy to know that he could expose the senator.

"I don't care that you know of the senator. He's a filthy pig, but still he is powerful."

Jimmy apparently was just warming up, and Charles wondered if he should pull off the road or keep driving. Jimmy rambled on.

"Pigs don't sweat. They keep it inside; hold all the toxins within their skins. The senator is a pig. He is evil but he holds it all in. He got elected and why, because he held his poison in. Me, I'm not like a pig. I'm more like a snake. Do you know why?"

Charles could think of a thousand things to say, but he had learned that there was only one way to respond to killers.

"You're fast and deadly like a snake. You don't hold your poison in. You release it when the time is right."

Jimmy laughed.

"Very good," he said, "but there's much more to a snake than its poison. Soon you will understand what I mean."

Without warning, Jimmy became quiet again.

Charles's mind raced as he considered his options. What would Jimmy want to hear? How could he keep him on the phone? Then like a giant light bulb turning into a blinding searchlight, Charles hit himself in the head for being so stupid.

If Jimmy was half as smart as Charles had given him credit for, he had probably already tracked his location from the cell phone he was using.

Charles took the next exit off the road. Jimmy laughed.

"Why have you taken that exit?"

Charles shot back a curse word.

Jimmy stopped laughing and demanded, "Where is Le? Where are you hiding her?"

Charles remained quiet, but he was still mad at himself for his ignorant oversight. Jimmy now had him where he wanted him. That's when he began to dig in deeper. He told Charles his mother's name, address, and phone number.

Charles pounded his fist into the seat cushion. Even though it had been only a short amount of time since his encounter with Jimmy, the information about his mother could destroy him.

"If you touch my mother, I will kill you," Charles screamed into the phone.

Jimmy began to talk in his faraway voice again.

"Killing too simple. It's just a surprise for one minute, and then it's over. I've always believed that true suffering is to be alive, but for the rest of your life you'll wish you were dead. I will ask you one last time, where is Le?"

Charles still didn't answer. He couldn't answer. He knew his mother wouldn't permit him to answer.

Jimmy began to egg Charles on, and in his threatening voice, he said, "The worst thing is to hear an old lady scream. I have made many old ladies scream. It's not pretty. Do you want to hear your mother scream, Charles?"

Charles swallowed hard. His fist tightened around the steering wheel. His mom was innocent. She hadn't been involved in any of his cases other than to offer advice. To see her hurt and tortured was something he couldn't let happen.

He hung up the phone and dialed his mom. The phone rang several times and then the answering machine came on. Charles yelled into the phone for her to get out and go somewhere safe, but there was no response.

Chapter 50

Charles became frantic as he thought about what could happen to his mom. His face twisted into a scowl as he envisioned Jimmy putting his hands on her. He hoped the reason she hadn't answered her phone was that she was in church and not at home. It was Friday and this was about the time when she would normally be in a prayer session. That brought him a little peace, especially knowing that his mother never missed her prayer session.

She believed that the world needed more than just a few prayer warriors. She always told Charles that she had to do whatever she could to help out. If she ever missed a day, the church would most likely call him first, and then they'd send someone to her home to make sure that she hadn't fallen or hurt herself.

Charles pushed the gas pedal further to the floor, and now the speedometer read 90 mph. His car had reached that speed before, but he was being reminded that when he took the corners at high speeds, the car had almost tipped over. He prayed on the way, feeling that a lot of words weren't necessary, and that he wanted to get straight to the point.

"Lord, save my momma," was all he said.

He felt that after all she had done for God, the least he could do was save her from harm. He looked at his watch and realized that it was nearly time for her to be heading home. She always turned off her cell phone in church. On many occasions, she had told Charles that no matter what the problem was that God always came first.

If Charles could make his car go any faster, he would do it. As he sped along the roadways, he rocked back and forth and tried not to panic. He thought long and hard and tried to remember the church's phone number, but he couldn't. He hated himself for not having it memorized or locked into his phone. Twisting the numbers together in his mind, nearly closing his eyes as he drove, he tried to reach back deep into his memory to produce the magic combination.

As if by divine intervention, he got it and quickly dialed the number. But to his disappointment, all he got was a recording on the answering machine that gave the hours of the church services and the pastor's name. Charles left a frantic message in hopes that someone would somehow get the call.

He then thought to call his mother's friend, Shelia Waston. Shelia was like an aunt to him and as a sister to his mother. She was a small, dark-skinned woman with deep piercing eyes. Years of pain and hurt had been replaced by the love she received in the church. Perhaps that was why they were such good friends. Charles looked through his contact list on his phone. He remembered putting her number in a long time ago, but hoped that it hadn't somehow gotten deleted.

When he found the number, he called. The phone rang twice before a soft and hushed voice answered.

"Hello?"

"Mrs. Waston!" Charles screamed on the other end.

"Hello?" she said again, as if it was a bad connection.

"Mrs. Waston," Charles said once more, screaming nearly at the top of his lungs.

He instinctively reached down, and turned off all the knobs on the car radio as though they were the cause of the interference.

After a moment, he heard her say, "Yes," which confirmed that she had heard him.

Charles quickly tried to tell her who he was, but between the static of the phone and her inability to hear, it was difficult. She began to speak over his voice as if he was not on the other end.

"Do you know what time it is?" she asked him. "Don't you know that I'm in church?"

Charles felt like throwing the phone at the car's dashboard. His level of patience was being challenged, and his frustration level was rising due to the lack of communication.

He yelled, "I'm sorry for disturbing you, but I have to speak to my mother. It's an emergency."

Mrs. Waston asked, "Who did you want to speak to?"

Charles yelled out his mother's name again and then there was silence. In the background, Charles heard women speaking and praying unto the Lord. At least that was a good sign.

Mrs. Waston came back to the phone again and asked, "Who is this?"

Charles shook his head in anger, clinched his teeth, and then tried to calmly yell out his name. She finally understood who he was and began talking for a few minutes about how she hadn't seen him in such a long time.

"What's been going on in your life?"

Charles said, as calmly as he could, "I have to speak to my mom. It's an emergency."

Mrs. Waston finally understood and said, "Oh, I see. She's in the middle of her prayers. I'll tell her to call you as soon as she finishes praying."

Charles yelled, "Don't hang up! I have to speak to her right now. It's very important. Her prayers will have to wait."

Mrs. Waston became quiet, as if in shock, and then she replied, "Prayer waits for no one. The world is in the mess that it is because of the lack of prayer. Everyone's always in such a rush."

Charles shook his head, agreeing with her, as if she could somehow magically see what he was doing and expedite his need to speak to his mother.

"Mrs. Waston," Charles said, now holding back his anger, "I have to speak with my mother. I don't care who the hell she is talking to, I want to speak with her right now."

Charles heard Mrs. Waston gasp loudly. Her once pleasant voice became extremely indignant and harsh.

"Your mom is praying over someone right now. A Chinese fellow just came in and really needed prayer. If this is not a life and death situation, then she will have to call you back later."

Just the thought of Jimmy being in the church and having his mother praying over him was more than Charles could bear. He screamed into the phone for her and his mother to get away from the man, but Mrs. Waston hung up the phone in the middle of his sentence.

Charles felt like he was going crazy. His head was pounding. Evil thoughts filled his mind. He looked at the speedometer and pushed the gas pedal further to the floor.

Jimmy must have been near the church the whole time that Charles was speaking to him on the phone. No wonder he sounded so smug.

He couldn't believe that his own mother was praying over the man who had tried to kill him and had threatened to harm her. Charles looked into the distance and realized that he was still a mile away from the church. Calling the police would put everyone in jeopardy. He just had to get there before his mother was finished praying.

No doubt Mrs. Waston would talk about the way Charles had screamed at her on the phone. Charles knew his mother was smart enough to put two and two together, but she just might not know the threat that was standing directly in front of her.

Time always seems to tick in slow motion when you have to be somewhere fast. A car can seem like the slowest thing on the face of the earth when compared to a speeding bullet or the sound of a scream.

Charles visualized his mom and prayed that she could somehow hear his thoughts, and that somehow God would tell her what she needed to know.

His car nearly tipped over as he rounded the last corner before he arrived at the church. It was a simple nondescript church located in a business complex. The only thing that separated it from the other buildings was a sign that stood on the front lawn. "Come all who are weary and brokenhearted." It was simple and to the point.

Charles jumped out of the car with his hand on his gun. He couldn't afford to burst in the front door and create a chaotic reaction. Normally on a Friday night there were several elderly women praying and even some men. Any one of them could get hurt by stray bullets.

Charles quickly glanced around the exterior of the building. He was looking for anyone lurking or someone sitting in a nearby parked car. Several late model Cadillacs lined the streets, but nothing appeared out of the ordinary.

Running hunched over, he ran to the side of the building near a window. He inhaled and peered inside. Just as he'd thought, his mom's prayers were long, and she still had Jimmy on his knees, apparently praying for him. One of her hands was raised in the air, and her other hand was resting on his head. Mrs. Waston stood near her, holding onto her purse with her eyes closed.

Several other women surrounded Jimmy, each with their hands extended. He was being delivered by God, as his mother would say, and Charles felt he was going to be the deliverer.

Chapter 51

Harold looked at his wife. Sadly, he didn't feel anything for her anymore. He knew she wanted to leave him, and all he could think about was that she would run into Xavier's arms. He wished he would have just shot him when he had the chance, but he couldn't face going back to jail. If it was a matter of life or death, and if he had to go back to jail, he'd rather kill himself. Bad things happened, but he couldn't go back to the way things were.

Miriam began to sway back and forth. The loss of blood had taken its toll. For the moment, her bleeding had stopped, but she'd lost enough blood that her face and skin were as pale as a ghost. Harold stared at her and then looked away. He knew he loved her, but he didn't want to *be* in love with her. He didn't want to feel anything when he finally put her to sleep.

Turning to look at her again, Harold asked Miriam, "You never stopped loving him, did you?"

She could barely comprehend his words as her eyes began to roll to the back of her head. Light and darkness played a game of tag in her mind. She could see Harold, but it was as if he were in a faraway fog. To her, he was a demon sitting next to her on the bed.

Miriam tried to move, but her strength was gone. The only thing that remained were her thoughts. She closed her eyes and thought about Xavier. It seemed like a long time since she had thought about him until recently hearing the news reports of what had happened to him. She knew that she still loved him. He was the one that got away, and now she wished that somehow he would ride in and rescue her. She knew it was a dream and a fantasy, but it gave her peace.

Harold reached over and began to shake her. He didn't want her to die yet. In fact, he preferred to keep her alive for his own amusement. He fantasized about placing his hands around her neck one final time just for the sheer pleasure of feeling life slip out of her body.

He shook her again. For a moment, her body twitched.

"Wake up, baby," he said, as if nothing was wrong. "Don't quit on me, yet."

Miriam tried to focus but deep within her soul, she was tired, and she didn't want to talk to him. He had shot her, choked her, and he wanted to kill her. She had no desire to suffer anymore at his hand.

Harold shook her again, this time more violently. She looked like a rag doll flopping around in his grasp.

All she could murmur was, "Let me die."

Harold turned her face towards his and gave her a kiss on the cheek.

"Baby, I almost forgot to tell you what I saw on the news tonight. Your dumb boyfriend fooled around and got himself shot. He's darn near dead. So you see, I can't let you die. I don't want this to be some romantic ending where both of you die together. We'll wait for a better time."

Miriam didn't understand what he was talking about, but she heard that Xavier had been shot. She wondered how it had happened. Then she wondered if Harold had something to do with it.

Harold smiled with a look of satisfaction knowing that she had heard what he said. He leaned over and looked at her blood-soaked blouse.

"Let me take a look at this wound."

He began to undress her, but he couldn't resist inflicting enough pain on her body so that she could feel it, but not enough to make her pass out. After a few moments, he sat her up on the bed. All she was wearing was her bra, which revealed a blood clogged hole near the top of her breast where the bullet had entered and shot through her back.

Black and blue marks covered most of Miriam's arms and back. Her pale white skin looked almost foreign next to the bruised areas on her body. Harold looked at her and then got up and walked to the bathroom. He returned with a bottle of alcohol and a rag. He walked up to Miriam and opened her mouth. Her eyes were fixed on him, not sure of what he was doing. But she had no strength to respond.

He began shoving the rag in her mouth as she barely struggled to fight back. Her struggle was nothing more than a whimper and a thought. He then poured the alcohol down the front of her chest and watched as Miriam's eyes widened when feeling the pain. She began to scream, but her sounds were muffled by the rag. Her body went into convulsions, and a moment later she didn't move at all. She had passed out.

Minutes passed but yet time seemed to stand still. Miriam didn't know how long she had been out of it, and she didn't care. In fact, she felt totally depressed that she had even come back to life. She knew Harold would be waiting for her, and that he would be ready to torture her one more time. Her arm still throbbed but didn't feel nearly as bad as it had before. She remembered feeling a sharp pain, and then nothingness.

Lying motionless on the bed, it felt like there was a tight bandage pulling against the bullet wound. She tried to move, but Harold's hand instantly held her down.

In a fake, sweet voice, Harold whispered, "Lie still and rest."

Miriam didn't want to rest. She wanted to die or somehow run away from him. Mental images of scenes from her past flashed in front of her eyes. If only, she thought, if only I could get one more chance, I'd do my life differently. She strained against his grip but his hands pushed her back onto the bed.

"Rest, my darling, rest," he said in a decisive tone.

Chapter 52

Charles hesitated for a moment, while trying to devise a plan in his mind. One idea was to storm into the church and shoot Jimmy on the spot. The consequences to that were that Jimmy was too close to his mom, and Jimmy's reaction could be fatal for everyone in the church.

Charles untucked his shirt and placed his gun underneath his belt. He decided that the best way to handle things was to walk in and wait until Jimmy became aware of him.

He walked cautiously toward the front door of the church, hoping that he'd reach the entrance before anything bad happened.

He tugged on the door handle and slowly opened the door, prepared for anything. He silently thanked God for long prayers while he solemnly walked towards his mom, not wanting to bring any attention to himself.

Everyone appeared to be deep in prayer except Mrs. Waston. She spotted him right away. Her looked revealed that she was eager to give him an earful about the way he had spoken to her earlier. Charles raised his hand indicating for her to be quiet, but she ignored him.

She purposely moved into position and blocked the path toward Jimmy. Charles quickened his pace to meet her halfway. Although she walked with a cane, she moved surprisingly fast for a woman of her age. They met halfway and Charles whispered for her to move. Once again, her hearing failed her. She reprimanded him about the language he had used with her on the phone.

Jimmy appeared to become restless; no doubt that he sensed Charles was close by. Charles's mom stopped praying. She opened her eyes and looked straight at him. Although apparently finished praying for Jimmy, she acted like she was still in the spirit. She smiled at her son as an acknowledgment of her love for him.

Jimmy arose from his kneeling position on the floor and faced her. His back was to Charles. Then as quick as a speeding bullet, Charles saw his mother's face turn dull and her look was frightening. No one else seemed to be aware of what was going on. But Charles sensed that Jimmy was pushing a pistol into her skin.

"Mom!" Charles shouted, which caused everyone in the front of the church to turn around and look at him.

Someone saw the gun that was pointed at Carolyn's stomach, and what happened next was like a chain reaction of screams and prayers.

Jimmy grabbed Carolyn by the throat and turned her around to face Charles.

He then raised his gun in the air, and screamed, "Everyone get in front of me. Now!"

Mrs. Waston had an expression on her face as if to say that she had no clue about what was going on. Apparently she hadn't seen the gun, but what she did see were women in the church who all had frightened looks on their faces. She slowly turned around, and that's when she saw a man pointing a gun at her best friend's head.

She screamed out, "Oh, Lord," in a voice that was both strong and loud.

Her reaction and the alarming tone in her voice were unexpected and shocked everybody, including Jimmy. At that very moment, Mrs. Waston grabbed her heart and started to drop to the floor. Charles sped to her side, bent over, and caught her before she hit the floor. He wasn't sure what happened next, but he heard Jimmy screaming.

Then Jimmy dropped to the floor while apparently suffering from violent convulsions. Mrs. Waston looked up at Charles and smiled.

"I'm okay. Thanks for catching me," she said.

Charles wasn't sure what was happening. Things seemed to be occurring like a well-orchestrated military maneuver. Charles stood up and watched his mother walking towards him. She held a stun gun in her hand. Then she looked at Mrs. Waston, and they both began to laugh.

"You did it, Carolyn. I'm proud of you," Mrs. Waston said in a loud enough voice that everyone in the church heard.

Quickly, Charles ran over to Jimmy and cuffed him with both hands behind his back. He checked Jimmy's pulse to make sure he was still alive. Then he turned to face his mom.

"How? What?" he couldn't form the words.

Several women laughed.

Carolyn shook her head and looked at Charles as though he was still the same ignorant child that she had raised before he became a grown man.

"Baby, momma ain't so stupid, and the God I serve is the God of the most high."

Like a chorus, the women responded with a resounding, "Amen!"

Charles still didn't understand, but he thanked God anyway.

Carolyn came up to him and told him, "Son, before I came to church, I was praying, like I always do. But this time, the Lord told me to be alert and watchful. I knew that meant that I was to be prepared for anything. So I put my stun gun in my purse. The Holy Spirit let me know that Jimmy was a fraud."

Then along with the women surrounding her, they all laughed, as if knowing the secret code to something that Charles had no clue about.

Then Carolyn said, "Asian men don't come into a church full of old black women looking to find God."

Charles asked Mrs. Waston, "But if you were in on this, too, what was the deal with you falling to the floor? That scared me."

"I faked a heart attack, that's all," she said, laughing. "I was trying to create a diversion like I'd seen those actors do on television. I didn't know Carolyn would be the one to take him down. I thought that was your job."

"But do you both even know how much of a dangerous situation you put yourselves into? You might have been killed. This isn't funny."

Carolyn interrupted his soapbox speech, and said, "Charles, stop being so disrespectful."

Although every bone and emotion in his body was twitching to go after Jimmy again, he tried to push the thoughts out of his head. He needed to focus on the positives, and not what could have happened.

The question that came to Charles's mind was what he should do with Jimmy, especially since he was no longer a cop. Charles rubbed his eyes. He wasn't sure where all of this was going, but he knew that whatever actions he took, would impact everyone in the church. More than that, this whole ugly mess included his mom, whom he loved more than life itself.

Charles's mom put her hand on his shoulder, and whispered, "It'll be okay, baby. God is protecting us."

Charles wanted to argue, but after what he had just witnessed, it was hard to argue against a group of senior women taking down a killer in a matter of seconds.

Charles looked at Jimmy sprawled out on the floor. His first instinct was to kick him in the face. Even though Jimmy's body had stopped shaking from the shock of the stun gun, he was still out cold.

Carolyn saw the expression on her son's face, and like she had always done, she began to help her boy out with the case.

"Charles!" she said, staring at him and waiting for a response.

Charles didn't answer.

Again, she said, "Charles!"

He just stood there with a faraway look on his face, and then suddenly he was back.

When she saw him respond to her, she said, "We're okay, Charles. You just need to learn to thank God."

Charles gazed at his mother's face, and then he broke down in tears. As much as he wanted to turn it off, and return to his stature of a hard-core cop, he couldn't. He wasn't sure why the tears were flowing, except possibly something deeply emotional had triggered it.

As if gaining a new perspective on the reality at hand, he noted that his mom was all right, and for the moment, Jimmy was not a threat to their safety.

Within seconds, Charles felt warm hands being laid on his head, shoulders, back, and chest. The ladies in the church were comforting him. Some were praying out loud, and some could be seen with their eyes closed and their lips moving. Charles felt the love of the village of women who protected each other as well as everyone who came into their care.

Carolyn lifted Charles's head and said in a soft voice, "You need to get back to work."

Charles didn't want to leave. He hadn't broken down and cried like that since he was a child. Like a warm blanket on a cold wintry night, he didn't want the comfort of the women to go away.

Carolyn gently shook him and said, "You have more work to do."

It was a truth that Charles didn't want to hear, but looking at Jimmy, he knew what he had to do.

Chapter 53

Carolyn lifted her stun gun in the air and told Charles, "Don't worry about Jimmy. We'll keep him and wait for the police."

Charles wasn't too keen about the idea of leaving a killer with a bunch of elderly women, but his mother was insistent that he should continue with what he had started out to do.

Carolyn looked at him again, more sternly this time. It was as if she wanted to make sure that he had gotten her point.

"I told you not to worry. The moment Jimmy moves, I'll hit him with my stun gun again. Don't forget, the word of God and angry black women are a powerful combination," she said, smiling, to give him some encouragement.

Charles shook his head indicating he didn't agree with her, but she turned him around and pointed him towards the door, like a little kid.

"I'll tell the police what happened," she said, calling after him. "This man came into our church to rob a bunch of old ladies. He had a gun and everything, but luckily, we were prepared. Charles, you were never here!"

Charles had to admit it was a good story and close to the truth. All the women would agree with his mother's story. It wasn't lying in their eyes; just seeing the truth from a different perspective. It would be enough to keep Jimmy locked up at least overnight.

With a sigh and a slumped shoulder, Charles walked toward the church's front door. As he passed Mrs. Watson, she smiled.

Then she warned him, "Watch your mouth."

Although she sounded mean, Charles knew it was her way of saying that everything would be okay, and that she'd look after Mom. Charles smiled and walked back to his car.

Driving to the address that was written on the paper, he kept wondering if he had made the right move. He would never be able to forgive himself if anything happened to his mother. Trying to calm his thoughts, he imagined his mother hitting Jimmy with the stun gun again. There was no doubt in his mind that she would use it the moment he started to move. Charles knew that Jimmy was quick, but more importantly, he was a killer. He said a quick prayer and asked God to protect his mother.

Several times he found his foot on the brakes, thinking about turning around and going back to the church. He knew the church was fairly close to the police station and they should have someone out there in a matter of minutes. Once they found out it was his mom, he figured they would really put a rush on things. She had been like the team mom for his unit. They loved her as if she were one of their own.

The night skies were known to play tricks on the mind when a person was trying to hide in the darkness. Charles wondered how Xavier was doing. He also wondered why this case meant so much to him. He was already in trouble. Being involved in this case would only get him into more trouble.

He really couldn't envision a happy ending, but he felt that he had to follow through. That's what Xavier had told him when he was young and wanted to drop out of school. Xavier's words were something he had modeled his police career on: Never give up and follow through.

The address written on the paper indicated that Charles would have to make a left turn. That's when he saw the house. He wasn't sure what to expect, but in a way, the home fit the picture. There was nothing special about it. Late at night it looked like every other home with a light at the front door.

Charles turned his car key to the off position and sat silently for a moment. He parked near the curb of another home a few feet away from the address he had been given. He closed his eyes and tried to think.

Everything had gone so fast, and he didn't have a plan. That wasn't a good thing. Charles liked plans. He wondered what excuse he could make to justify walking up to the home of complete strangers in the middle of the night. What could he say before asking a bunch of questions?

Charles thought about turning around before it was too late, but it was now or never. He looked at his watch. It had just turned 10 o'clock. He got out of the car, and began walking to the front door.

Chapter 54

Charles knocked on the front door. He figured the only thing he could do would be to trust his gut. He knew there was nothing he could say that would explain why he was knocking on someone's door this late at night. It wasn't the way he liked to operate, but his mother reminded him to finish the job, and that's exactly what he was determined to do. Since everything else had worked out well today, he figured he had nothing to lose.

Harold had just finished talking to Miriam when he heard a knock on the front door. He jumped, not sure who would come unannounced at this hour of the night. He wondered if someone had seen something and called the police.

He glanced at Miriam who appeared to have passed out again. He figured that she wouldn't cause any commotion for awhile, but he still couldn't afford for anyone to see her.

The knock on the door came again. He hurried to put her under the blankets. Miriam moaned, which made him wonder if she would suddenly regain consciousness. She only moaned for a second, however, and he wrote it off in his mind as just being a reaction to the bullet wound. But whoever was at his front door, he had to get rid of them fast.

Harold caught a glimpse of himself in the mirror and noticed that he looked like a wild man. He wiped the sweat that was forming on his forehead. Then he tucked in his shirt and smoothed his slacks. Inhaling deeply, he exhaled and hurried towards the door.

Peering through the side window, he noticed a tall black man standing still, looking straight ahead at the door. The man appeared to be wearing regular clothing, but to Harold, the man had a stoic look to him. The guy could be a cop, he reasoned to himself, but it was unlikely. Harold glanced back at the bedroom making sure Miriam wasn't stirring or making any noise.

"Who is it?" he yelled in a stern voice, trying to sound as though he was being awakened from a peaceful night's slumber.

"Charles," he said, knowing that his name would have no meaning to the man on the other side of the door.

Harold demanded, "What do you want?"

He wanted to sound a little bit rougher to get the point across that he was irritated about being disturbed late at night.

Unprepared for the idea that had just popped into Charles's head, he hesitated and then said, "I'm here to talk to you about Xavier."

Harold's body began to immediately tense up. He could feel his anger welling up inside him.

He shouted to Charles, "I have nothing to say. I'm ordering you to leave me and my wife alone."

It didn't take Charles all the years of being on the force to know that Harold was hiding something. Nevertheless, he still didn't have a valid reason for standing on the front porch so late at night.

Charles opened his mouth to speak but nothing came out. He wanted to tell him that he was a policeman, but he'd already used that trick. He knew it would just cause more trouble. He also thought about using Angela's name, but he didn't want to involve her more than she was already involved. It would be like blowing the whistle on her, and he didn't want to do that.

By the sound of Harold's voice, Charles figured that he had a temper, and a man with a temper was unpredictable. He couldn't risk anyone else's life. His only option was to turn and walk away.

Humbly, Charles said, "I'm sorry for disturbing you so late at night."

Harold stood at the door. He had brought his gun with him and had withdrawn it from his pocket. The barrel was pointed at the door, and he was determined to shoot if he had to. He had done it before and figured he'd say that the person on his porch had tried to break in and he shot him in self-defense.

Harold smiled knowing it would be an easy case to prove. A large black man at his front door at 10:00 at night would be reason enough for anyone to shoot, especially in his all-white neighborhood.

He waited for the slightest jiggle of the door knob, but it never came. In a way, he was disappointed, but he wasn't relieved.

Harold waited a few more minutes and didn't move from his spot behind the door. Then suddenly, he became aware of his surroundings and listened for Miriam. He hadn't heard any noise coming from the bedroom, but he still didn't trust her. He walked to the bedroom, not sure what to expect.

To his utter astonishment, his heart nearly stopped when he saw that the bed was empty. He glanced around the room, went into the bathroom looking for her, and he even checked the closet. She wasn't there. That's when he noticed that the bedroom window was wide open.

Harold ran to the window and peered out into the darkness. He didn't see her. But he was sure she was gone. When he examined the window sill, droplets of blood were visible. The scent of her body lingered in the air.

He became frantic at the thought of everything that he had told her and what she knew. Like a crazed man, he ran to the front door and threw it open. Had she staggered to the front of the house and met up with the tall black man? Harold stood on the porch, and then ran down several stairs and onto the lawn, but he didn't see Miriam anywhere.

He quickly ran back into the house and slammed the door behind him. Then he grabbed his stomach at the sick feeling that threatened to make him want to vomit. If she had taken his black book, he would have to find her and kill her.

He threw open the closet door in their bedroom, and dove for the secret hiding place where he had always kept his black book. It had been there before he tucked Miriam in bed, and before he had heard the knock on the door.

To his disappointment, the black book wasn't there. Harold pounded his fist on the floor and began swearing in a loud and vicious voice. She had taken it.

He stood up and paced in circles in the bedroom, not knowing what to do.

"My whole life is in that book!" he shouted to the walls. "Everything is documented in those pages. She wasn't supposed to take it."

In his mind, he saw himself writing about Xavier and how he had stalked him. He remembered the events of how he laced the envelope that he had sent him to sign autograph cards. He had written about all the drugs he had used on Miriam's roommate all those years ago. Everything he had ever done was documented in that black book.

If it got delivered into the wrong hands, it could totally destroy him. Anger rose up in him beyond his control this time. Now there'd be no turning back. One way or another, he had to take care of all the evidence, including Miriam. Like someone being shot from a cannon, he charged towards the front door.

Chapter 55

Charles felt like giving up. Everything he tried seemed to come to a dead end. He wasn't even sure how long the police could hold Jimmy, and now his thoughts turned to his mother's safety.

Although he tried not to be cocky, failure was something he didn't like or tolerate. He consoled himself by saying that things happened and he couldn't win every battle. Still, he would never get used to the pain of defeat.

Over his shoulder he heard a faint sound. Quickly his mind tried to process what it was. It sounded like an animal, perhaps a small cat. He cautiously turned, with his gun ready in case he needed it.

In front of him stood an attractive woman dressed in jeans, wearing no shoes, a bra, with nothing else covering her, and she was clinging to a book that she held close to her chest. She looked like a frightened child, her eyes wide and dazed.

She mouthed the word, "Help," and then dropped to one knee.

Charles made a move towards her but she forced herself up and met him halfway. He wasn't sure what to make of her situation, but he removed his sports coat and placed it over her shoulders to cover her. He noticed the bandage in the front and back of her shoulder.

"You okay?" he asked, instinctively sounding like a rookie policeman.

Of course he knew she wasn't okay, but it was the only thing he could think to say.

"He's crazy, and he's trying to kill me. We have to get out of here!"

Charles didn't know who she was, but he was smart enough to know that they both had to get out while the getting was good.

His car was only about twenty feet in front of them. He moved her quickly to the passenger side. Before he opened the car door, he scanned their surroundings for potential danger. Everything seemed quiet until the front door opened in the house that he had just left.

Harold rushed out with his gun pointed straight at them. He was screaming like a mad man. Instantly, both men locked their gazes upon each other. Charles had seen that look before, and he knew that he had to move fast.

Harold glanced at Charles and then at the passenger side of the car. That's when he saw Miriam's head. He became enraged and fired a single shot. The echo of the gunshot rang loud in the once-silent neighborhood. Lights immediately flicked on and no doubt someone was dialing 9-1-1.

Miriam screamed and put her head down between the car seats.

Charles hollered, "Stop shooting. I'm a police officer. Put your gun down!"

Harold squeezed off another shot that missed Charles by only inches. The bullet made a thudding sound as it lodged itself in Charles's car.

Quickly, Charles looked inside to make sure Miriam was okay. She was shaking and curled up in a ball like an abused child, but she seemed to be unharmed.

Once more Charles identified himself by saying, "Stop! I'm a police officer."

In his mind, this wouldn't be an easy task, but if the man continued to shoot at them, then he would have to kill this mad man who was running toward him.

Although Harold's shots were close, his aim was uncontrolled. Charles had been in this type of situation before and had trained to fire under pressure. The only danger was that Harold might get lucky or that someone else might get hurt.

Crouched behind the front of his car, he took his time and aimed. Harold was no more than twenty yards away.

Once more, Charles yelled, Freeze!" but Harold continued to walk and shoot.

Charles squeezed the trigger and shot him. The force of the bullet knocked him off his feet. His body hit the ground hard. Charles stood up while still pointing the gun towards Harold's body.

He aimed for the arm, but a few inches in either direction could have resulted in death. Glancing quickly at the car, he saw Miriam still in the same position. Hopefully she was okay.

Charles yelled to Harold, "Throw the gun down!"

Harold didn't respond verbally or to Charles's demands.

This was the part where people always got killed. The rule is to never assume that your victim is done until you are sure he is no longer a threat.

Charles trained his gun on Harold's head. If he moved, he would be dead.

Chapter 56

Charles looked at Harold. Although he looked peaceful enough lying on the ground, he still hadn't seen the gun.

He yelled at Harold, "Throw out your weapon," but there was no response.

Yelling once more, he took a step closer. There was still no movement from Harold. Charles looked at his gunshot wound or at least where the blood was coming from. It looked like a clean shot, but the bullet could have gone in at a strange angle or moved around and taken his life.

Hesitating, Charles walked a little closer and kicked Harold on the leg. His body absorbed the kick, but still he didn't respond. Charles wasn't sure if Harold was dead, but he lowered his gun just a bit and moved to get a full view of the victim.

Charles heard the police sirens as they screamed in the distance. In just a matter of minutes, they'd arrive and he'd at least have a backup unit to assist him. With an incomplete story of who these people were, and what was at stake, all he knew was a man had been shooting live rounds at him, and that a wounded woman was lying down in his car trying to avoid getting hit by stray bullets from the crazy man.

Charles thought about the woman. He knew he couldn't take his eyes off the man who was trying to kill him, and yet he wondered if she was still crouched down in the seat suffering from some sort of shock. His question was answered when he heard her voice to the side of him.

Softly she asked, "Is Harold dead?"

Charles knew he was messing up, especially if this Harold guy wasn't dead, but he turned and said, "Get back in the car!"

The next thing Charles heard was a loud bang and then he felt a warm sensation filling his body. His gun flew out of his hand as he dropped to the ground. He'd been shot.

Lying on the cold cement, Charles cursed himself for letting his guard down. He had been hit, but he didn't think it was too serious. Pain was a problem, but as far as he could tell, the bullet hadn't injured any major organs.

Miriam moved back and hid behind a nearby tree, unsure of what her husband might do to her again.

Charles tried to roll up. He knew that time was of the essence. He also knew that Harold would be standing up, and that his gun would either be trained on him or the lady. Charles forced himself to look up at the front barrel of a gun pointed directly at him.

Harold stood up, but he was shaking uncontrollably, and blood was oozing from his mouth.

He began to scream, "Who the hell are you?"

Charles laughed and said, "As I mentioned before, I'm a police officer!"

The news didn't sit well with Harold. The expression on his face was snarly.

Charles said, "Look, man, you don't want to kill a cop. I don't know what's going on here, but shooting a policeman will get you life in prison."

Harold's face scrunched up as if to show that he was in pain, but Charles wasn't going to fall for another distractive ploy of his. He decided to push the guy's buttons.

"The police should be here any second. Don't make a mistake."

Harold looked at him with a blank stare. Charles decided to stick with the fear tactic.

"Harold, do you know what goes on in prison? You don't want to go there, especially for life."

Harold began to visibly shake. Charles figured something had happened to him and he could use this to their advantage. If he could keep Harold's mind occupied long enough, they'd be safe until the police units arrived.

"Harold," he said.

Harold looked at him but also through him. It was as if he was reliving something from his past, but Charles didn't care where he was at as long as he didn't shoot. He decided to make his move and get into his mind.

"Put the gun down, and I'll tell them that you cooperated. I promise. Nothing will happen to you."

Harold's head dropped slightly, but not enough for Charles to do anything.

"This is your chance, Harold. It's a one-time offer. Listen, I hear sirens. They're almost here. Don't make it worse on yourself, Harold."

Harold kept the gun trained on Charles. He was breathing hard now and sweating profusely.

"Put the gun down, Harold!" Miriam shouted as she emerged from behind the tree.

Her voice was strong or at least strong for a woman who had just been shot.

Harold's face showed anger and then rage. He pivoted and with two hands, held the gun and aimed it at Miriam. Then in an instant, the sound of a gunshot rang through the night air. Harold's head was ripped apart and blood spilled onto Charles.

Miriam stood in a frozen stance holding Charles's gun that he'd lost when Harold had shot him. She had just killed her husband.

Squad cars arrived and police officers rushed to their sides. They ordered her to put the gun down on the ground. Miriam did as she was told.

Charles tried to identify himself, but his words fell upon deaf ears. Flashing lights and men yelling told him it would be safer to place his hands above his head and lie flat on the ground. He complied with their wishes. He didn't want to end up like Harold.

The police were quick and efficient. Two men had their guns trained on Charles. Another man eased up behind him and searched him for a weapon. Charles tried to announce that he was a fellow officer, but they secured their positions first. Apparently, he'd have time later to tell them who he was and what had happened.

Pain and fear overtook Miriam. She began crying and screaming. Two officers had to force her arms over her head. Then they forced her to lie face down on the ground. That's when they handcuffed her wrists behind her back.

The police weren't gentle, and the fact that she was a woman meant nothing to them. She was still a potential danger to everyone at the scene. Charles didn't fare any better. They handled him roughly, too.

The bullet in his leg still burned with the heat of impact. Charles bit his tongue, and closed his eyes. He'd have to endure the pain, and he wondered how he had gotten himself into this mess.

As he listened to the familiar sounds of police officers doing their jobs at a crime scene, he thought about his mom and wondered if she was safe and if Jimmy was in jail.

Chapter 57

It seemed like a mad house to Charles. Here it was almost midnight and reporters, television camera crews, and people from out of nowhere milled around to be part of all the excitement. The police chief tried to do damage control as he gave a statement periodically, but it did little good to take the attention off of Charles.

The good news was that Miriam had taken Harold's black book and it listed all the information the officials needed to close at least part of the case. Harold had put something on an envelope that he knew Xavier would lick to seal it. He had sent letters to Xavier before, as a test, to see if he would lick the envelopes.

He took his time to test the way they were sealed when Xavier would send something back. When Harold checked the so-called glue that bonded the flap to the envelope, he knew it was spit that had sealed the edges shut and not just a glue stick.

When Xavier killed those people in the beginning of all the trouble, he didn't even realize that he was driving his car. That's how powerful the drug was that Harold had put on the envelope.

Although Harold had shot Charles in the leg, the bullet had passed straight through. The doctors told him that he'd spend a month or so on crutches, but that he'd be okay.

* * *

While still in the hospital, Charles made sure that doctors were attending to Miriam. Now his one final stop for the evening was to visit

Xavier, his hero and mentor. He didn't know if he'd ever see him again if his condition worsened and he died.

Unsteady on his crutches, he limped slowly down the hallway towards Xavier's room. He had heard that he was still in bad shape from the gunshot incident. His condition had improved from intensive to critical, but he was still in danger of dying at any moment.

Charles moved towards the door. He braced himself to see his hero. Time and the gunshot had taken their toll on the once-athletic body of Xavier. Charles had seen that type of damage before but not with someone he cared about.

A lone police officer guarded the door. Charles knew that Xavier still had a lot of problems to deal with even if he survived. There were a lot of unexplained things that had to be figured out.

Frank was dead and Xavier had written a suicide note that had been found at Xavier's house. It was theorized that Frank must have walked in on Xavier trying to kill himself and Frank tried to stop him. There must have been a struggle for a second and then Frank was shot. Xavier must have been out of his mind when he realized that he had shot his best friend. That's the reason police used to explain why Xavier had taken off into the woods and resurfaced, looking for food and water in the senator's house.

Officials figured that Xavier didn't know he was on the senator's property. It was a theory that might have been believed by a jury, however, when Miriam showed up with Harold's black book, all previous theories were under scrutiny.

A lot of things didn't seem to make sense to Charles, but at the moment, he didn't want to think about any of it. He only wanted a face-to-face meeting with the man he called his hero.

He inhaled deeply and walked into the room. Xavier was lying in bed, not moving, and silent. All that could be heard were the sounds of the machines running that were monitoring his progress and keeping him alive.

One thing that Charles hated the most about hospitals was the smell of disinfectant and sickness. People often said that the smell in hospitals reminded them of death. But for Charles, the smell of death didn't bother him. It was the absence of smell that got to him.

Life was known for smells and scents, but death was empty, void of anything that could make a scent. The smell of food cooking in the kitchen, or the smells of sweat on the basketball court were scents that Charles could identify with. But for him it seemed like when he was in the hospital he couldn't identify any smells that represented life. To him, life was missing in the hospital. Charles hated that.

He entered Xavier's room as quietly as possible with crutches and tiptoed to the side of his bed. He didn't want to awaken Xavier. However, after standing in the room for over a minute, he realized that he didn't have to worry about waking Xavier up. He apparently was under a lot of medication and wouldn't be talking to anyone.

Standing next to Xavier's bed, and staring at the sick and ashen colored face of his hero, he had a hard time dealing with all of the tubes that protruded from every part of his body. It was making him sick to even comprehend what that man had been through.

Charles wanted to leave the room and walk out. He'd seen sick people before, but seeing his hero lying there almost dead was more than he could handle. For a fleeting second, he got a glimpse of what his ex-wife probably had to deal with on a daily basis—repeatedly she had told him that she lived in fear. She had said that she never wanted to see his body all beaten up and him on the verge of dying. All she had wanted was for him to get out of the business and live his life. But he couldn't do it.

Gritting his teeth, Charles forced himself to look at Xavier. For a moment, there was silence and then Charles, with tears spilling down his cheeks, spoke to Xavier. He had never divulged any of his deepest feelings before, but he felt it was safe there. He thought it was finally okay to let his walls down.

Charles began, "Xavier, you're the only person who I ever looked up to. I always wanted to be like you. When you and I stopped communicating with each other, I had to live with the constant, daily feeling of total emptiness. I hate to say it, but I guess you were like a dad or big brother to me."

Charles stopped talking for a moment. He looked around the room trying to locate a box of tissues. He grabbed a handful with intensity and wiped his wet cheeks. Then more tears came, and out of total helplessness, he laughed as he wiped his face again. He sighed deeply and continued talking to his hero.

"I never had a chance to tell you that I bought a dog. I named him after you. His name is X. I hope you're not offended."

For several more minutes, Charles shared his innermost thoughts and feelings with Xavier, yet he never opened his eyes. He was just connected to all of those machines with tubes poking out of his body. If anyone had been witnessing or listening to Charles's one-sided conversation, they would've thought that Xavier and Charles were two long lost friends who had just been reunited.

As quickly as Charles had begun his conversation with Xavier, he was done, and stopped talking. He stood tall, squared his shoulders, and took a deep breath. It was time for him to build up his wall again and go back into the world. He had solved part of the case but there was so much more to be revealed. His gut told him that Jimmy's involvement and connections went much further and deeper than anyone knew.

* * *

Just about the time that Charles was ready to leave Xavier's room, he heard a tap on the door. He turned around and saw Le standing next to Angela in the doorway.

"They told me you might still be here," Angela said. "How's your leg?"

Le chimed in, "I'm so glad to see you alive."

"Hello, ladies," Charles said, rubbing his leg as if to indicate that it was okay but still causing him a bit of pain. "Let's take this out in the hall."

With one final glance at Xavier, Charles escorted the women into the hall as he closed the hospital door.

Angela was first to speak, "We need to talk to you in private."

"Okay," Charles answered.

"I figure it would be best if we just drove around and talked," Angela said, speaking her words with a machine gun delivery approach. "I don't know what kind of undercover agents are lurking, or if someone has planted listening devices that we don't know about. It's just safer this way."

It was strange to hear her talking about the secrecy. He thought they would be safe in the hospital, but he agreed to her plan and went along with the flow.

To Charles, both women looked beautiful, but he was drawn to Le. She had also been part of the problem and one of the reasons for Xavier being in the hospital. Le held her head down as if she were a child about to be scolded for doing something wrong.

"What do you know about Jimmy?" he asked, directing his concern towards her. "I'm kind of concerned about my mom's safety."

They both didn't answer the question directly, other than to say that his mother was okay and safe. Again, Charles knew there was more to the story, but he waited for them to fill him in.

As Angela drove around the city, Le told Charles that she had gone to the police and had given them a confession stating that Xavier hadn't tried to attack her. She had implicated Jimmy.

In her statement, she said that Jimmy had forced her to say that Xavier had tried to attack her. Then she testified about his prostitution ring and all the evils that he had done to her and her family. She didn't mention the senator, because she feared that no one would believe her.

With only a brief pause after Le had finished telling Charles what had happened, Angela interrupted.

"Charles, have you heard the news?"

"I haven't been listening to the news, or even turned on my radio. I didn't want to hear what another reporter was trying to speculate about Xavier's case. I just wanted to visit Xavier in case he passed away."

Charles shook his head and Angela looked disappointed.

"Jimmy is dead," she blurted out.

Charles didn't know how to react. He looked at Le.

"I thought you just said that the police took him to jail?"

"They were taking him, and then as the story has it, he tried to escape after killing someone. The ensuing fight led to the officers killing him. They're doing an investigation," Angela said. "They also don't believe it was an accident, but so far, they've come up empty."

"Good God!" Charles exclaimed in a tone that was saddened by the death of the man who could explain everything.

He looked in the back seat at Le, wondering what her reaction was to the news. She was holding her head in her hands. Charles couldn't tell if she was too shocked to say anything, but it didn't matter anymore. Jimmy was dead.

Looking at Angela, Charles waited for the rest of the story.

Angela appeared suddenly nervous, and then she said, "Charles, I've spent time with Le and there's a lot more."

Charles rolled his eyes as if to say, "Please enlighten me."

Angela continued, "Jimmy forced Le to say that Xavier tried to rape her, but he was just following orders."

Charles jumped in, "Working under whose orders?"

Angela looked annoyed at the interruption, but kept talking.

"Jimmy was a bad guy, but he worked for…" She paused for a moment, and then let it out. "He worked for Senator Stevens."

Charles's face went pale. It was as if he had just seen a ghost. He yelled at Angela, unaware of the strength of his voice.

"Senator Stevens is one of the most powerful men around," Charles wailed.

Clearly, Angela was alarmed and even shocked at his tone of voice, but she responded to him in the same tone.

"Absolutely," Angela hollered. "Le was his kept woman and Xavier just happened to be at the wrong place at the wrong time."

Charles looked in the back seat at Le. She was nodding her head yes.

"Le panicked when she heard Xavier talking to the police and especially when he handed her the phone. She didn't want to talk to the police. That was one of her rules."

"That's probably why the senator stepped in and assigned Jimmy to keep Le captive," Charles commented, talking more to himself than to the women.

"Jimmy was his boy," Angela said. "I'll bet he was the one who had Jimmy killed by the police."

Angela looked at him with a confused expression on her face, but Charles answered the look by telling her, "We don't know how far and wide the senator's reach is."

"Because I got away," Le said.

Charles interrupted, "Please, he didn't die because of you."

Angela turned a corner and continued taking quick glances into the rearview mirror. Charles hadn't missed that.

"Now things are starting to make sense," he said. "Senator Stevens shot Xavier. He apparently didn't have time to finish the job though, because the police showed up too early. Thank God that the police car must've been in the neighborhood when the call went out. They arrived within minutes."

Angela made another right turn, and then she began to speed up.

Charles asked, "What's going on?"

Angela said, "There's a car following us."

Charles quickly glanced into the side mirror to see how much distance was between them. He figured he would know if they were being tailed or if Angela's mind was playing tricks on her.

"You're right," he said. "We're being followed."

Charles moved to grab his gun, but he remembered he didn't have it. Angela accelerated the gas pedal even more.

In a commanding voice, Charles said, "Stay calm."

He felt fairly confident that whoever was following them wouldn't do something right away. It would be too suspicious if something happened while they were all together in the same vehicle.

Le still sat quietly in the back seat. She didn't look up, speak, or move.

Charles knew the area they were driving in and told Angela, "Make a left at the next light. Just take it easy and relax."

Charles put a hand on her shoulder and he could feel her body's tension. Her eyes were wide with fear. She'd been a reporter and he knew that she'd probably taken on tough cases. But now her reporter's credentials meant nothing. She was just plain scared.

All it would take would be one bullet, one stray bullet, and she could become the headline in tomorrow's newspaper.

"Ladies!" Charles shouted. "I need you to stay calm. Can you do that?"

Straight ahead Charles saw a large shopping mall with stores such as Nordstrom and Neiman Marcus. The parking lots were filled with cars. Charles figured the mall would be a good place to get lost.

To Angela, he said, "Circle around and try to find a spot close to the front and near one of the entrance doors."

As fate would have it, a spot opened up near the entrance of the mall. Unfortunately, another car was also racing to get to the same parking place. Charles could see that Angela was a competitor and even more so when her life was involved. She sped up and then hit the brakes just enough to fit into the spot.

The driver in the other car flipped everyone off and screamed some profanities, but it was a small price to pay for safety.

All three of them jumped out of the car and ran for the mall except Charles who hobbled along as fast as he could go on his crutches.

Tires screeched behind them and two men jumped out of the car that had been following them. They ran towards them just as Angela, Le and Charles disappeared inside the mall.

Charles grabbed Le's hand and led her in the direction he wanted to go. Angela, however, went in another direction. It didn't help that Charles was maneuvering through the mall on crutches. But he didn't dare stop to look behind them. Hop, hop, zig, zag, Charles made his way through the mall as fast as he could.

Chapter 58

Charles and Le reconnected with Angela inside one of the busy department stores.

He said, "I want the two of you to stay together while I maneuver around to get behind the guy who was following us. Do you understand? I mean it. Stay together and don't try to come up with some wild plan."

Angela grabbed his hand. Fear exposed itself across her face.

"I want all of us to stay together," she said.

Charles said, "I know, but that's not a good strategy for us right now."

Charles took Angela's hand and squeezed it gently. He was not trying to be the hero. He just wanted her to gain strength from his strength.

"No one will hurt you, I promise."

Angela nervously smiled and then pulled her hand away from Charles.

"I know it will be okay," she said. "Be safe."

Charles turned to his left and began to quickly hobble away. If only he didn't have these crutches, he thought. He gave a quick glance over his shoulder and to the right he saw a young man. The guy appeared to be in his 30s. He was dressed in black from head to toe. He was moving swiftly between the racks of clothes.

It was the same man that Charles had seen following them. He could tell that he must have caught a glimpse of Angela and Le as he began to pick up his pace.

Charles held his breath as he maneuvered around to the back of the guy. There wasn't a lot he could do in the mall, but he could find out who this guy was and why he was following them.

Charles put his crutches to the side and walked as silently as he could behind the man in the black outfit. Pain shot through his leg as he fought hard to walk quietly applying as much pressure as he could on his other leg. Then he put his hand in the middle of the guy's lower back, amazed that he had made it without being detected. He assumed that noise in the mall and all the excitement of the moment allowed him to get close without being exposed.

"Don't move. I have a gun," Charles whispered in the guy's ear.

The young man froze and his body tensed up immediately. Charles could sense that the tension was not from fright. He was about to pounce Charles.

"Keep walking," Charles demanded, as he led him toward the men's restroom.

While they were walking, he felt along the stranger's body and found a gun. It was something he knew could be there, but he had hoped it wasn't.

Reaching in, he took it and slid it behind his belt that was covered by his shirt. His leg was beginning to throb but he decided to will himself to keep going forward. He couldn't show pain or injury, because once inside the restroom, he'd become an easy target.

A quick flashback of when he was a kid overcoming pain helped him once again pretend that he was Xavier. It gave him the needed strength to keep going. He remembered seeing Xavier play with severe injuries, and he used the same willpower.

Charles continued to lead him towards the restroom. They entered and he hoped there'd be a lock on the restroom door. But luck wasn't with him. This was a new and modern mall that had open entrances and a turning walkway into the stalls.

Quickly, Charles glanced at the setup in the room and made sure that they were alone. The room was empty. Not to his advantage was that the restroom walls were lined with mirrors.

The guy immediately noticed the blood oozing out of Charles's leg. Probably figuring he could easily take Charles, the guy turned around quickly and with the open palm of his hand, he hit Charles square in the nose.

At first, Charles's head reeled backwards and he didn't feel anything other than the pressure of his nose starting to swell. But within seconds, pain shot from the inner parts of his eye sockets to the tip of his nose. Blood came squirting out as if being released from a high pressure dam.

Charles's eyes began to water. Then he felt his head spinning. A quick kick into his already injured leg and then a swift move towards his head sent the gun flying. Whoever this guy was, he was good. Charles leaned up against the sink and the water came on automatically.

"Who are you?" Charles yelled as the stranger walked quickly towards him.

The guy didn't answer. He just stood there looking silently confident yet deadly. He took slow deliberate steps toward Charles.

Charles spat blood at his assailant. The stranger wiped his face. Charles could see that he was angered.

Staggering back, Charles felt the bathroom stall door against his back. He was feeling lightheaded. Blood was oozing out of him faster than he could wipe it up. His leg and his nose were throbbing.

It would only be a matter of seconds before the opponent in front of him pressed his advantage on either one. Black spots danced in front of his face, and then he remembered. He had the gun.

He started to reach under his shirt remembering that he had the other gun, when suddenly a male shopper walked into the restroom. A look of horror swept across his face as Charles could only imagine what things looked like.

Blood was all over the floor and sink. He was backed up against the stall while a white man dressed in black clothing was moving in on him.

A weak gasp of air left the mouth of the unexpected guest. His eyes bulged with horror. Then he turned and ran. Charles hoped that he was a good citizen and would go get help, but he couldn't bank on it.

He quickly pulled out the gun and hit his assailant on the head while he was distracted by the stranger. The blow was hard but only enough to knock the stranger down to one knee. Charles raised the gun and hit him again. This time he went down.

If someone had walked in at that moment, they would have sworn that Charles had shot the man lying on the floor. They also might have thought that it was the stranger's blood covering the walls.

Without a second thought, Charles rifled through the assailant's pockets. He removed the guy's wallet and looked at his identification. He was packing an ID and a badge that said he was a Secret Service agent.

Chapter 59

Charles quickly wiped his face with several damp paper towels. He tried to clean up his appearance, but it was hard to do. There were large splashes of blood on his clothing that couldn't be disguised.

However, as fortune would have it, the agent was wearing a jacket about Charles's size. He put it on and it seemed to cover most of the blood stains. The worst thing that could happen now would be if the security guards came rushing in. They'd probably shoot him and ask questions later.

Charles looked at the man lying on the floor. He was motionless. He thought about splashing water on the guy's face, but he didn't have time to interrogate him to get more info. Whoever was driving the assailant's car was probably inside the mall looking for his partner.

Besides, Angela and Le might still be in danger. After he retrieved his crutches, he rushed out of the restroom and tried to get lost in the crowd. He wanted to slow down, but he didn't want to bring any attention to himself. As he gimped along, he began whispering for Angela and Le.

He didn't see them or even know where they were, but he moved in the direction he figured that two scared women might travel.

He hoped they were hiding, but he needed to find them and fast. Charles raised his voice a little bit more and waited to see if it brought any type of movement from people in the crowd. Then he began to yell their names, and that's when Angela and Le ran up to him.

Angela asked, "Are you okay?"

Charles grabbed both their hands and they all took off running. The mall was a good start, but they needed to go someplace where they could talk. He knew that home was out of the question. If the senator could have him followed, he would know everything about him. He also worried about his mom and his child. The senator was a powerful man. In fact, if Xavier died, then he would have gotten away with murder. Charles wanted to make sure that didn't happen.

All three jetted down the hallway trying to get outside. Although the mall was crowded, it would only be a matter of time before someone found the unconscious agent on the restroom floor. Then the place would become a mad house.

No one could afford to go to jail right now. They needed time to think and time to plan things out. Charles went outside first. The coolness of the air brought him hope as he grabbed the two ladies and hobbled towards the car.

Quickly Charles looked over his shoulder and saw fear in Angela's eyes. Le remained expressionless as if running was something she had been doing all her life.

The car, a metal place of refuge seemed within their grasp. But like everything else that day, it was an illusion; something to be denied. The squeal of tires filled their ears as the assassin's car whirled around the corner.

Charles immediately tried to get the women into the car. He hurried to the driver's side, but he forgot that it was Angela who had been driving. When he tried to retrieve the keys, he realized it was too late.

A gun was pointed at them and the man on the other side of the vehicle was motioning for them to get out. Angela started to scream having never been in a situation where death looked her in the face. Le, on the other hand, still remained silent as if in some type of trance.

In a moment, they were out of the car. Charles was sure that the people driving and walking past must have seen what was happening. Hadn't anyone seen the gun?

He held his hand out as if to say, "Don't shoot," Charles wanted to let his assassin know that he wouldn't put up a fight. He surmised that if they were supposed to be dead, they would have already been shot.

Entering the other car was like stepping into a chariot of death. The car, although a new model Lincoln, seemed void of life. No music was playing, and the tinted windows blocked all incoming light.

Charles asked, "Where are you taking us?"

Their assailants just pointed and indicated that Angela should drive. Charles plotted in his mind that if there was any move he could do to save the day, he would. But it appeared that everything had been well orchestrated by their assassins.

He sat behind Angela who had a gun pointed at her head. Le sat in the front seat still with a stoic look on her face. If Charles made any move against the assassin, Angela would for sure take a bullet in the head. Depending on how well he was trained, Le might also take a shot.

A tap on the shoulder, and a finger pointing in a certain direction was the only thing leading the way. They drove for a few hours and then arrived in front of a beautiful home. Dogs barked loudly as the assassin tapped Angela on the shoulder to let her know to stop.

Charles knew this was not a good sign. Wherever they were, they had seen enough. They could each retrace their steps if they wanted to, and that wasn't good.

The assassin signaled for Charles to get out of the car and then the rest of them should follow. The gun was trained at Charles's head as the man signaled for him to ring the doorbell. Angela and Le followed along with the quietness of children who knew they'd get punished if they even made the slightest sound.

Charles rang the doorbell, not sure what to expect. An older, well-dressed man opened the door. To his left side a huge dog stood at attention, but it didn't bark. It just showed its teeth to let everyone know that one wrong move and you'd be all his.

Cold blue eyes stared straight into Charles's eyes. He had seen his type before. At any given time those same eyes would look alive and full of life. Someone might think that his eyes could be trusted, but today, they were eyes of death.

Le stepped back in fear, as Charles and Angela put the whole picture into focus. The man who stood before them was the senator.

He moved to the side allowing room for the three of them to enter. Charles resisted at first but felt the hard butt of a gun on the back of his head. He dropped to the ground for a second, only to come face to face with the snarling dog. If the choice was having his face bit off or getting shot, Charles would choose the bullet.

He jumped back up and moved into the house. Angela tried to grab his arm to help him, but her own fear made her unable to do anyone any good. Fear covered her body like a blanket of snow and she had the worst case of frostbite.

Charles tried to give her a look of comfort, but this time, he couldn't hide his own doubts.

Chapter 60

Charles thought about power. Even though the senator was small and fragile, he appeared large and strong. Charles thought about himself, Le, and Angela. They were powerless, especially when someone with power could control if they lived or died.

That made him angry.

"What in the hell do you want with us?" he yelled.

The senator laughed out loud. His voice was cold, but it was also the voice of a man who was getting what he wanted.

"To be honest," he said, "I'd like to see all of you dead, but right now, it seems to be a problem."

Charles glared at him. If he could get away with it, he'd spit in his face.

With a belligerent retort, Charles said, "Then I guess you've got a problem."

His response was answered with another hit across the head.

The senator moved in close to Charles, but then went past him. Next, he moved closer to Angela. He put his hand lightly against her face. She grimaced and pulled back. He smiled at her and then moved in even closer. Now he was right in front of her face.

"You're just like that nigger," he said, pausing briefly. "What's his name, Xavier?"

Angela raised her hand as if to slap him, but her sudden actions made the senator's dog growl. She put her hand back down, reluctantly.

As the senator moved from person to person, it was like he was greeting voters at a political campaign. Now he stood in front of Le. His facial expression changed instantly as he grabbed her by the hair and pulled her closer to him.

With a snarly voice and pursed lips, the senator reprimanded Le, "One job, just one that I asked you to do for me. I gave you a home, money, and anything you ever wanted, and this is the way you repay me?"

Le stepped back, and her hair slipped out of the senator's hand. But he moved surprisingly fast and grabbed her by the neck. Then he threw her against the wall. He moved in and kicked her again and again and again, like someone would do to their most hated enemy.

Charles just couldn't stand by and do nothing, so he made his move. As he stretched out his hand to grab the senator, he was welcomed by the pain of his hand nearly being torn off. It was a quick bite, but blood flowed profusely from the puncture wounds. Charles saw this as maybe being his only chance. It was up to him to make his move. He tried to size things up.

His obstacles were a dog, a well-trained man with a gun, and the senator. He listed them in the order of complexities. He reasoned that the senator would be the least of his worries. He'd have to stop the gunman first, and then take care of the dog. He'd handle the senator last.

Charles moved his hand in a wide sweep. Blood sprayed across the face of the gunman. That's when Charles made his move as the startled gunman wiped his eyes. Fear of being infected by some sort of blood-borne disease was greater than protecting the senator. Using his good hand to grab the gun, he positioned his body so that he could use his elbow to deliver a quick blow.

The assassin staggered backwards, which gave Charles the opportunity to focus the gun on the charging dog. He squeezed the trigger. Two quick muffled rounds fired off, and the dog dropped to the floor, dead.

The senator fell to his knees and held onto his dead dog. What had taken only seconds, had taken away a lifetime for the senator's best friend. Charles didn't know if he could hold the assassin any longer. His good hand was all but useless, and he was losing his grip. If he had to die, he'd at least know that he had caused pain to the senator. That gave him a bit of pleasure.

With the next blink of his eye, Charles was thrown to the floor and was staring into the gun barrel pointed at him.

The senator spewed out several obscenities, spit, and then yelled to the assassin, "Kill him!"

Charles had run out of options. His hand and arm felt numb as he prepared himself for death.

The mind can work faster than any computer. In microseconds, Charles thought about the life of his son without his influence. He thought about his mom outliving him and the pain she would feel. Mostly, he had regrets. No matter how strong his will was to fight back, and no matter what his heart's desires were, he was a realist. He knew that this was the end.

Charles prepared for his death, but it was interrupted by two angry women. The fear that once held Angela at bay now became fuel for her rage. She would have done any linebacker proud as she ran shoulder-first into the assassin. Her attack was enough to throw him off. He stumbled backwards and lost his balance.

Le clawed at his face and then his eyes. Angela, appearing like a seasoned street fighter, hit him straight in the balls. He dropped to the floor near Charles, making it easy for him to greet the assassin with a strong knee that finished him off.

Now after all the mess, the only thing that remained to take care of was the senator. He now faced two angry women and Charles holding his bloody hand.

Blood continued to pump onto the floor from the dog bite wounds, and Charles began to feel a little lightheaded. He was a walking mess—a dog bite, a gunshot wound in the leg and several blows across the head. He looked like a poster for military war victims.

Looking at his hand, he figured the dog's bite had hit an artery. He needed medical help right away, or he would bleed to death.

Chapter 61

Charles began to see spots. Little black dots jumped in front of everything he saw. He felt like he was going to black out. He could see Angela's and Le's faces and their mouths moving, but he couldn't hear anything. It was like watching a silent movie without the words.

He felt his energy slipping away. He needed help, and he needed it fast! He forced himself to try to remember his training. 'I need to slow my heart rate down,' he told himself. But he was scared which only made him hyperventilate. He tried to yell, but his voice failed him. He felt trapped inside his body. All he could do was watch the people in the room.

The senator, although old, was fierce. He moved quickly and pushed Angela against the wall. She fell against it with a hard thud, and then she tried to swing back, but he must have had some training, similar to Jimmy's. He blocked her punch and hit her square in the mouth. Angela was down and out.

Charles fought to stay awake. He wanted to help, but it was impossible. It took everything he had just to keep his eyelids open. The senator turned to Le. She froze as she watched him walk toward her with relentless determination.

Lifting his hand, he slapped her hard across the face. The blow staggered her, but she remained on her feet. Defiantly, she squared her stance and faced him. He backhanded her again across the face. Again, she stumbled, but she didn't go down. It had now become a game of willpower, and Le looked as though she was up to the challenge.

Her tiny body seemed like a blade of grass being swayed by the wind, but it still was unmoving. The senator balled up his fist and hit her with the same force that he had hit Angela with. It sent her to the floor, but still, she arose once again to face him.

Charles had never seen anything like what he was witnessing. As small as Le was, she was tough. Blood flowed out of her mouth, and her eye was beginning to swell, but she still faced the senator. He took the confrontation as a challenge. With a cocky look, he was determined to win.

He hit her in the stomach and threw several punches across her face. Each time she went down, she would rise back up. Charles could see that the senator was wearing down. Soon, his energy would be depleted if the battle continued for much longer.

Although Le was a bloody mess, she was winning. The senator stopped and looked at her, angry, but tired.

With a quick glance around the room, he saw the assassin's gun on the floor near him. Charles saw it at the same time. He made one last ditch effort to help. He pushed himself off the floor, and landed, full body, onto the gun. With his good hand, he grabbed it and held on tight. He tried to remain strong and focused, but everything went black.

Senator Stevens tried to separate Charles's body from the gun, but couldn't. He had no strength left.

Even in an unconscious state, Charles somehow managed to hold onto the gun. Sweat poured off the senator's face as he continued to try to pry the gun out of Charles's hand.

His mistake was that he had forgotten all about Angela. Apparently his naive thinking told him that she'd do nothing while he struggled against Charles. But Angela knew that if he retrieved the gun, that he'd kill her.

To his surprise, Angela kicked him in the back, as hard as she could. A loud thud sounded as he rolled over in pain. Angela kicked him again and again, which sent him into a coiled-up ball position. She rushed over to Charles and pried the gun out of his hand. As if Charles knew good from evil, his hand relaxed, and Angela was able to take the gun with ease.

Standing erect or at least as tall as her badly beaten body would allow her, Le took the gun from Angela, aimed it at the senator and shot three rounds into him. Each time the gun recoiled, she walked closer to his body. The final fatal shot was near point blank range.

The senator was dead and Charles felt his body drift off to sleep. Le glanced at him and for the first time he saw her smile.

Chapter 62

There was darkness and there was peace. Charles drifted further and further into emptiness. He was beginning to embrace the feeling, but suddenly a voice called out to him. It was the lone voice of a man telling him to wake up. Charles resisted. He was enjoying his peace.

His life had been hard and sometimes troubled. This darkness was comforting. Another voice came to him, but this time it was softer. It was the voice of a woman. Charles knew that voice. He had heard it before, and he searched his memory trying to place it.

"Charles, I love you," the voice said and then there was silence.

On and off again he continued to hear voices. Sometimes they seemed familiar, and sometimes like strangers, but each time, it was a voice calling him. Now he wanted to see who the voices belonged to. He wanted to remember.

Willing himself with all his might, Charles opened his eyes. For a moment, blinding light caused him to close his eyes again, but he knew that he couldn't be denied. Summoning all of his willpower once more, he forced his eyes open to see what was before him.

Sitting next to him, at his side, was his mom. She had been praying for him. By the looks of her, she hadn't slept in days. Like a warm blast of sunshine on a cold and damp day, she became his strength once more. He focused on her, even though he couldn't move.

Then with what felt like every ounce of energy he had, he whispered, "Hello."

Charles's mother smiled. She raised her hands in the air praising God. Tears began to flow down her face. Her baby boy was alive and conscious.

Charles continued to look around the room. He saw Alice standing at the foot of his bed. She smiled at him. Her eyes spoke volumes of how much she loved him. Charles realized how lucky he was.

She touched his foot and, like a transponder, she filled him with her own loving and positive energy flow. He was alive now and his mind was becoming clearer. He loved his son, loved his mom, and loved Alice. He promised himself that this time things would change. He would stop hating his ex, and he'd love and cherish those around him.

"What about X, my buddy and best friend? I miss him."

Alice, knowing him sometimes better than he knew himself, smiled, and said, "Don't worry about X, boo. You know I got your back. I didn't hear from you and figured I needed to take care of X, one way or another."

The tail end of her statement wavered off almost into a soft whisper, as she thought about the possibility of not ever seeing Charles again.

Charles licked his dry lips and asked, "What happened?"

His mom was the first one to grab his hand.

She said, "Everyone was so worried about you. You'd lost so much blood and nearly died. Le called 9-1-1 and they came to the senator's house with an ambulance."

Charles tried to remember that night, but in a way he knew he was blocking it from his memory. He remembered the senator. He remembered Le and Angela. He remembered getting bitten by the dog. His hand began to throb at the thought of everything that had transpired.

Scanning the room of familiar faces, he searched for the two women who had saved his life.

Alice, said, "Angela's doing a story on everything. She's been on TV nonstop. Le's still in police custody, but that's only because she's the one who shot the senator. Once everything is revealed, they'll set her free."

"The men following us?" Charles asked weakly as he tried to wrap his mind around everything.

"They were some of the senator's private goons who did a little side work beyond their government pay. They didn't die, but they'll be in prison long enough to wish they had."

Charles never believed in happy endings. He wouldn't even admit it to his mom. Until today, he wondered if he'd go to heaven after he died. Beyond all that, he was curious about one other important fact that no one had mentioned.

"I want to know about Xavier. Is he okay?"

The room became instantly silent as no one spoke. Then Charles noticed a smile on Alice's face. But she said nothing, and just left the room.

Charles was puzzled but still weak. He wanted to sit up but his head was spinning. He also didn't understand why Alice had left.

"How long have I been here? I mean, how long have I been unconscious in this place?" he asked.

His mother answered, "One week, one day, and seven hours."

Everyone laughed, including Charles.

"That's my mom," he said.

Then the door to his room opened, and Alice reappeared. A broad smile was plastered across her face as she pushed Xavier into the room, seated in his wheelchair.

Both men looked at each other, and in their silence was the respect of warriors. Xavier gave Charles a nod, and Charles returned it with a weak smile.

Then he drifted off to sleep. At long last, he had found his peace and his happy ending. He dreamt of a new job and taking his dog for a walk.

Epilogue

Miriam gave the black book she held onto so tightly to the police, it explained everything Harold had done. It was enough to clear her name and also clear Xavier's name.

That black book was like gold to Xavier. It revealed Harold's meticulous notes detailing the time he spent researching Xavier, and developing a plot to destroy the man he thought violated his wife.

Apparently, Harold sent several envelopes to Xavier with collectors' cards for him to autograph. He timed how long it took Xavier to return the cards. He even examined each one to determine if Xavier licked the envelope or used glue.

Xavier was a creature of habit that promptly signed, licked, and returned each envelope within a day or so. Like Miriam, Harold took advantage of a man who was kind and principled to a fault, an almost fatal fault. Drugging Xavier was easy once he knew his habits. Loading the envelope with some heavy duty narcotics, he waited with the hope of Xavier doing something stupid.

Harold wished Xavier embarrassed and even dead. In truth, he couldn't have envisioned a scheme that included the deaths of Warren and Martha. The tourists' murder by Xavier's Hummer was the nail in the coffin Harold built for his wife's former lover. Or so his dead soul desired.

If Harold accomplished anything, then it was killing any opportunity Miriam had to reunite with Xavier. Yes, her own evil deeds destroyed the relationship years before but no amount of repentance would make her fantasies of a relationship come to life.

Miriam visited Xavier daily. She understood that there could never be anything between them, but felt it was her duty to make sure he was okay. Vowing to be only a memory in his life, she visited until the moment Xavier stirred out of his coma. True to her word, perhaps for the first time in her life, Miriam disappeared.

Le was reunited with her family, who found the honor in her dishonor. She hadn't allowed Senator Stevens to exploit her for any other reason than to give them a good life. They decided that to be forgivable, especially after Angela's story caught the attention of people willing to pay Le thousands of dollars to share her experiences. The money enabled her to care for her family, and in the process, Le unearthed a calling. She fought passionately to spare other women the same indignities as they pursued citizenship. Thanks to Angela and a caring church community, she would be just fine.

Thanks to Le and Xavier, Angela's reporting finally received the recognition it deserved. The twisted plot involving Xavier's life won multiple awards and for the first time Angela no longer had to chase a story. Stories ran right to her as she joined the investigative reporting elite.

Xavier awoke from a coma to a changed life. Although cleared of all charges, he still carried the guilt of the two people he killed with his car and the death of his friend, Frank. The deaths were irreversible changes, the weightiest of all he endured. He couldn't bring himself to ask God why him. Xavier refused to believe himself to be victimized in light of the innocent lives taken.

The press hounded him with stories both factual and fictional. All of the unwanted attention was an inconvenience as he adjusted to the aftermath. He could not have paid for that type of publicity when he was in the NFL.

It was once said that a hero is a person who rises to the top in spite of their circumstances. Xavier's character was even more fine-tuned as he chose to live a quiet and simple life; sending his earnings from appearances and other minor investments to the family of Martha and Warren. He couldn't think of a better way to honor Frank's faithful spirit.

In the meantime, Charles honored Xavier's faithfulness to him, as well as his heroic spirit. Convalescence had this funny way of making him sit still, which he hated, though he used the time to re-think every aspect of his life.

One thing for sure, he knew that God had reunited him with his hero for a reason. For the first time in his life, he was willing to be patient until the reason was revealed.

-The End-